**Praise for the Novels
of Vicki Lewis Thompson
The *Babes on Brooms* Romances**

Chick with a Charm

"I love this series! These witchy characters are hilarious. . . .
I can't wait to see what Ms. Thompson has in store for
her readers next! . . . If you have read anything by Ms.
Thompson before and liked it, you will like this series
too!"   —The Romance Studio

"Vicki Thompson can definitely te̶   really
gets you to know and love the chara̶   atch-
ing and waiting for another one."

                                                             ̶views

"The fast-paced story line is laced   t, and
whimsy that makes for an enjoya̶   ard to
put down."   —̶   eviews

"A funny installment of the Ba̶   series,
Chick with a Charm delights w̶   rs and
elegant writing that will make r̶   rab the
rest of the series!"   Fiction

Blonde with a Wand

"Extremely readable . . . terrific writing, and great character development. . . . Readers will fully enjoy this con-
fection."   —*Romantic Times* (4 stars)

The *Hexy* Romances

Casual Hex

"A romantic tale that's sprinkled with magic and rein-
forced by love . . . a fast-paced read, and a great addition
to the enchanting world of Big Knob."

                                                             —Darque Reviews

continued . . .

"An enjoyable lighthearted story.... Fans will enjoy this jocular jaunt." —*Midwest Book Review*

Wild & Hexy

"An excellent addition that makes me eager for more! ... You never really know what might happen in the small town of Big Knob, but you won't want to miss a thing. A must read!" —Fallen Angel Reviews

"There was so much going on in this book that I really didn't want it to end ... wonderfully fun ... a keeper for sure!" —Fresh Fiction

"Pure FUN from first page to last!" —The Romance Readers Connection

Over Hexed

"A snappy, funny, romantic novel." —*New York Times* bestselling author Carly Phillips

"Filled with laughs, this is a charmer of a book." —The Eternal Night

"The same trademark blend of comedy and heart that won Thompson's Nerd series a loyal following." —*Publishers Weekly*

"Thompson mixes magic, small-town quirkiness, and passionate sex for a winsome effect." —*Booklist*

"Vicki Lewis Thompson pens an enchanting tale for her amorous characters." —*Darque Reviews*

**Further Praise for
Vicki Lewis Thompson and Her Novels**

"Count on Vicki Lewis Thompson for a sharp, sassy, sexy read. Stranded on a desert island? I hope you've got this book in your beach bag."　　—Jayne Ann Krentz

"Wildly sexy . . . a full complement of oddball characters and sparkles with sassy humor."　　—*Library Journal*

"A riotous cast of colorful characters . . . fills the pages with hilarious situations and hot, creative sex."
　　—*Booklist*

"Smart, spunky, and delightfully over-the-top."
　　—*Publishers Weekly*

"[A] lighthearted and frisky tale of discovery between two engaging people."　　—*The Oakland Press* (MI)

"Delightfully eccentric . . . humor, mystical ingredients, and plenty of fun . . . a winning tale."
　　—The Best Reviews

"A funny and thrilling ride!"
　　—Romance Reviews Today

"A hilarious romp."　　—Romance Junkies

"Extremely sexy . . . over-the-top . . . sparkling."
　　—*Rendezvous*

"A whole new dimension in laughter. A big . . . BRAVO!"
　　—A Romance Review

Also by Vicki Lewis Thompson

Chick with a Charm
Blonde with a Wand
Casual Hex
Wild & Hexy
Over Hexed

A
Werewolf in Manhattan

A WILD ABOUT YOU NOVEL

Vicki Lewis Thompson

A SIGNET ECLIPSE BOOK

SIGNET ECLIPSE
Published by New American Library, a division of
Penguin Group (USA) Inc., 375 Hudson Street,
New York, New York 10014, USA
Penguin Group (Canada), 90 Eglinton Avenue East, Suite 700, Toronto,
Ontario M4P 2Y3, Canada (a division of Pearson Penguin Canada Inc.)
Penguin Books Ltd., 80 Strand, London WC2R 0RL, England
Penguin Ireland, 25 St. Stephen's Green, Dublin 2,
Ireland (a division of Penguin Books Ltd.)
Penguin Group (Australia), 250 Camberwell Road, Camberwell, Victoria 3124,
Australia (a division of Pearson Australia Group Pty. Ltd.)
Penguin Books India Pvt. Ltd., 11 Community Centre, Panchsheel Park,
New Delhi - 110 017, India
Penguin Group (NZ), 67 Apollo Drive, Rosedale, North Shore 0632,
New Zealand (a division of Pearson New Zealand Ltd.)
Penguin Books (South Africa) (Pty.) Ltd., 24 Sturdee Avenue,
Rosebank, Johannesburg 2196, South Africa

Penguin Books Ltd., Registered Offices:
80 Strand, London WC2R 0RL, England

First published by Signet Eclipse, an imprint of New American Library,
a division of Penguin Group (USA) Inc.

First Printing, January 2011
10 9 8 7 6 5 4 3 2 1

Copyright © Vicki Lewis Thompson, 2011
All rights reserved

SIGNET ECLIPSE and logo are trademarks of Penguin Group (USA) Inc.

Printed in the United States of America

Without limiting the rights under copyright reserved above, no part of this pub-
lication may be reproduced, stored in or introduced into a retrieval system, or
transmitted, in any form, or by any means (electronic, mechanical, photocopying,
recording, or otherwise), without the prior written permission of both the copyright owner and the above publisher of this book.

PUBLISHER'S NOTE
This is a work of fiction. Names, characters, places, and incidents either are the
product of the author's imagination or are used fictitiously, and any resemblance
to actual persons, living or dead, business establishments, events, or locales is
entirely coincidental.
    The publisher does not have any control over and does not assume any re-
sponsibility for author or third-party Web sites or their content.

If you purchased this book without a cover you should be aware that this book is
stolen property. It was reported as "unsold and destroyed" to the publisher and
neither the author nor the publisher has received any payment for this "stripped
book."

The scanning, uploading, and distribution of this book via the Internet or via any
other means without the permission of the publisher is illegal and punishable by
law. Please purchase only authorized electronic editions, and do not participate
in or encourage electronic piracy of copyrighted materials. Your support of the
author's rights is appreciated.

For my agent, Robert Gottlieb, who challenged me to write this story and whose continued support provides a lifeline in this wild and crazy business of publishing.

ACKNOWLEDGMENTS

Writing is always a pleasure, but thanks to the enthusiastic response from my editor, Claire Zion, it's also a joy. As a bonus, I get to work with her assistant, the ever-cheerful Jhanteigh Kupihea. I also benefit from the skills of the art department at Penguin, which creates such fantastic covers for my books. On the home front, I'm blessed with my assistant/daughter, Audrey Sharpe, who keeps me from going off the rails, and my spoiled cat, Eve, who keeps me humble.

Chapter 1

"Wanting her was dangerous. She was not of his kind, and if she learned what he was, she could put the pack at risk. Yet desire waylaid him each time he caught her scent."

Aidan Wallace listened intently as Emma Gavin—her cute, blond self tucked into a red dress—read from her latest book, *Night Shift*. Emma always kicked off a book tour with a reading in Manhattan, and Aidan had attended the last three. The first two times he'd come as a fan intrigued by this petite twenty-eight-year-old who seemed to have an uncanny understanding of werewolves. Most writers got it all wrong.

But her accuracy had a downside. For this Wednesday night event, he wasn't here as a fan. Instead he was attending in his role as chief security officer for the Wallace pack. Howard Wallace, the alpha and Aidan's father, worried that a rogue werewolf might have been feeding Emma information. If she'd made contact with somebody on the inside, that kind of leak had the power to destroy the pack.

Three months ago, Howard had directed Aidan to put her under twenty-four-hour surveillance. So far he'd turned up nothing, but his father wanted him to stay on the job. When Emma left on her book tour, Aidan would follow, although trailing her from place to place without being spotted would test his skills.

He would manage. With business interests that stretched from Park Avenue to Broadway, from Wall Street to Times Square, the Wallaces couldn't afford a security breach. New York City tolerated a diverse population, but even New Yorkers might panic if they learned that a sizable chunk of the city was owned by werewolves.

"She wanted him, too. Her breathing changed and her pupils widened whenever he was near." Emma paused and ran her tongue nervously over her lips. She never seemed at ease during these events.

That didn't surprise him. After observing her for three months, he knew she'd rather have been alone in her loft, curled up in a cozy chair with a book or her laptop. Besides, she had to be exhausted after pulling that all-nighter to meet today's deadline for the next book in the series.

Aidan figured that if she was getting inside info from the werewolf community, she would have contacted her source sometime during the past few days, and most definitely last night, when she was pushing toward the finish. She hadn't. So what explained the on-target nature of her stories? Lucky guesses?

Aidan had pondered that while reading *Night Shift* recently. He'd been privy to an advance copy because his father and the publisher were old drinking buddies. No wonder Emma had chosen this passage for tonight's presentation. It captured the basic appeal of the series—a takeoff on *Beauty and the Beast* that had fans sacrificing grocery money to buy her books in hardcover.

The fantasy of a male werewolf mating with a human female was a popular one. Aidan would like to believe he wasn't drawn to it, that he viewed the subject intellectually. That wasn't quite true.

But tonight, with Emma standing there in a silk dress, which lovingly draped over her breasts and hips, he couldn't allow himself to fantasize. His groin tightened, and he glanced away, irritated with his automatic response to her. Arousal was a reaction he couldn't afford, especially given his genetic flaw: Unsatisfied arousal caused him to begin to shift.

He concentrated on the uncomfortable nature of the metal folding chair. The manufacturer hadn't created this chair with a six-four, two-hundred-pound werewolf in mind. The seat was too small and the back, too low. Mentally complaining about the chair did the trick, and he was able to return his attention to Emma.

She stood in front of a table stacked high with her books, and a young brunette in a black suit hovered nearby. Aidan pegged her as somebody from the publishing house who'd come along to facilitate the signing gig.

If he took her, there would be no turning back. A werewolf mated for life.

As would he. The crown prince of the Wallace pack was expected to choose well and cement either a financial or political alliance with one of the other great werewolf families based in North America. His brother, Roarke, might have more leeway, but Aidan's path was preordained.

Barring some misstep, he'd end up with Nadia Henderson, daughter of Leland Henderson, alpha leader of the pack based near Chicago. Aidan and Nadia had known each other since they were young, and he liked her. She didn't excite him sexually, but that wasn't the point. Uniting the New York and Chicago packs through marriage would create a powerful dynasty.

Because Emma stirred him more than any human female he'd ever met, he was wary of her. At thirty-two, he was fast approaching the time when he'd have to commit to Nadia, and he prided himself on honoring his commitments. Love and passion, the kind Emma wrote about, wouldn't factor into it.

Distracted by that thought, he missed the end of the reading and the beginning of the autographing session. A line had formed by the time Aidan stood, and the woman in the black suit had stepped in to slip promo material into each copy before handing it back to the buyer.

Holding the hardback he'd purchased earlier in the evening and folding his topcoat over one arm, Aidan headed to the back of the group. He hated lines, but he would stand in this one because it would give him a rare chance to talk with Emma face-to-face. Maybe he'd learn something important.

He hadn't sensed any other werewolves in the crowd, which was a disappointment. He'd thought her informant, if she had one, would want to attend the launch of her book tour. *Apparently not.*

He recognized a few faces from the previous two signings. Her mother was here, of course. Betty Gavin had taken a chair in front and was near the head of the line.

Her blond hair was mixed with gray, and she carried a few more pounds than her daughter, but the resemblance was striking. She worked as an administrative assistant for a group of lawyers. Aidan had checked her out thoroughly, too, and hadn't found anything suspicious. Obviously she thought her daughter had hung the moon.

Aidan settled in to wait and tried to block out the sensory overload created by a pack of humans. Perfume, aftershave, and deodorant assaulted his nostrils, while a cacophony of voices, cell phone chimes, background music, and shuffling feet battered his eardrums.

He longed for the stillness of the forest or the hushed ambience he'd achieved in his Central Park West apartment with triple-paned glass and yards of moss green carpet. A flat-screen in every room ran continuous forest-scene footage to give him the illusion of the deep woods—even in the heart of the city—and he kept a jungle of plants healthy with the help of a plant sitter.

Silence was another thing he appreciated about Emma. She didn't make unnecessary noise, except once in a great while when she'd crank up the volume on her iPod speakers and dance around her Greenwich Village loft. She knew some sexy dance moves that he'd have been wise to forget about.

She didn't wear perfume, either, which allowed him to pick up her true scent. Unfortunately, he was drawn to it. He understood the power of pheromones and recognized that he had a significant problem with Emma in that regard.

Her beguiling aroma reached out to him, penetrating the maze of competing scents, taunting him from thirty feet away. He'd met her up close only twice before, both times when she'd autographed books at this store.

The first time she only smiled and thanked him for coming. But the second time she'd asked enough questions to find out he was a member of the well-connected Wallace family. She'd seemed a little surprised, yet pleased, that Aidan read her books.

He figured she'd already spotted him tonight. After all, he was one of a handful of men in the audience. He'd bet he was the only one who knew how she took her coffee—no sugar, two creams—or what color sheets were on her bed—hunter green. Seeing her tonight was a completely different experience for him now that he knew so much about her. He'd have to be careful to keep all that intimate knowledge under wraps when he spoke to her.

For three months, he and his staff had monitored her activities through wiretaps and hidden cameras in her loft. He'd personally followed her whenever she left her apartment for lunch dates with her mom, her agent, or a girlfriend.

Her lifestyle wasn't all that different from many women in their late twenties. She was an environmentalist, which prompted her to take public transportation to save fossil fuels. She drank organic coffee, but she drank too much of it, which had turned her into an insomniac. Or maybe it was all the organic chocolate she ate along with the coffee. More than once he'd cringed as he'd realized her dinner had consisted of those two items.

But he understood the food, or lack thereof, more than he understood her choice of boyfriend. As he moved closer to the signing table and the pull of pheromones grew stronger, his thoughts understandably turned to her sex life, or what passed for her sex life.

The way he figured it, a woman who could dance, a woman who could write creative sex scenes that left him hard and aching, would require a dynamite lover. Instead she had . . . Doug, who was also her CPA. Doug might have been world-class when it came to preparing her tax returns, but apparently he didn't know jack shit about pleasing her in bed.

Doug had spent the night at Emma's loft exactly four times in three months. Aidan had balked at putting a camera in her bedroom, both to respect her privacy and protect his sanity. But the audio from the living-room camera had picked up the sounds of a couple having sex in the bedroom. Sad to say, he hadn't detected much excitement. Doug seemed to have the energy quotient of a stale bagel.

Emma deserved somebody more inspired, somebody more ardent. Aidan wondered whether she was so busy with her career that she simply lacked the time to search out a better alternative to Doug. Then, too, her taxes were probably complicated, and a good CPA was hard to find.

As Aidan contemplated Emma's sorry excuse for a sex life, Betty Gavin walked past him, holding her signed book.

She paused. "Aren't you Aidan Wallace?"

"Guilty as charged."

Betty smiled and held out her hand. "I'm Emma's mother. She told me you read her books. I think she's proud of that."

Aidan shook her hand and took note that Betty had a firm grip. His contacts had assured him that, in the office where she worked, she was a force to be reckoned with. "Your daughter's a gifted writer."

It was the right thing to say. Betty beamed as if he'd handed her an Academy Award, and her blue eyes, so like Emma's, glowed with pride. "She's amazing. I don't know where she gets all those ideas."

That was the very question that had the Wallace pack so agitated, but he couldn't say that. "I guess she's just creative."

"Yes, she certainly is." Betty looked over toward the bookstore entrance. "I was so hoping Doug would surprise her at the last minute and show up." She glanced at Aidan. "That's her boyfriend. But he had a Rotary meeting tonight."

"You'd think he'd want to be here." *No, shit—he should be here.*

"You would think so, wouldn't you? Emma just finished a book early this morning, and she likes to celebrate after turning in a manuscript. I wish I could stay and party with her, but my office called an early meeting, and if I don't head home I'll sleep through it."

"Maybe her boyfriend will show up." Aidan wondered how tuned in the guy could have been if he didn't know about Emma's habit of celebrating when she met a deadline.

"Maybe he will. Anyway, I have to go." Betty patted his arm. "It's almost your turn, anyway. Thanks for coming to her signings. I know she's thrilled about that." She walked away clutching her book.

Aidan figured she'd paid full price for it, too, because she wanted to support her daughter's career. He admired that kind of loyalty.

Just then, the woman in front of him walked away with her signed book, which left him as the only autograph seeker in the vicinity. Emma's scent hit him full force, and he steeled himself against the urge to reach across the table and pull her right out of her chair and into his arms.

That the thought crossed his mind was a warning signal. Years of training had subdued his animal instincts, but no amount of training would eliminate them completely. He would be careful.

"Aidan Wallace!" Emma smiled as she stood and held out her hand. "I saw you in the audience, and I was hoping you'd stick around."

Aidan put down the book in order to take her hand. "Had to get an autograph before you head off on your tour." Her hand was ice-cold, and he unconsciously sandwiched it between both of his. *Not good.* He released her hand and cleared his throat. "Congratulations on your new book."

"Thank you, Aidan." Her blue eyes sparkled in welcome, but her makeup couldn't disguise purple smudges underneath those incredible eyes.

She needed a vacation, not a book tour. He thought of his ancestral home near Sitka, Alaska. The remote lodge, surrounded by cozy log cabins, was his favorite retreat in the world, and he had the insane urge to take her there so she could rest. Ah, but they would do more than rest. And there was the rub.

So instead he made pleasant conversation. "I hear you're headed off to Chicago in a few days."

"Right!" Her enthusiasm didn't ring true, but if she dreaded the tour, she couldn't very well mention that in front of her publisher's representative. She turned to the woman in black. "Jenny, this is Aidan Wallace. Aidan, Jenny Dunn handles PR for the company and was kind enough to come with me tonight."

"It's the least I could do, considering how hard Emma works." Jenny shook hands with Aidan. "It's nice to meet you, Aidan. I've seen your father a few times in the office."

Aidan nodded. "He and Roger Claymore go way back."

Emma braced both hands on the table as she gazed at him with a bemused expression. "I didn't realize your father and Roger were old friends. Your father should have snagged you an advance copy of the book."

"He did." *All in the name of research to supplement Emma's growing file.*

"And you're still buying one?" She pushed it gently back toward him. "You don't have to do that."

"Yeah, I do." He gave the book a nudge back in her direction. "The copy I read was one of those softcover deals." And he'd marked it up looking for clues that she'd hooked up with the werewolf world. "I want an autographed hardback for my bookshelf."

Jenny nodded in approval. "Very cool."

"Yes, it is." A soft light came into Emma's eyes as she looked at him. Then she sat down and picked up her pen. "I'm honored to have a place on your bookshelf."

Aidan felt a stab of guilt and quickly reminded himself that he'd been a fan before he'd started spying on her. He really did want an autographed copy for the section of his bookshelf devoted to her, but coming to the reading tonight had been primarily to see whether any werewolves showed up.

Jenny began gathering bookmarks and flyers from the table. "I hope you two won't think I'm rude, but my daughter has a cold, and my husband's home with her. If you're okay with it, Emma, I'd like to get back and check on them."

Emma glanced up, her pen still poised over Aidan's open book. "Of course! Go! And thanks so much for being here. That e-mail I got late this afternoon freaked me out a little, but I'm fine, now."

Aha. Aidan was proud of his casual response, considering the alarm bells clanging in his head. His crew had been monitoring her e-mails several times a day, but since nothing interesting had popped up, he'd told them to cut back to once in the morning. "Crazy fan?"

"I guess so. Some guy claims he's a werewolf. Wants to show me what a real werewolf is like."

Holy shit. Aidan did his best to stay calm. "Sounds like a nut."

"Or some lonely soul trying to get a date." She

smiled at him. "I guess he imagines I actually believe in werewolves."

That was news he could use. "I take it you don't?"

She went back to autographing his book. "The day I start believing in the fantasy I created is the day they'll have to chase after me with a butterfly net."

Aidan mentally sighed in relief. He was good at reading people, and Emma seemed perfectly sincere. She couldn't very well have a mole inside the werewolf community if she didn't believe in werewolves. His job was over except for one thing—she might have attracted the attention of a rogue, after all.

"That e-mail was sort of creepy, though." Jenny tucked all the publicity materials into a satchel and hooked the straps over her shoulder. "We can still send somebody with you on tour. It's not too late, and Roger's completely okay with that."

Send me. Aidan saw a golden opportunity and vowed to take advantage of it.

Emma shook her head. "That's a waste of money. You've lined up media escorts at each stop. The hotels are secure. I'm not worried."

"Has anybody done a reverse trace on the e-mail?" Aidan wanted to get his hands on it in the worst way. He could notify his tech guys to pull it up, but going through Emma might be the simplest. A plan was forming in his mind.

"We tried," Jenny said. "Nothing came up."

Aidan didn't want to appear too eager, even though he was chomping at the bit. "I handle security for Wallace Enterprises. I might be able to figure it out for you."

"You're a security expert?" Emma gave him an assessing glance. "Somehow I thought you were on Wall Street."

"I have a cousin who is, but I went a different route."

"I'm thrilled he's in security," Jenny said. "If you'll give me your e-mail address, Aidan, I'll send over what Emma forwarded to me. The guy's probably a harmless kook, but if we could pinpoint where he is, that would be valuable."

Aidan pulled out a business card from an inside pocket of his suit jacket and handed it to Jenny. "Considering my dad's history with Roger Claymore, the service will be gratis." He'd play this as if he needed Jenny's cooperation to get that e-mail.

"You should charge your regular fee." Emma finished the autograph and closed the book. "If they were going to send somebody along on the tour, they can certainly afford your expert advice."

"It won't take long enough to justify a bill." Aidan was still planning to turn this into a bodyguard assignment. Although he didn't consider Emma weak, she was ill prepared to confront a werewolf. No good could come of it, either for her or for the packs living in various North American cities.

"I appreciate the offer." Jenny accepted the card and tucked it into her pocket. "I'll send the e-mail first thing in the morning. Emma, take a cab home. I realize you're a subway kind of girl, but no more of that until we figure this out."

"I have a car and driver," Aidan said, knowing she wouldn't approve of his luxury town car. "I'll see that she gets home safely."

Emma glanced up at him. "Thank you, but that's not necessary."

"Em." Jenny sent her a pointed look. "A security expert, who also happens to be a Wallace and who loves your books, has offered to run a trace on that e-mail for free, and now he's prepared to get you home safely. As a representative of your publisher, I insist you accept that offer."

"Okay, but I think it's kind of silly."

"Humor me."

"All right."

Jenny nodded. "Thanks, Em. Talk to you tomorrow. Nice meeting you, Aidan." With a wave, she walked away.

"There you go." Emma pushed the book back across the table. "And you certainly don't have to chauffeur me home tonight. You must have a million things to do that are more important."

"Can't think of any." He put on his topcoat before picking up the book. "Are you ready to go?" He was still sorting through the possibilities of the e-mail. The sender could be a nutcase or a werewolf willing to betray his pack to impress a woman, which made him a werewolf nutcase. Either way, his behavior could be unpredictable.

She sighed, and her shoulders dropped. "Truthfully, I'd love a ride home in a luxury car instead of a taxi. I doubt your car will be emitting any more greenhouse gases than the taxi, and it's been a long day."

Following a long night. He'd kept track of her through most of it, and she'd spent the wee hours finishing her manuscript instead of sleeping. "Let me call Ralph." He pulled his BlackBerry from inside his jacket and speed-dialed his driver. "Yes, I'm ready. Down by the front door. I have a passenger to drop off in the Village."

Then he cringed. He wasn't supposed to know where she lived. He hoped she was too tired to notice the slip. Now he had to hope Ralph would remember to ask her for the address as if he didn't know it. If Aidan had been in wolf form, he could have sent Ralph a telepathic message, but in human form he had to rely on his cell.

"I do appreciate this." Standing, Emma grabbed her coat and purse from a neighboring chair before walking around the table to join him. "I love meeting readers, but my cheeks hurt from smiling."

"I'll bet. Let me help you with your coat."

"Oh." She looked a little disoriented but handed it over and set her purse on the table so he could slide the coat over her arms and onto her shoulders.

Although manners had been heavily ingrained in Aidan since a young age, he wasn't in the habit of lying to himself. Manners hadn't been his main reason for helping her with the coat. He'd wanted the chance to move closer, to let his fingers brush the red silk of her dress, to feel the warmth of her body swirl as the coat went on.

None of that fit into his plan to be careful. When she lifted her blond hair off the nape of her neck to settle it over the coat collar, he stared at that vulnerable spot and swallowed. He wanted her too much. He should turn this job over to one of his capable staff members. But he knew he wouldn't.

"Thank you." She glanced back at him. "You have an old-world charm about you, Aidan. It's nice."

Nice. If she only knew the thoughts he was having, the growl of primitive need he was choking back. "I'm sure you're tired. We should get going."

"I *am* tired." She picked up her purse and started toward the front of the store. "But I can hardly complain. My books are doing well, and this kind of success doesn't come along every day."

He followed as they wound their way through the book aisles. "I've often wondered if readings are stressful for writers." And Dougie-boy hadn't shown up to give her moral support or take her out afterward for a little celebration. The more he learned about the guy, the less he liked him.

"The extroverts don't mind them, I suppose, but for introverts like me, it can be a challenge sometimes. So how did you know I lived in the Village?" she asked over her shoulder.

Apparently she wasn't *that* tired if she'd picked up on his slip. He'd have to lie. "Must have read it in an interview somewhere."

"That's possible. I've asked reporters not to mention stuff like that, but sometimes it gets in, anyway. Fortunately, I don't have a huge problem with people pestering me."

"I promise not to pester you." *Another lie.* He planned to stick to her like fur to polyester. He doubted the e-mail she'd received had come from anyone in the Wallace pack. The Wallaces had some interesting family dynamics, and not everyone got along, but nobody would take the chance of sabotaging the whole operation.

He suspected the rogue, if that's who had sent the e-mail, belonged to another pack, and if so, Aidan planned to get himself assigned as Emma's bodyguard for the entire book tour. His father could talk Roger Claymore into it by giving the publisher a smoking rate for Aidan's services.

There was a good chance that when Emma left for Chicago, Aidan would be on the plane with her, unless someone in the family figured out that he craved this woman. Then he'd have to take himself off the case.

He rebelled at that idea, even as he acknowledged the wisdom of it. He didn't trust the job to anyone else, and he was determined to protect Emma from any potential threat. Including himself.

Chapter 2

Somewhere between leaving the autograph table and stepping into the frigid cold of a New York February night, Emma must have clicked over from tired to over-tired because she was suddenly wide-awake. Or maybe it was the extremely masculine presence beside her that had recharged her batteries.

She'd always realized Aidan was hot. No woman could help noticing those shoulders, which filled out his custom-made suit without the benefit of padding. Because she'd seen him only in a suit, she had to guess whether he had a nice butt, but she'd be willing to bet he did.

He had the kind of jaw that usually showed up in shaving commercials, a strong nose, and a high forehead. She suspected he was easily as intelligent as he looked. Thick hair the color of chocolate and eyes the shade of warm caramel added up to one yummy guy.

But he'd given no indication he was interested in her personally. She was probably the only one who'd been affected by their brief contact when he'd helped her on with her coat. She doubted he found anything cozy and intimate about sharing the backseat of his town car with her, either.

She'd expected him to wear some pricey cologne, but it must have been subtle, because she didn't recognize any particular brand. She had the inappropriate urge to bury her nose in the side of his neck.

She wouldn't, of course, because she was with Doug, even though he was currently on her shit list. Surely he could have chucked his Rotary Club meeting so he could be here tonight. It was her first signing since they'd moved their relationship from professional to personal, and his excuse—that he already had an autographed book—didn't sit well with her. He could have bought one for his mother.

True, Emma hadn't been much of a girlfriend the past couple of weeks, with her deadline looming. She wasn't sure how great a girlfriend she was, period, considering how much quality time she spent writing and how little quality time she spent with Doug. Maybe a writer wasn't meant to have a boyfriend. Maybe he was justified in missing the signing.

But she hadn't had a chance to tell him about the creepy e-mail from the guy who thought he was a werewolf. Then again, Doug might not take it seriously. She kind of liked that Aidan Wallace—who had to be worth a gazillion dollars—did.

She definitely liked the mode of transportation Aidan provided. On principle she was opposed to a megaexpensive car dedicated to ferrying one person all over Christendom, but sinking down onto the butter-soft leather, she'd almost moaned in delight. Tomorrow Aidan would trace the e-mail and she'd be back on the subway, as always. Tonight Jenny had practically forced her to ride like royalty, so she'd ditch the guilt.

The older man in the front seat wore a sweatshirt and jeans instead of a chauffer's uniform, but chauffeuring was clearly his function. He pulled the car smoothly into traffic. "What address in the Village, Aidan?"

The guy spoke like a friend instead of an employee, and Emma's little democratic heart warmed. Money shouldn't give anyone the right to act superior, in her opinion. She leaned forward to give him the address. "It's—"

"Wait." Aidan laid a hand on her arm. "I just realized something."

So had she. She didn't want to go home yet. His lingering touch, even through her wool coat and silk dress, was wildly exciting. Awareness sizzled in all her pleasure centers, and now she was *really* awake. She hadn't had this kind of instant reaction to a man in ages. In fact, she'd told herself that she'd outgrown such craziness, even though she wrote about it all the time.

He glanced at her, his eyes in shadow. "You might not want me to know where you live."

She almost laughed. If it weren't for Doug, she'd show him exactly where she lived and invite him in for coffee. Maybe all he admired was her writing talent, but given time, that might change.

"I could call a limo service instead of taking you home personally," he said. "That might be better." The dim light of the car's interior emphasized the rugged line of his jaw and brought out the chiseled beauty of his cheekbones. He looked mysterious, sexy, and damned near irresistible.

Oh, baby. "I don't care if you know where I live. I just—" She hesitated as she debated the wisdom of saying what was on her mind. She'd have loved to go somewhere for a drink to celebrate the twin victories of meeting her deadline and launching a new book. When Doug had crapped out and her mother had begged off, she'd thought of suggesting drinks to Jenny, but Jenny had a sick kid at home.

That left her in the company of Aidan Wallace, a certified hunk who had voluntarily shown up at her signing, and for the third time, too. It wasn't even ten yet, but she doubted he had other plans for tonight or he wouldn't have been so willing to offer her a ride home.

"Just *what*?" he prompted.

If she suggested having a drink with him, she'd have to tell Doug about it. He might not love the idea. But Aidan was a fan, who certainly wasn't hitting on her in any way, so this was business, sort of, wasn't it?

No, it wasn't. She was momentarily crushing on a gorgeous man who loved her books. Even if Aidan wasn't attracted to her, her interest in him was no longer casual. Acting on that interest wasn't fair to Doug, even if he had skipped the signing.

She sighed. "Never mind."

"Emma, are you afraid to go home? Is it that e-mail?"

"No, it's not the e-mail." She didn't want to turn this into a silly game of twenty questions, so she settled on a partial truth, omitting her ill-advised attraction to him. "Finishing a manuscript always makes me feel like celebrating, but what I need is a good night's sleep."

He smiled. "Who says you can't have both?"

My conscience. But her conscience was no match for the magnetic pull of Aidan Wallace. "Good question."

Aidan leaned toward the front seat. "Drop us off at Jessie's, Ralph."

Ralph hesitated for a fraction of a second. "Sure thing."

Emma wondered briefly about that hesitation, but the decision had been made, and she wasn't planning to reverse it. Aidan thought she should celebrate, and celebrate she would. *Within the bounds of propriety, of course.*

She found Aidan's take-charge attitude familiar and finally realized why. He behaved like one of her heroes. Of course, to really qualify he'd have to be a shifter who could become a wolf whenever he wanted to.

She smiled to herself, thinking of how he'd laugh himself silly over that. But telling him was out of the question. It would be a blatant attempt to flirt, and she wasn't doing that.

She'd never heard of a nightspot named Jessie's, but that meant nothing. She didn't get out much. Now there was a huge understatement. Her life had settled into a boring rut, and that was bad for a writer. She needed grist for the mill.

All righty, then. Her guilt could take a long jump off a short pier. She wasn't simply having a social drink with a very attractive man who could serve as inspiration for her next book. She was also collecting grist for the mill while enjoying the life of a bestselling author, whatever that was supposed to be.

She'd always imagined herself moving to Key West and living like a real writer should—drinking booze in smoky bars and hanging out with all the clever people. Maybe having a glass of wine with a member of an influential New York family was a start.

Ralph swung the car over to the curb, and Aidan opened the door. "Thanks, Ralph. I'll call when we're ready to leave."

"We won't be long," Emma added as a sop to her still-niggling conscience.

"Take your time. It's a beautiful night." Ralph's manner was relaxed and easy, as if he didn't mind waiting around.

Emma concluded the man must be both well paid and well respected, and her estimation of Aidan, already hovering at good, moved into the excellent range.

Aidan exited the car with the same fluid grace with which he'd entered it. He held out his hand to Emma. Anticipation thrummed in her veins as she placed her hand in his and absorbed his warmth and strength. She wondered whether he had a girlfriend, which was a totally inappropriate thought because *she* had a boyfriend.

Once he'd helped her out of the car, he released her hand, which was the right thing to do. They were mere acquaintances, after all. This wasn't a date, and she'd do well to remember that. He was humoring her desire to party a little.

"This way." He lightly touched the small of her back to guide her toward a black enameled doorway.

When he used a card-key to open the door, he verified her suspicion that he was taking her to a private club. No wonder she'd never heard of it.

The black enameled door opened into a small lobby, decorated in grays and blacks with a splash of red here and there. On their right was a narrow stairway carpeted in red, but no sign indicated where it led.

"Jessie's is upstairs." Aidan gestured for her to climb the carpeted steps. "I think you'll like it."

She had no doubt she would. So far, Aidan's world had seduced her with luxury, and she expected the same from this exclusive club. Soft jazz filtered down to her as she climbed the stairs. She was aware of Aidan behind her, his footfalls amazingly light considering his solid build.

She'd never realized until tonight how graceful he

was. She felt like a klutz in comparison, but then, she'd never claimed to be coordinated. Aidan would be a marvelous dancer. *And a marvelous lover.* The thought had no business showing up in her head, but there it was, taunting her with possibilities.

At the top of the stairs, a silver-haired man in a tuxedo moved out from behind a tall reception desk and shook Aidan's hand. "Aidan. It's good to see you."

"It's good to be back, Sylvester. This is Emma Gavin. She writes—"

"The werewolf books." Sylvester eyed her with obvious curiosity. "This is indeed a pleasure. I've read them all."

"Really?"

"I find them fascinating," Sylvester said. "So detailed."

"Fortunately, I was blessed with a good imagination."

"You certainly were." Sylvester exchanged a glance with Aidan. "Table for two?"

"Please." Aidan helped her off with her coat.

His touch produced the same electric charge as when he'd helped her put it on. She would have to get over that. While Sylvester hung their coats on a rack behind the desk, she gave herself a talking-to.

Her self-talk continued as she followed Sylvester through an arched doorway. *Having a drink with Aidan is a onetime deal, and she . . . whoa.* Had they somehow wandered into an alternate universe? The club seemed to be nestled in a forest, a forest on the second floor of a brick building in the middle of Manhattan.

She couldn't help staring. "Wow."

"I thought you'd like it." Aidan sounded pleased.

"I love it." She wasn't sure how the owners had managed the effect, but the trees arching over the small dance floor seemed real, as did the ones scattered around the perimeter of the room.

Tiny white lights winked like fireflies in branches, which curved to create intimate bowers for each rough-hewn table. To her right, a live jazz trio played on a moss-covered knoll.

Sylvester led them to a table near the back of the room and pulled out Emma's chair.

"Thank you, Sylvester." She glanced back at him. "This is quite a place."

He smiled at her. "A waiter will be over soon to take your order. Enjoy." He laid an affectionate hand on Aidan's shoulder before leaving them.

Aw. Emma didn't need more reasons to admire Aidan, but she was getting them anyway. He obviously inspired friendship and respect among his associates. "Thank you for sharing this place with me," she said. "I thought we'd just find a little tavern somewhere, but this is breathtakingly beautiful."

"There's more. Look up."

She did and was dazzled by the night sky, complete with stars, peeking through the foliage. The effect was so real she would swear someone had slid the roof back, except they were in the heart of the city, where the lights blocked out the stars completely.

Aidan settled into the chair across from her. "What would you like to drink?"

She continued to gaze upward as she tried to figure out how they'd created the effect. "Chardonnay is fine."

"That's it? Nothing more exotic?"

She met his gaze. She always ordered chardonnay, and if she intended to break out of her rut, she should experiment with a different drink. "Any suggestions?"

"The bartender makes great coffee martinis."

"Oh, my God, I have to have one. I *love* coffee."

"I know."

"How would you know that?"

He blinked. "Uh, don't all writers drink coffee?"

"Not necessarily. Some guzzle gallons of tea, and others survive on Coke. The clichés aren't always true." But she thought it was cute that he had such a definite idea of how a writer should behave.

Aidan signaled a waiter and ordered them each a coffee martini.

"This is wonderful." Emma was grateful for her interesting surroundings because without them she was likely to stare at Aidan the whole time. "It's like a movie set."

"We called in some film people to help with the staging."

"*We?* Oh, wait, I should have guessed that right away. Private club, your favorite hangout. Of course it belongs to Wallace Enterprises."

"Yeah, it does. I—" He stopped speaking and glanced toward the arched entryway as a tall blond guy with a build similar to Aidan's walked into the club. "Looks like you're about to meet my little brother, Roarke."

"Is he in security, too?"

"No. Roarke's an anthropology professor at NYU."

Emma studied the man who was headed straight toward their table. None of her college professors had looked like that. Roarke might be younger than Aidan, but he wasn't *little* in any sense of the word. She could see the family resemblance in his square jaw and strong nose. "No slackers in the Wallace family, are there?"

"Not so you'd notice." Aidan rose from the table to greet his brother. "This is a surprise."

Roarke didn't smile. "I know." Barely disguised tension radiated from his powerful frame.

Aidan didn't seem to notice. "I'd like you to meet Emma Gavin, the author of the werewolf books."

"Nice to meet you, Emma. I've heard plenty about your books." Roarke still looked grim.

"Good things, I hope." She wasn't sure what to make of Roarke's stern behavior.

"Very good. Sorry to interrupt, but I need to see Aidan for a minute in the foyer."

Something was wrong. Maybe some security issue had come up, something only Aidan could handle. And yet, Roarke had sent her a wary glance before leaving with Aidan. Crazy as it sounded, she had the feeling that she was part of the problem.

Roarke spun around to face Aidan the moment they were out of the room. "What the hell are you doing?"

At the challenge in Roarke's voice, the hairs on the back of Aidan's neck rose and he fought back a snarl. Reacting like a wolf wouldn't help matters any. He kept his response mild. "What I was assigned to do."

"You were assigned to watch her, not bring her into our private club! I counted at least six Weres in that room." He turned to Sylvester, who leaned casually against the reception desk, arms crossed. "Sylvester makes seven."

"So? We're allowed to bring business contacts in here. We've always done that."

"She's not a business contact. She's a threat to our survival."

Aidan worked to control his temper. "If Dad would wait for my report instead of sending you over to chew my ass, he'd discover that Emma is no danger to us. She doesn't believe in werewolves."

Roarke's green eyes glittered. "I suppose she told you that."

"She did."

"And you, despite your obscenely high IQ, believed her."

"I did. I do."

Roarke blew out a breath in disbelief. "Come on, Aidan. She can't be making all that up."

"Just because you and I aren't that creative doesn't mean she isn't. But the problem goes beyond that. It's possible a rogue has contacted her by e-mail and plans to confront her in person."

"Did you consider that *she* contacted *him*?"

"No. We've kept a close eye on all her Internet activity. This is something new, and if it is a rogue, I'll make sure she never meets him."

Aidan could have said, *We'll make sure she never meets him*, but he was no longer willing to share responsibility for Emma's safety. He would be in charge, which was the only way he could guarantee she'd be all right and the pack's anonymity would be protected.

Roarke's belligerence faded. "Have you seen the e-mail?"

"Not yet, but I will. In fact, now that you've brought that up, let me take care of something." Pulling out his phone, he sent a brief message so his tech crew could start the reverse trace.

As he put the phone away, he glanced at Roarke. "Tell Dad I'm here tonight because I'm trying to win her confidence. I'll know soon what we're dealing with, and depending on what I find out, Dad might need to get me assigned as her bodyguard for the book tour."

"Aidan!" Roarke sighed. "Talk about a potential train wreck!"

Aidan's jaw tightened. "Why?"

"You're not the one to do this."

"Of course I am. I'm the most highly trained security specialist we have."

"And you want her."

Aidan tried to stare his brother down, but it was no use. Roarke's senses were as finely tuned as his, and they were brothers, only nineteen months apart. The minute Roarke had walked into the club, he'd known.

So Aidan said the only thing he could. "I'll control it."

"What, your johnson?"

That brought a snort from Sylvester.

Usually Aidan rolled with his brother's cracks, but tonight he wasn't amused. "The situation, Roarke. I'll control the situation."

"You know that's easier said than done. Having sex with a human is risky in any context, but it's especially dangerous with this author chick."

Aidan's lips curled back from his teeth. "Don't talk about her like that."

Roarke groaned. "Damn. You've gone alpha. Next you'll be marking her front door with your scent."

"Bite me."

"I'm tempted. Look, Aidan, don't go on this book tour. Okay? If she has to be watched, send somebody else."

"I don't trust anyone else to handle it."

Roarke threw up his hands. "I see my little intervention came way too late. Dad should never have assigned you to this gig. I'll bet he hasn't ever cracked one of her books, has he?"

"I doubt it, but what's that got to do with anything?"

"She writes good sex."

"That's not—"

"Sure it is, Aidan. I picked up a copy of *Night Shift* today and flipped through it. The woman knows her stuff. On top of that, the studly hero is—wait for it—a werewolf. You're Emma's dream guy. Who wouldn't get sucked in by that ego trip?"

Clearing his throat, Sylvester stepped from behind the reception desk. "I think Roarke has a point. I've read all her books, and if I were twenty years younger . . ."

Aidan knew then that he was in big trouble. Sylvester was a beloved uncle. Yet Aidan had the urge to go for his throat simply because the older man had indicated a sexual appreciation of Emma's work.

Aidan raked a hand through his hair. "You're both right. I need to take myself off this assignment. And I will after we trace the e-mail. Maybe it's just a kook. Any of the guys can handle a garden-variety kook."

"Then my work here is done." Clapping Aidan on the shoulder, Roarke headed for the stairs. "I knew you'd come to your senses, bro," he said over his shoulder. "You're too smart to let a woman screw up everything."

Aidan wasn't so sure about that. His genius IQ made him very good at his job, but it didn't seem to be helping him overcome his gut reaction to Emma. And because he couldn't seem to overcome it, he'd have to assign someone else to guard her. He wondered whether he'd be able to do that.

Chapter 3

Their drinks had arrived, and at first Emma wondered whether she should wait until Aidan returned to take a sip. But the frothy martini, decorated with three coffee beans, called to her. Depending on the problem Aidan had with Roarke, she might not get to stay, and she wanted to know what this new drink tasted like.

Not surprisingly, it tasted like heaven. She was definitely Googling the recipe when she got back to her loft. Or maybe Aidan, who owned the joint, could get her the exact recipe, because she didn't want a variation of a coffee martini. She wanted this one.

She took a longer sip. Chances were slim she'd get to come here again. If she told Doug about it—and she *would* tell Doug, she vowed for about the third time—she could predict the result. Because he was a man with manly instincts—although they were sometimes obscured by a preoccupation with the tax code—Doug would show up at her next signing so he could meet Aidan Wallace.

That could be interesting. The two men were about

the same height, but that was where the resemblance ended. Aidan had the body of a star quarterback. Doug had the body of a star . . . bridge player. She admired Doug for his mind, which was a perfect left-brain complement to her overly active right brain. But she'd never kidded herself that his body was a wonder to behold. It was okay—not fat or skinny—just sort of there. Functional.

Until tonight, she'd considered herself more evolved these days because she no longer required sculpted muscles in order to date a man. She took another sip of her drink as Aidan walked back toward their table. Apparently she was regressing to her teen years, because watching Aidan move gave her goose bumps.

"Sorry about that." Aidan returned to his seat. "Family stuff." He seemed quiet.

"Do we need to leave? I mean, if there's something you should take care of, I certainly understand."

"No, no. Roarke just had some things to tell me." Yet he definitely seemed subdued by the conversation.

She was curious, but she couldn't start quizzing him. She didn't know him well and didn't know his family at all. "I'm afraid I started without you. The coffee martini's great."

His smile returned. "Glad you like it." He took a drink of his and nodded. "Frederick does a good job at the bar."

"Does Frederick ever give out his recipes?"

Aidan shook his head. "No recipes. The guy mixes drinks instinctively now, and he probably couldn't tell you how to make this even if he wanted to."

"Then it's Google time for me, but guaranteed it won't be the same."

"Sorry."

The silence that followed that single-word response told her all she needed to know. That would have been his cue to mention bringing her back again sometime, and he hadn't said a word. She knew about Doug, but Aidan didn't, so something else was stopping him from pursuing the relationship.

Imagining what that might be was too depressing, so she wouldn't think about it. "The music's nice, too."

He studied her for a moment. "Would you like to dance?"

The question startled her, especially after she'd concluded that he had no interest in her whatsoever, other than her writing ability. "I wasn't dropping hints. You invited me for a drink, and that's what we're having. Please don't feel obligated to dance with me because I mentioned the music."

"I didn't ask because I feel obligated."

She checked his expression for sincerity. His light brown eyes were warm, and that cute little half smile had reappeared. *Talk about your mixed signals*. Now he *did* seem interested.

She had a horrible thought. What if he was the kind of man who was into conquests? She knew absolutely nothing about his personal life or his track record with women. He certainly had the physique and charisma to be a Don Juan. What if he planned to seduce her tonight and then mark her off a master list he kept in his head? *Bestselling author: check.*

Well, she had a built-in braking system for that kind of man. "I'm seeing someone."

"I figured you must be." His eyes glowed with good humor.

Now she felt gauche and unsophisticated. People danced all the time without heading straight for a bedroom afterward. He did have beautiful eyes. "Not that I think you meant anything by asking me to dance. I just thought you should know."

"So you don't want to dance?"

That was the problem. She'd love to dance with this man, who might or might not be trying to take advantage of her. If he had sex in mind, she wouldn't let things go that far. And it was only a dance.

And yet telling Doug that she'd had a drink with a fan after the signing was one thing. She wouldn't even have to mention that the fan was male, actually. But if she admitted that she'd also danced with said fan, the man-fan thing would become known and the incident would begin to look suspicious.

But the evening would never be repeated, either. She knew that because he hadn't offered to bring her back sometime for another coffee martini. So this would be her one and only opportunity to have a close encounter of the rhythmic kind with Aidan Wallace. Chickening out might make her feel less guilty about Doug, but she'd regret missing the experience of dancing with this hot guy.

Research. She'd nearly forgotten that she'd decided to make tonight all about research. What if the heroine in her next book decided to go dancing with the hunky hero? Sure, Emma could put her imagination to work as to how that would feel, but firsthand knowledge would definitely help.

"I'd love to dance," she said.

"Good." Standing, he took off his jacket and hung it over the back of his chair. He was even more magnificent without the jacket, which had somewhat disguised his pecs. The gray silk dress shirt, open at the collar, fit him like a dream.

She gulped a little more of her martini for courage

before standing and walking ahead of him to the dance
floor. Once there, she turned, prepared to be swept into
his strong arms.

Or not. The band switched numbers, launching into a
tune with a fast, driving beat. Emma glanced at Aidan,
who shrugged and smiled. Then he stepped onto the
floor and initiated the sexiest hip action she'd seen outside of *Dancing with the Stars*.

Adrenaline pumped through her system as she followed suit with a grin of delight. She had a few moves
of her own, and recently they'd been confined to the privacy of her apartment. Back in the day, she'd enjoyed
the club scene, but her intense career didn't give her the
time to party. Besides, she didn't have the right partner.
Doug was willing to dance, but his sense of timing left
something to be desired.

Aidan had the rhythm of a born athlete. If he made
love the way he danced—*Uh-oh, better not go there, girl.*
She quickly pulled herself back from the edge of that
perilous cliff of supposition. Instead of picturing Aidan
naked in tangled sheets, which she would not do, she
channeled her sexual energy into her dancing.

It was a decent plan, but ultimately a flawed one. She
couldn't dance without watching Aidan or she was liable to bump into him. She already felt less coordinated
than he was, and turning the dance floor into a mosh pit
wouldn't be cool.

Therefore she became aware of each swivel of his
hips, each thrust of his pelvis. She found herself mirror-
ing him in the same way she might if they were horizontal on an innerspring. They weren't touching, and yet she
felt his heat burning all the way to the forbidden zone,
the place she was supposed to keep safe and warm for
Doug.

Nothing was safe from a man like Aidan. She'd naively thought she could control the situation tonight. *Fat chance.* If this kept up, somebody would have to turn a fire hose on them.

But the music stopped, leaving them breathing fast and laughing as they gazed at each other. Before Emma could gather her wits, the band eased into a slow number.

Aidan closed the distance between them and drew her into his arms. The top of her head would have fit under his chin if she'd allowed herself to snuggle in. She resisted the impulse and gazed up at him. "Nice dancing."

"Same to you." He guided her in a lazy waltz, his thighs brushing hers. His touch was steady and gentle as he telegraphed his movements with subtle pressure against the small of her back. As with any talented dancer, he made his partner, aka Emma, look and feel good.

She'd never danced with such effortless pleasure in her life. He was weaving a spell that was a mixture of blatant sexuality and romantic tenderness. Women probably fell all over themselves to become a notch in this man's belt. Assuming he was a notches-in-the-belt kind of guy.

Conversation might help keep her out of trouble, though. "No fair," she said. "You've had lessons."

"Not formal lessons." He brought her a fraction closer, causing her breasts to settle against his firm chest. "I learned at family gatherings."

"You dance at family parties?" The idea of a family dancing together enchanted her almost as much as the thought of the party itself. She didn't have parties with relatives. Her family consisted of her and her mom. An aunt lived out in California, and Emma had some cousins there whom she barely knew. Her dad had left when she was a baby and had never been heard from again.

"It's a family tradition to have music at our events, so of course everybody is expected to learn to dance."

"That's nice." The closer he held her, the less she felt inclined to make conversation. He felt so damn good. Worse yet, he smelled good, too. She still couldn't identify his cologne, but she desperately wanted to nestle her cheek against his chest and breathe in that heady male fragrance. She longed to be seduced.

But she'd hate herself in the morning, so she resisted the snuggle urge. The alternative wasn't much better. She was left looking up into his caramel-colored eyes like a lovesick teenager, which was pretty much how she felt. Aidan was rich, handsome, and a terrific dancer. What woman wouldn't want all that in her bed?

"Do you have a girlfriend?" The second the words were out, she wanted them back. No doubt her face was turning red. *Lovely.* "Cancel that. Forget I asked. It's none of my business."

"No, I don't have a girlfriend."

By now they were plastered together from chest to groin. She could feel the steady thump of his heart, and . . . yes, his obvious arousal. Easing away from him would be the smart way to handle this. She'd always been a smart girl. But she'd never come up against— literally—the likes of Aidan Wallace. Now that she was in his arms, she never wanted to leave.

When the music ended, he studied her without loosening his hold. "I suppose you should be getting home."

Wanna come with me? "I suppose."

Something flickered in his eyes, as if he were wrestling with a problem. Then the sparkle disappeared, and his grip loosened. "I should probably be getting home, too. I'll call Ralph."

So that was that. When he released her, the cool air

of reason caressed her heated skin. Whether he was a playboy or not, he'd obviously decided against playing with her. Time to end this encounter, whatever it was. Time for Cinderella to climb into her pumpkin coach and leave the ball.

Dancing with her had been a bad idea, but Aidan had figured he was about to be pulled off the case and he'd wanted to see her dance in person just once. Fortunately, she'd missed seeing him signal the band to play a fast number. She probably thought that was an accident.

No, he'd engineered the whole sequence, and now he had only himself to blame for his present sexual frustration, which could lead to some embarrassing and potentially dangerous consequences. As he rode back to her apartment with her in the cozy rear seat of the town car, the backs of his hands prickled and his tailbone itched.

He'd inherited a rare genetic condition that showed up only every second or third generation. If he happened to be in human form when he was aroused with no prospect of satisfaction, his body strained to shift instead, as a kind of compensation. An orgasm could calm him immediately and stop the process, but that wouldn't be happening anytime soon.

He should have sent Emma home in the town car by herself. He could have called Roarke to come and get him. Then again, maybe not. If Roarke had been driving his Ferrari and using the fuzz buster, he'd probably made it back to the family estate and was enjoying a recreational run through the woods by now.

Okay, so Roarke might not have been available, but there had been other options for Aidan, like commercial limos. Still, he'd felt the need to see Emma safely home to her apartment. Once they were closed inside the backseat together, though, and his teeth ached with the need to sharpen and grow, he realized he was screwed, and not in a good way.

Worse yet, his chauffeur must have sensed that the air was thick with unmet sexual needs. Any werewolf would be able to pick up on that. That explained why Ralph kept his eyes on the road ahead and hadn't attempted conversation. He might have thought coupling was about to happen in the back of the town car.

Aidan needed a distraction, and he needed it now. He glanced at Emma. "Do you have your phone with you?"

"My phone?" She seemed startled. "Yes, I do, but I turned it off before the signing and never turned it back on. Why?"

"Can you access your e-mail on it?" He knew damned well she could, but he wasn't supposed to know, so he had to play the game and ask.

"Yes, but—oh, I get it." She unzipped her purse and pulled out her BlackBerry. "You want to see the e-mail from the creepy guy."

"Just to get an idea of how hard it'll be to trace." *And to keep me from grabbing you and kissing you until you let me do whatever I want right here in the backseat of the town car.*

That was the other part of the equation. Judging from the way she'd danced with him, the slightest bit of effort on his part would make her forget all about Dougie-boy. Knowing she wanted him while he could do nothing about it made the pressure to shift even worse. The beginnings of a pelt rubbed against his silk shirt.

"Sure. Just a sec." She turned on the phone and waited for an Internet connection. Seconds later she handed him the phone. "Here it is."

He gazed at the small screen and forced himself to

concentrate on the words there instead of allowing her scent to pull him into a sensual whirlpool from which there would be no escape. Once they started down that road, they wouldn't stop until they'd wrung each other out. The dancing had told him that.

If he'd wanted her a little less, he might chance making love to her tonight. That had been his criterion from his first sexual encounter, at the age of sixteen. He'd indulge only if he knew they could both walk away at the end of the affair. He'd been able to tell his Were lovers he would have to make a political match someday and therefore couldn't get serious. They'd always understood that.

For his human lovers, and he'd had a few, he'd chosen women who were too focused on their careers to think about settling down with one guy. They'd been attractive and sexy, but not a single one had affected him the way Emma did. And he hadn't even taken her to bed yet.

Yet. The word flashed like a neon sign in his brain. Had he actually thought such a ridiculous thing? The word *yet* implied that he saw taking her to bed as inevitable. He didn't. Damn it, he *didn't.*

He could beat this attraction, no matter how strong it seemed now. Just because he wanted to rip that red dress from her body and explore every inch of her soft skin didn't mean that he would. Just because he longed to stroke her pert breasts until—

"Can you see it okay?" she asked. "I can make the text bigger if you need me to."

"Thanks, but I can see it just fine. I'm thinking." His eyesight was far better than she would ever know. And he hadn't lied. He had been thinking, just not about the e-mail in front of him. As a result, his pelt had grown even thicker. When he transformed, his fur was deep brown tipped with silver, and he was afraid that some silver fur might be sticking out of the open neck of his dress shirt already.

Once again he focused on the e-mail, and this time he was able to actually read the damned thing.

Hey, babe, I can tell from the way you write about werewolves that you dig them. Girl, you need to get it on with a real werewolf, and I'm the one to show you the ropes. Write back and I'll meet you whenever and wherever you say. Until then, think of me as always—
Ready Fur U

Aidan growled.

"Aidan? Are you okay?"

Shit! He'd growled, and she'd heard him! He made a big production of clearing his throat before he turned to answer her. "I felt like I had something stuck in my throat. It's gone now."

She laughed. "You clearing your throat sounds a lot like a Doberman guarding the front door."

She couldn't know how close she'd come to describing exactly how he felt. Some asshole was trying to make contact with her for the purpose of sex. Aidan no longer cared whether the guy was a werewolf or only pretending to be so he could meet her. Aidan would track him to his lair, wherever that might be, and put him out of commission.

Emma's laughter faded. "You're looking really fierce right now. In fact, you're scaring me a little."

Immediately he offered her his most winning smile and hoped to hell his canines didn't look too frightening yet. "Sorry. It's just that I hate guys who use the Internet to harass women."

"Do you think you can find out where he is?"

"Absolutely. And I don't want to wait until tomorrow to start the process." As Ralph pulled up in front of her building, Aidan reached inside his suit jacket and took out another card. "If you'll send the e-mail to that address, I'll get on it tonight." Unwittingly he'd created a great cover for the fact that his guys were already working on the trace.

"Now that we're at my place, why not come up to my loft and use my computer? I'll make coffee."

God, did she have any idea what she was saying? He thought maybe she did. Lust shone in her blue eyes. She knew exactly what she was saying, and Doug had mentally been kicked to the curb.

He clenched his back teeth together to keep himself from saying yes. . . . Yes to the invitation, yes to the coffee, and yes to the sex that would definitely take place if he stepped foot inside her apartment. He might be able to accomplish the deed without her noticing that he'd become unusually hairy.

But he wouldn't do it. Roarke was going to be so proud of him. "Thanks, but you need sleep, and I can work better on my own equipment." Saying that nearly killed him, but he felt noble as hell.

"But—"

"Seriously, it's important to accomplish this, and it'll all go faster at my place." Which would be his office instead of his apartment, but she didn't have to know that. "I'll e-mail you the results when I'm done so you'll have the information in the morning and can pass it on to Jenny."

"Okay." The word was drenched in frustration and disappointment.

Hell, she seriously wanted him to spend the night

with her. And he wasn't going to. Roarke should give him a damned medal.

"We'll wait here while you let yourself in and go upstairs," he said. "Leave your phone on, and if there's any problem when you get up there, call me." He pulled his phone out of his jacket and turned it on. "I can be there in no time."

She gazed at him. "Sure you won't come up?"

His tail was growing and beginning to bush out. "I'm sure."

"Then I probably won't see you again until the next book comes out."

"Guess not." He doubted he'd be at her next signing. He could get a book autographed through Roger Claymore. That would be a safer option.

"Thanks for a terrific evening." Before he could stop her, she leaned forward and kissed him full on the mouth. Then she scrambled quickly out of the car, out of his reach, and closed the door.

His mouth felt branded by hers, and he wanted more, much more.

Ralph chuckled. "Guess you have something stuck in your throat again."

"Listen, Ralph, old buddy. You'd growl, too, if you—"

"Yeah, I know, Aidan. You get major points for not going up there."

"Mmm." Aidan kept his eye on her window until he saw the light go on. Then his phone rang and he immediately answered. "What?"

"Just wanted you to know that everything's fine. Good night, Aidan."

"Good night, Emma." He disconnected the phone and closed his eyes. "Drop me off in the park, Ralph. And step on it."

Ralph quickly navigated into traffic. "The park's risky. Let me take you north to the estate."

"No. Can't afford the time." Aidan gritted his teeth and fought the shift that was coming whether he wanted it to or not. "I want to make sure the guys are working on that e-mail trace."

"You're the boss." Ralph wove in and out of traffic.

As they neared the park, Aidan began pulling off his clothes. "If I run for a while, I should be able to shift back in an hour or so. Wait for me."

"Will do." Ralph drove into Central Park and cruised along slowly. "How's this?"

"Good. Not much light. Give me three minutes to finish shifting, and then come around and open the door for me."

"All right." Ralph didn't sound happy about it, but he would do what Aidan asked.

In exactly three minutes, the back door of the town car opened. Aidan leaped out and began to run, his paws scattering the remnants of snow left on the ground. He would run until he was exhausted. Maybe then he wouldn't want Emma with the fierceness only an alpha male could feel toward a woman who'd awakened his instinct to mate.

Chapter 4

Doug called at eight, waking Emma from a hot dream that involved Aidan and a grassy knoll. Aidan was licking up drops of the coffee martini he'd poured all over her naked body and she was . . . delirious.

She would have loved to find out what happened after that, and now she'd never know. She must have sounded as annoyed as she felt, because Doug immediately became contrite.

"Bad turnout last night, huh?"

"No. Why would you think that?"

His tone changed. "Because you're in a crappy mood."

"You woke me up, Doug. I haven't had coffee yet."

"Woke you up? It's past eight."

Barely. Emma rolled her eyes. Doug kept regular hours and had never quite adjusted to the fact she didn't. "I slept in."

"Did you and your mom stay out late last night, then?"

"No, Mom had to leave right after the signing, so I

went for a drink with one of my fans." There, she'd said it. She hadn't exactly told the truth, the whole truth, and nothing but the truth, but she'd thrown out a piece of information that was correct as far as it went.

"I'll bet you made her evening, too. See, if I'd gone, you wouldn't have felt free to do that, and I'm sure you girls had a great time sipping umbrella drinks and talking about sexy werewolves."

If Doug had called at nine, after Emma had brewed herself some coffee and consumed a cup or two, she might not have reacted so adversely to that patronizing remark. But he'd called at eight, when she was involved in a most excellent dream of passion and sexual adventure with a man who made her current boyfriend look like a dweeb. She was at least a quart low on caffeine, and come to think of it, her boyfriend *was* a dweeb.

"You know what, Doug? I just decided we should take a break from each other."

"What?"

"A break. A hiatus. A sabbatical. It's perfect timing because you're heading into tax season and I'm leaving on a book tour Friday morning."

"Emma, don't do this. I know you wanted me to show up last night, but the meeting was important. A couple of members are thinking of giving me their corporate business, and that would be huge."

"This isn't about last night." And it really wasn't. It was about this morning. Well, it might be about last night, but not in the way he thought. She might not be able to have Aidan Wallace, but she could start looking around for someone who was more exciting than Doug.

Because of her heavy writing schedule, she'd allowed herself to settle for someone who was near at hand, even if he did virtually nothing for her sexually. That wasn't fair to her, and it wasn't fair to Doug.

"Emma, let's have lunch today. We'll talk it out. I promise to come to the next book signing you have here in town."

"I'm not free for lunch, and I mean it, Doug. I don't think either of us is invested in this relationship the way we should be. Let's take a step back. After tax season is over, if we decide to continue seeing each other, we can talk about what we each want in a partner." Unfortunately for Doug, she now wanted muscles on her man.

"You don't want to see me until after April fifteenth? That's impossible."

"Why?"

"We have to review your tax picture."

She almost laughed but caught herself before she did. Laughing would be mean. The fact remained that he was more worried about her 1040 than their future as a couple. "Doug, you've been doing my taxes for five years. I don't think we need to review them in person."

"It's better if we do."

"You could be right." Privately she thought Doug liked using the sessions to parade his knowledge and pass out what he considered gold-plated advice. He got to be the authority and the big cheese during those meetings. She'd never enjoyed them much.

"Then let's set up a time."

"Let's not." She hoped he wouldn't screw up her taxes on purpose, but she didn't think he would stoop that low. "We can communicate by e-mail. Have a great tax season. I truly wish you the best."

"Wait. You can't just do this."

"It's for the best. Good-bye, Doug." Then she disconnected the call. When he immediately called back, she didn't answer. She did, however, listen to the message he left.

Emma, is it that time of the month?

Yep, he was a dweeb.

Aidan and his team had spent several hours on the e-mail trace, and then he had managed to grab some sleep at home. Now he was headed back to the Wallace building in lower Manhattan to report his findings to his father. Ralph picked him up, as usual.

Technically Aidan should have been exhausted, but the challenge of this case and his concern for Emma kept his adrenaline pumping. A good run always helped, too. His recreational romp through Central Park had been without incident.

Few people with any sense wandered around in there late at night anyway. Anyone at the park at that hour likely wouldn't be the kind of person who ran to the police for any reason, let alone because he or she'd seen a large brown-and-silver wolf loping through the trees.

Still, it had been a risk. Anything that called attention to the pack constituted a risk. Yet he'd been forced to do something that would allow him to work off his sexual tension so he could shift back into human form. Once he'd felt that beginning to happen, he'd bounded back to the town car so that he could use the privacy of the backseat to shift and then dress in the clothes he'd left there.

The sun was shining brightly the next morning when Ralph pulled up in front of the fifty-story building that housed Wallace Enterprises on the top two floors. "Want me to wait for you?"

"That's okay. I'm thinking you could use some time

off. If I need a ride anywhere, I'll get one of Dad's drivers."

Ralph smiled. "Thanks. I'll take you up on that. Maybe Fran and I will have lunch uptown and go to a matinee."

"Good idea. Have fun. I'll be in touch tomorrow." As Aidan entered the tall building and headed for the elevator bank, he realized he envied his driver, who'd been married to Fran for almost thirty years. They still loved each other, still enjoyed simple things like lunch and a movie. Aside from the fact they were both werewolves, they lived a fairly typical middle-class life.

Most of the time Aidan was happy about his privileged position in the Wallace empire. But a less privileged position would mean he'd be free to mate for love and not political expedience. He might look forward to a marriage like Ralph and Fran's.

He still wouldn't be able to choose a human like Emma, though. Sex with humans was common, but marriages were almost unheard of. A Were would never be able to keep his or her wolf status a secret from a spouse, so the spouse had to be trusted with the sensitive knowledge that a werewolf community existed. Understandably, that made the rest of the pack extremely nervous.

Because of Aidan's strong attraction to Emma, one that was mate-worthy, he'd have to steer clear of her, and he would, right after he fixed the current problem. Stepping out of the elevator, he walked across thick green-and-brown patterned carpet. Weres preferred something that reminded them of grass and the spongy texture of the forest floor.

Plants abounded here in the lobby. Aidan glanced at the giant flat-screen running videos similar to his that featured trees and waterfalls. Visitors thought the Wallaces were eco-conscious, and they certainly were that. But the decor was a matter of personal sanity more than a statement about conservation. Being surrounded by images of nature soothed his father and any other members of the pack who felt overwhelmed by the noise of the city.

From the lobby Aidan moved through the open double doors leading to the receptionist's office.

Gabrielle, a thirty-five-year-old Were who'd moved to New York from the San Francisco pack, looked up from her computer as he arrived. A redhead in human form, she transformed into a russet she-wolf. She was stunning either way, and had caught the eye of several members of the Wallace pack. But she'd recently ended a relationship in San Francisco and wasn't interested.

"He's expecting you, Aidan. Go on in."

"Thanks." In a detached sort of way, he noticed that he wasn't interested in flirting with her, either. When she'd taken the job, he'd thought they might enjoy a no-strings-attached affair, but she hadn't been ready for that. He'd continued to be friendly in hopes that she'd change her mind. But after an evening with Emma, he realized he didn't care whether Gabrielle changed her mind. At some point, he'd have to rid himself of what was becoming an obsession with the lovely Ms. Gavin, but he couldn't expect to do it until he'd finished the business at hand.

Opening the hand-carved door into his father's office, he allowed his eyes to adjust to the dim light. Howard Wallace didn't appreciate the floor-to-ceiling windows that graced nearly every Manhattan office of any size and importance, including this one. He didn't give a damn about the skyline, but he liked being up here, away from the traffic noise.

The office was scented with evergreens and peat moss because they were here in abundance in various planters around the room. Foliage covered the windows so that only a few rays of sunlight penetrated through the dense array of greenery. Aidan loved the feel of his dad's office and had used many of the design elements in his own apartment.

His own office was on the floor below this one, but his team used it more than he did. His job kept him on the move, which he happened to like.

Howard rose from his massive, yet rustic-looking, desk and came around it to embrace his son. A barrel-chested man in his late fifties, Howard still had all his hair, although it was snow-white. The pack alpha was a sight to behold when he transformed into a magnificent creature with snow-white fur. His striking appearance was legendary in the Were community.

Howard stood back to look at his son with obvious fondness. "What do you have for me, Aidan?"

Aidan knew that benevolence could change to stern censure under certain conditions. He hoped that wouldn't happen today. "A delicate situation, I'm afraid."

"Let's sit." Howard gestured toward a group of black leather chairs circling a low table in the corner of his office. "Do you want something to drink? Anything to eat?"

Aidan tried to remember when he'd done either. The few sips of a coffee martini might be the extent of it since an early dinner the night before. But he knew that his father's two-floor suite of offices included a kitchen and a world-class chef. And at the mention of food, Aidan discovered he was starving. "A roast beef sandwich would hit the spot."

"Say no more." Howard crossed to his desk and

picked up the phone. Moments later he returned to the circle of chairs and took a seat next to Aidan. "Gabrielle will see to it."

"Thanks, Dad." Now that Aidan had admitted to his hunger, he felt the contractions of his very empty stomach.

Howard shook his head. "I notice you're still in the habit of working straight through without eating. I admire the single-mindedness, but it's not good for your health. Your mother would raise a bigger ruckus than I, so be glad it's me who's telling you this."

"I'll try to do better."

"Good. If you pass out in the middle of an assignment, you won't be doing anyone any favors." Howard settled back in his chair. "Now tell me about Emma Gavin."

For one unsettling moment, Aidan thought his father had guessed Aidan's secret yearning for the talented Ms. Gavin. He took a deep breath and told himself that was crazy. Roarke wouldn't have said anything, and nobody else knew besides Sylvester. Sylvester wasn't a snitch, either.

"Our initial suspicions were wrong," Aidan said. "She not only has no inside source—she doesn't believe that werewolves exist."

Howard's gray eyes narrowed. "Are you absolutely sure of this?"

"Yes." He'd thought about it some more. If Emma had any idea that werewolves were real, she would have sensed the changes happening to him last night in the backseat of the town car. When humans believed that werewolves were a reality, it was as if they'd broken a secret code. If she'd known that code, she could have identified him easily.

"So we don't have a problem, after all."

"Not quite true."

Gabrielle knocked on the office door, and Howard invited her in. She brought a tray containing a fragrant sandwich and a bottle of Aidan's favorite mineral water. He was touched that she'd noticed such a small thing.

As she set the tray on the circular coffee table, she leaned down far enough to provide a glimpse of cleavage while glancing at Aidan from under her lashes. Damn, *now* she was ready to flirt with him, when his hormonal urges were all focused on a certain author of werewolf fiction.

"Thanks so much, Gabrielle." He smiled at her.

"Anytime." Her voice held that low, throaty quality that telegraphed sexual interest. "Anything else, Mr. Wallace?"

Howard looked at Aidan. "Anything missing, son?"

"Nope." Aidan unfolded the cloth napkin and laid it over his lap. "This is great."

"Then I guess we're good, Gabrielle. Hold my calls until Aidan leaves, okay?"

"Of course." With one last sultry glance in Aidan's direction, she left the office.

Howard blew out a breath. "I think she's coming out of hibernation. Just for the record, I don't care what happens between you two so long as it doesn't disrupt her work. And it goes without saying that she's not an acceptable mate for you, so it would have to be a temporary thing."

"I know that."

"Still, I can't expect you to be celibate, for God's sake, so go ahead, but don't mess up my office routine, please. Gabrielle's been reliable so far, and I'd hate for that to change."

"Dad, I'm not interested in Gabrielle." Aidan picked up half of the sandwich. "Right now I have work to do. My team pulled an all-nighter, and we found out a lot. Someone from the Chicago pack has contacted Emma and wants to show her what a real werewolf is like."

Howard nearly came out of his chair. "The hell you say! Leland's bunch? I'll call him right now."

"I wouldn't do that, Dad. It's Leland's son, Theo."

"Oh, dear God." Howard scrubbed a hand over his face. "That changes everything."

"I figured it would."

"Theo Henderson has delivered trouble to Leland's doorstep for all his nineteen years. Everyone sees it but Leland. He insists Theo's high-strung and he'll grow out of it. Leland never did believe that Theo was the one who broke into the zoo, drugged a couple of wolves, and dressed them in Armani."

"I didn't hear about that." Aidan put down his sandwich, no longer hungry. Once every hundred years or so a Were came along who chafed against the rule of concealment. These militant Weres advocated full disclosure followed by complete domination of all humans. "Do you think Theo has visions of a werewolf revolution of some kind?"

"I hope for all our sakes he's just a mixed-up kid. How Leland could have raised two such different Weres is beyond me. Nadia's a credit to the community, but Theo seems determined to make problems."

"Has he done anything else I should know about?"

"At Halloween he always insisted on dressing as a werewolf, and he's mouthed off a few times about how he resents not being able to shift whenever he feels like it. He's risked getting caught more than once."

Aidan couldn't fault Theo on that score, after his own inappropriate shift last night. But if Theo was doing it intentionally, that put him in a different category. "This isn't sounding good."

"No, but Leland wouldn't believe Theo's headed down revolutionary road, and I don't want to be the one to suggest it to him, considering that I have high hopes that Nadia will become your mate someday. You'd make a stunning pair."

Aidan ignored the weight of responsibility that settled over him with that statement. He recognized that Nadia was attractive. In her human form, she was tall with long dark hair that reached halfway down her back. In wolf form, she was glossy black with gray eyes. At the moment, the only eyes he cared to gaze into were blue.

"So I'm hoping you have some ideas for dealing with this Henderson pup," Howard said. "Ideas that don't involve confronting Leland. I see that as a last resort."

Aidan took a deep breath. "All right. I need you to contact Roger Claymore and have me assigned to travel with Emma as far as Chicago."

"I'll do that. Good plan."

"If you give the okay, I'll let her publisher know that the possible stalker is from there. I'll monitor the Chicago gig and intercept Theo if he should show up. I'll gently remind him that he's putting the entire werewolf community at risk and send him back home. I think I'll be very convincing."

Howard nodded. "I'm sure you will be." He stood. "Let me call Roger right now. When does Emma leave on tour?"

"Friday morning. She'll spend Friday night, all day Saturday, and Saturday night in Chicago. When she leaves there, I'll have neutralized the threat. I'll come home, and she can continue on to Denver for the rest of her tour."

"Excellent. I know you'll keep this on the down-low, as they say these days. It goes without saying that the less Emma knows about the Henderson-Wallace connection, the better."

"Right."

"I feel good knowing you'll be handling this, son."

Aidan squashed any feelings of uneasiness. He was the logical person for the assignment, because as the firstborn of the alpha, he carried the authority of the entire Wallace pack. He would be the most effective in shutting down Theo Henderson. Roarke might not approve of this trip, but Aidan could control himself. It was only two days. *And two nights.*

Chapter 5

"Jenny, it's ludicrous and unnecessary." Wearing gray sweats and a black wool sweater, Emma paced the hardwood floor of her loft as she clutched her BlackBerry to her ear. "You're telling me he's only nineteen, which means this is probably just a kid with a crush. I don't need a high-powered security expert like Aidan Wallace to fix this."

"I've lost control of the situation," Jenny said. "Howard Wallace has convinced Roger that Aidan needs to go. Because of Howard and Roger's long friendship, Wallace Enterprises is cutting Aidan's usual fee in half, and you know Roger can't pass up a bargain."

"Jenny"—Emma sighed in frustration—"how am I supposed to explain him to the bookstore folks? Won't they freak out if they think I'm in enough danger to need a bodyguard? Which I'm not, but having Mr. Muscles there will make it seem as if I could be kidnapped at any moment."

"Mr. Muscles." Jenny laughed. "That's good. Anyway, no worries about the explanation. I've canceled your media escort for Chicago. Aidan has your itinerary, and he'll become your escort for the Chicago gig. It's only two days, Em. You'll make my life a lot easier if you'll go along with this."

But what about my life? Emma couldn't imagine how she'd make it through two solid days with Aidan in tow. Last night had been embarrassing enough. She'd *kissed* him, for Christ's sake. She'd based that impulse on her firm belief that she wouldn't see him until the next book signing, and by then she'd have a sexy boyfriend to call her own, somebody who would stack up very well against Aidan Wallace, poster boy for Bowflex.

"Please, Em," Jenny said. "Howard's put the fear of God into Roger, and he's acting like a mother hen over here. Next thing you know, he'll decide to go along and monitor your Chicago appearances."

Emma closed her eyes in resignation. "Okay." So she'd have to be humiliated. She could only imagine what Aidan thought about this, being told to keep a grown woman safe from a love-struck teenager.

Damn, she'd made such a fool of herself last night, too. She'd practically begged him to come upstairs with her, and he'd turned her down. Twice. But had she attempted to retain her dignity in the face of his double rejection? *Nope.* She'd planted one on him, just so he'd know for sure that she craved his body.

Ayiyiyi. How could she face him at JFK on Friday morning? She had only one option—to play the cool professional who considered this whole exercise ridiculous. She did think it was ridiculous, but playing the cool professional in the presence of his hot body would take some doing.

*　　　*　　　*

Aidan arrived at the gate early on Friday morning. He hadn't seen Emma in the line going through security, and she wasn't in the gate area, either. He hoped to hell she wouldn't show up at the last minute, or worse yet, miss the plane. She had a tendency to run late, something he knew from those months of watching her.

He bought coffee and sipped it as he paced the gate area and cast frequent glances down the concourse. Nothing. He should have followed his first impulse and insisted on picking her up in the town car to guarantee she'd be on time.

They'd exchanged a couple of brief e-mails in which he'd suggested exactly that, and she'd refused the offer. Not surprising, considering the way he'd rejected her invitation on Wednesday night. She'd want to keep her distance, and that was all for the better, especially considering the plan he'd devised to make sure Theo backed off.

Posing as her media escort wouldn't be enough. Aidan had decided to present himself as her fiancé, but he had to make sure the masquerade didn't tempt him to get too chummy with her. If she remained aloof, that would help.

When the gate attendant announced boarding for first-class passengers, he pulled out his BlackBerry and called her. No answer. Damn it, this was not a good way to start out.

He caught her scent before he saw her, but then, there she was, striding toward the gate in three-inch black heels and pulling a wheeled computer case. Her blond hair bounced around her shoulders, and her black trench coat was unbuttoned. It flapped back to reveal a turquoise suit that hugged her curves in a way that made his mouth go dry. She wore a white lace camisole under the jacket, and the shadow of her cleavage was visible through the delicate lace. This would be a very long two days.

"They're calling for us to board," he said as she approached. In the thirty-six hours they'd been apart, he'd kidded himself that he'd overreacted to her on Wednesday night. *Wrong.*

"You switched me to first class!" Her blue eyes flashed with indignation. "I've been down at the ticket counter trying to change back to coach, but they'd already sold my original seat."

She smelled absolutely wonderful. "Jenny didn't tell you she rebooked?"

"No, she did not, and for good reason. She knows I'd have a fit."

He had to work hard not to laugh. Leave it to Emma to complain about an upgrade. "What's wrong with first class?"

"Everything! It's elitist and overpriced and a waste of resources because fewer people fit in that space."

Jenny had clearly wimped out and left him to deal with Emma's objections. So he would. Going first-class was in his blood, and besides, booking at the last minute meant he wouldn't have been able to sit with her in coach. Instead he would have been squashed into a middle seat in the tail section. Not his idea of fun, and inefficient, to boot. He needed to be right beside her when they deplaned. He wasn't letting her out of his sight until he'd made sure Theo Henderson wouldn't do something stupid. Buying two new tickets had seemed like the way to go. With Wallace Enterprises footing the bill, Jenny had agreed, although she'd mentioned Emma might not be happy about it.

Emma was definitely not happy. She stood in front

of him, throwing off sparks of irritation. But unless she wanted to give up on the Chicago part of her tour, she was stuck with him in first class.

"I'm sorry you're upset about the seats," he said. "But they can't be changed at this point."

"I suppose not. Most people would be grateful, wouldn't they?"

"I would say so."

"It just goes against my principles."

"Sorry. At least we're taking public transportation."

She stared at him. "Don't tell me you considered taking the Wallace corporate *jet*?"

"Jenny said you'd never go for it."

"That's a colossal understatement." She shook her head in obvious dismay. "The corporate jet. So you're actually slumming by taking this flight."

"Well, I wouldn't quite put it that way."

She heaved the sigh of someone whose burdens were too much to bear. "I suppose I'll have to consider this research. Shall we go?"

He swept a hand toward the gate. "After you."

She was all smiles for the woman taking tickets, but she remained cool toward Aidan as they made their way down the Jetway to the plane. Because Aidan and Emma hadn't boarded with the rest of first class, coach passengers were lined up ahead of them waiting to get on. That meant standing together in the Jetway as an awkward silence developed between them.

Aidan decided to break it before it became a solid block of ill will. "You'll only have to endure this for one leg of your tour," he said. "When you leave Chicago on Sunday, you'll be in the seat Jenny reserved in the first place."

She glanced at him. "I didn't mean to be a brat about

it, but I don't like having someone manipulate my life without telling me. Jenny should have told me, but she didn't. I was wrong to take it out on you. I apologize."

"Apology accepted. And I confess that if I can't take the corporate jet, I'm all about first class. I don't fit into the coach seats very well."

"I guess you wouldn't. And considering how bogus the whole trip is for you, I can't expect you to make it crammed into coach, which would only add insult to injury."

"Who said it was bogus?"

As the line began moving again, he and Emma moved with it.

Looking over her shoulder at him, she rolled her eyes. "Come on, Aidan. Jenny told me he's *nineteen.* He read one of my books, and now he's enjoying a vicarious thrill by sending me e-mails pretending that he has special powers."

His senses sharpened. "Did you mean to say *e-mails,* as in more than one?"

"He's sent a couple more, both early this morning. Now that I know he's a kid, they don't worry me. I think your father and my publisher are making way too much of this, and now they've included you in the insanity." She walked toward the doorway of the plane.

"You didn't delete the e-mails, did you?"

"I thought about it, but no, I haven't." She walked onto the plane.

Thank God for small favors. He followed her. "Window or aisle?"

"Window. I love looking out."

That worked nicely for him. Even in first class, his legs felt cramped if he ended up by the window, so he always chose the aisle.

The flight attendant took Emma's coat and hung it up. For a moment, Aidan thought Emma would insist on hanging up her own coat, but then she relinquished it, thanked the attendant, and took her seat. She tucked her computer case under the seat in front of her and sat back.

Aidan's finely tuned hearing picked up a little sigh of pleasure, and he turned away so she wouldn't hear him chuckle. She might disapprove of first-class seats on principle, but her body loved being cushioned in that comfy leather.

Then he groaned inwardly as his hormone-soaked brain focused on that sensuous little body of hers nestled in the seat next to his. Hours ago, he'd convinced himself he could do this without danger of sprouting fur, and yet the backs of his hands were already starting to prickle.

He handed off his topcoat and tucked his own computer case under the seat in front of them. "Mind if I take a look at those two e-mails?"

"Be my guest." She called them up and handed her BlackBerry over as the flight attendant came by asking about coffee.

He smiled at the attendant and shook his head before going back to the screen and Theo's messages.

"Regular with just a tiny bit of cream, please," Emma said.

He glanced up. She'd been taking two creams for the past three months. "Why only a tiny bit?"

"Because cream is fattening, and I'm cutting back."

"You're dieting?"

"I always do after turning in a book. I tend to eat more when I'm on deadline, so this is how I balance it out." She fastened her seat belt.

He hadn't meant to watch her do that, but he couldn't seem to keep himself from observing how the belt rode low and tight over her hips, exactly as the flight attendant would instruct them to fasten them during takeoff.

Emma had terrific hips, in his estimation. She had terrific everything. He'd hate to see even an ounce disappear from that curvy figure. Then he heard himself say, against all good judgment, "But you're perfect."

Her eyes rounded. "Excuse me?"

"I . . . meant that you're perfectly okay now. I don't get the dieting thing."

"Thank you." She took a breath. "You confuse the hell out of me, Aidan."

"I'm not surprised. I confuse myself sometimes."

"The other night I thought you were interested in me, but then I decided you weren't. Now you seem interested again. I'm getting whiplash."

Aidan grabbed the first lifeline he could think of. "You said you had a boyfriend."

"So that's why you didn't come up the other night?"

When he looked into those blue eyes of hers, he had a hard time lying. "No, not really."

"I didn't think so."

He could tell her some of the truth, at least. "The fact is, I tend to have a one-track mind, and I was focused on tracing that e-mail. I knew if I came up to your loft, I'd lose focus."

"You're quite the dedicated guy, aren't you?"

"Guess so."

"I admire that, Aidan." She looked past him toward the aisle. "Thank God. My coffee's here."

"Your first cup?" He helped the flight attendant pass the steaming cup over to her.

"'Fraid so. I was a little rushed this morning."

He started to say that explained a lot about her quick temper, but stopped himself.

"Ah, manna from heaven." She closed her eyes and breathed in the vapors before taking a long, slow sip. "I think I'll live now."

He couldn't resist. "In coach they won't get coffee until we reach altitude and level off."

"Smart-ass." She smiled. "I understand the appeal of sitting up here. Maybe I'm afraid I'll get used to it. You know, get spoiled."

"Would that be so terrible?"

She studied him. "I think so. The money's coming in now, but I'm a self-employed writer. There's no guarantee the money will always be there. At this point, I haven't made enough to keep me in first-class seats for the rest of my life."

He stated what she had to be thinking. "Whereas I was born with a silver spoon in my mouth."

"Pretty much."

He nodded. "I'll own that. I'm probably spoiled." He thought about the house where he'd grown up, a ten-bedroom mansion filled with original art. Maids, cooks, chauffeurs. His father was an investment genius, and the family had weathered a couple of recessions without suffering.

"Don't get me wrong," she said. "I've noticed that the people you employ are treated with respect and consideration. I've heard that the Wallace family supports a whole raft of charities. I'm not dissing your situation. But it's different from mine."

She had no idea how different.

"My dad abandoned my mom when I was a baby, and she managed to raise me and keep a roof over our heads, but it was never easy."

"I met your mom at the signing. She seems like an intelligent woman."

Emma's eyes lit up. "She is. She mentioned that she'd stopped to say hello. Listen, about Doug, my boyfriend, I—"

The plane's engines revved up, cutting off the rest of what she'd been about to say. Knowing he'd have to shut down her BlackBerry any second, Aidan quickly glanced over Theo's two e-mails.

Hear you're coming to Chi-town, sweet thing. Looking forward to making that special connection, if you know what I mean. I'm still . . .
Ready Fur U

Aidan scrolled to the next one.

Hey, there! Weres do it on all fours! Think about it. I'm always . . .
Ready Fur U

Aidan ground some enamel off his back molars. Sure, Theo was just a kid, but even a kid could get himself and his fellow Weres into deep trouble. That was Aidan's intellectual evaluation.

But the e-mails affected him at a deeper level. Emma was not his mate, would never be his mate. And yet any sexual interest from another male aroused every possessive instinct he had. Maybe that wasn't a bad thing for the short term.

Theo might not cower before someone sent as Emma's bodyguard. But he would cringe in fear if Aidan presented himself as Emma's mate, a Were ready to defend her to the death. Aidan wasn't certain he could play that role and then abandon it again on Sunday. Doing so could end the problem with Theo, though. He'd have to think about it.

"Sir," the flight attendant said, "I'll have to ask you to turn off your phone."

"Right." He quickly put his cell number in a vacant speed dial position. Then he powered down the Black-Berry and handed it back to Emma as the attendant went through the seat-belt-and-flotation-device spiel. "You now have me on speed dial, letter z."

"Oh." She looked annoyed. "I guess that's okay."

"You can change it on Sunday afternoon."

"Don't worry. I will."

He settled back in his seat and tried to imagine himself running through the forest. Flying made him uneasy, which was another reason for choosing first class. Wolves weren't meant to be suspended thirty thousand feet in the air. Flying made his ears hurt and dried out his sinuses. When he flew alone, he drowned out the engine noise by wearing top-grade earphones tuned to a medley of forest sounds, but that wouldn't be happening today.

As they taxied down the runway, he gripped the armrests and swallowed. Visualization wasn't working for him this morning.

Emma must have noticed, because she glanced at him with undisguised curiosity. "Aidan, are you afraid of flying?"

"No."

"You are so! It's nothing to be ashamed of. Lots of people are spooked by the idea of being up in the air with no visible means of support."

"Thanks for that description." Aidan closed his eyes and clenched his jaw. Each time he did this, he promised himself he'd try hypnosis next time. But he never remembered until it was too late and he was headed for the airport.

"I've found the best remedy is distraction," Emma said. "So let's talk about something unrelated to flying. How about the weather?"

Aidan groaned. "Ice on the wings. I'd forgotten about that. We could end up with ice on the wings, and we'd go down like a rock."

"Okay, then politics. The world situation."

"Terrorists. Somebody could be on the plane with a bomb, and we'd never know. On a train or a bus, you have a fighting chance, but up in the air—"

"How about my love life? We could talk about that."

Aidan opened his eyes and turned his head to stare at her. "You're going to tell me about your love life?"

"See? You're already distracted."

"Go on." It did help to focus on her. He couldn't very well take her with him on every future flight, but for now, she was a great solution. "What about your love life?"

"You know that boyfriend I told you about?"

"Yes." He knew way more about Dougie-boy than she could imagine.

"We're taking a break from each other."

Ah. It shouldn't have mattered to him at all, but a surge of excitement told him it mattered, all right. "Since when?"

"Yesterday."

"Emma, if this has anything to do with me, that's not good, because I—"

"It does and it doesn't. It does because I had such a great time on Wednesday night that I realized Doug and I might not be right for each other. So I thank you for that. We needed to take a break."

"Look, if you're thinking we might hook up, there are several reasons why that wouldn't be a good idea." All he had to do was figure out which ones he could tell her without making her suspicious about his family.

She laughed. "You are so right about that. Several I can think of."

"What do you mean?" He'd thought he'd have all the reasons on his side.

"Well, I'll be the first to admit that my next lover will be physically more like you and less like Doug."

"That's flattering." He sincerely doubted her next lover would be physically anything like him.

"I can't deny that I'm very attracted to you physically. But I'm looking for someone who recycles the Sunday *Times*."

"I do that." Why he felt the need to mention it was beyond him. Besides, he only left instructions for his maid to recycle it, which might not count for as much in her book.

"I'm glad you do. Recycling is a small thing, though. I need someone who rides the subway and flies coach, someone who has to think twice before he buys a ticket to a Broadway play and has to save for months in order to afford a tropical vacation. The truth is, Aidan, gorgeous though you are, you're too rich for my blood."

Aidan tried to remember if any woman had said that to him in his life. *Nope.* None had. He had the impression that for most women, his money was an aphrodisiac. They liked the luxuries it could provide—exotic getaways, fine food, sensual spa treatments. He wouldn't date a woman who cared *only* about money, but enjoying the thrills money could buy wasn't a crime. Except to Emma, apparently.

"I do believe I've shocked you, Aidan."

"Could be."

"Distracted you pretty well, too, didn't I? Look out the window. We're airborne."

He leaned past her to check that out, and sure enough, they'd lifted above the layer of winter clouds suspended over New York City. Leaning closer to her wasn't such a good idea, though. Her scent filled his nostrils, and he remembered the way her lips had felt pressed against his on Wednesday night.

Turning slightly, he gazed into her eyes as a wave of lust moved through him. "Too rich for your blood, huh?"

Her breath caught, and her lips parted slightly. "Yes."

"And all along I thought you were too rich for mine." With a supreme effort, he leaned back in his seat and stared straight ahead while he fought against the arousal that was making the backs of his hands prickle and his tailbone ache. Shifting at thirty thousand feet would not be a good thing.

Chapter 6

Emma wasn't always so quick on her mental feet, but she'd executed a nice two-step that time. She'd managed to tell Aidan the exact truth and restore her sense of dignity in one fell swoop. Nice work if she did say so.

She still didn't know where he stood. Those mixed signals continued to be mixed. *No matter.* He knew where she stood, and that was a safe and sane distance away from him.

Discovering he was afraid of flying had given her another boost of confidence. Up to now she'd thought he was a perfect specimen, with no faults to speak of. A fear of flying didn't make him any less manly or yummy, but it did make him human.

Unsnapping her lap belt, she leaned over and pulled her computer case out from under the seat in front of her. Now would be a good time to flip open her laptop and present a picture of the working writer. She doubted she'd get much done sitting next to Aidan's hunky self, but he wouldn't know whether she was working or composing a letter.

Best of all, he wouldn't be inclined to start a conversation while she was typing. She was happy with the current balance of power, and another discussion might upset it. He affected her more than she wanted him to know, but the good news was that it cut both ways.

After booting up her computer, she had to come up with something to type and decided she might as well brainstorm ideas for her next book. She'd never considered whether werewolves would mind flying, but logically they wouldn't be very well suited to it. So far as she knew, no furry creature enjoyed the change in air pressure, the noise, or the smell of jet fuel.

She could create a plot that would require her hero to overcome his resistance to flying in order to save the heroine from something or other. Maybe she was a bush pilot in Alaska. That worked. She could crash-land in a remote area populated by a pack of werewolves. Maybe she'd be hurt in such a way that she'd have to teach the hero-werewolf how to fly or she'd be forever stranded there.

As the story outline took shape, she found herself on a roll. Instead of being distracted by Aidan sitting next to her, she was inspired by his solid presence and his scent. Yes, his actual scent, which she still couldn't identify, despite all these close encounters.

Aidan had taken out his computer, too, and was looking through some files. One quick glance told her it was some sort of spreadsheet. At some point she admitted that this was very nice, riding up in first class, where a person could get a glass of juice anytime. She liked having room to work on a laptop without being squished, and she most especially liked sitting beside a man who smelled as good as Aidan.

But she'd meant what she'd said. Despite enjoying

the heck out of this experience today, she was only gathering material for her research. She wrote about rich people, as well as middle-class and poor people. Hanging out with Aidan temporarily would help her write a more realistic rich person.

From the corner of her eye, she studied his hands. They looked strong and supple, with a light dusting of hair over the backs. His nails were neatly trimmed, maybe by a manicurist. He had no cuts or scratches on his hands and no visible calluses, which made sense. He was a businessman, not a laborer.

His cheeks were perfectly shaved, too, and his hair trimmed as if he had it done every few days. Wallace Enterprises probably had a barber on staff. The rich, or at least this rich family, appeared to be well-groomed.

"Like what you see?" His cheek creased in a smile.

"Sorry. I didn't mean to stare."

"That's okay." He glanced at her. "My ego loves it."

"I have a research question, in case I want to create a character who's rich."

Laughter danced in his golden eyes. "The PC word is *wealthy.*"

"Is that so? Then why was there a TV show called *Lifestyles of the Rich and Famous*?"

"Easier to market, maybe, but trust me—the word people with money actually use is *wealthy.*"

"I don't see what's wrong with *rich.* It's short, to the point, punchy. Hemingway would have liked it a lot better than *wealthy.*"

Aidan powered down his laptop and closed the cover. "Are you sure about that? Because if you use *rich* to mean that someone has a lot of money, what can you use to describe a thick wedge of chocolate cake with dark chocolate frosting?"

"Decadent."

"You're using three syllables when one syllable would do."

"Okay, then. *Moist.* And thanks a lot, because now I want some of that, and there goes my diet." She loved talking words, but she didn't meet too many men who would debate language choice with her.

"*Moist* isn't good enough. A sponge can be moist, but it sure as hell isn't rich."

"How about *intense*?" The conversation was becoming something of a turn-on.

He shook his head. "Not the same. If I tell you the chocolate cake is rich, then you can almost taste it."

"I guess." She remembered not long ago, when she'd told him he was too rich for her blood, he'd countered that she was too rich for his. Now that comment took on a whole other meaning, one that she'd do well to forget about. She had no doubt that if they ever ended up in bed, the experience would be exceedingly rich.

Good thing the world included chocolate, which she'd always found a decent substitute for hot sex. "You don't suppose they have any chocolate cake on the plane? I'm getting a real craving, here."

He reached up and pressed the call button. "Let's see."

But alas, they soon discovered the galley wasn't stocked with cake.

Aidan glanced at his watch. "We land in thirty minutes. Can you wait forty-five for that cake?"

"Obviously you haven't looked at the schedule. We go straight from the airport to a radio interview. There's no cake time in there."

"Sure there is. You'll have your cake and eat it, too."

"That's cute, Aidan, but we're not going to cruise

along Michigan Avenue looking for a deli and end up being late for the interview. I'm a big girl, and I'm supposed to be dieting. I can live without cake."

"But you don't have to." He gave her a slow smile. "You're with me."

Dear God, that smile was turning her into a pile of goo. She barely had the breath to respond. "What do you mean by that?"

"As I said, cake is rich. I'm wealthy."

"And proud of it, I see." She didn't want to be impressed by his cool confidence tinged with a certain amount of sexy arrogance. She didn't want to feel like Cinderella at the ball. But that pretty much described her situation. She could fight it, and him, or she could sit back and enjoy the view from the pumpkin coach.

The second option made more sense. But she'd have to be careful not to enjoy it too much.

The flight attendant came by and asked them to stow their computers for the landing, and she noticed that Aidan tensed up. Most people who were afraid of flying tended to dread the takeoff and landing the most.

If she drew him into another conversation, he might forget that they were in a descent. She'd meant to ask him something else before they got into the semantics of wealthy versus rich. What had it been?

Oh, yes. His hair. "I never asked my research question," she said.

He glanced over at her. "You're trying to distract me from the landing, aren't you?"

"Uh-huh."

"I appreciate that." Once again, his fingers gripped the armrests. "Go for it."

"Does your family have a hairstylist on retainer?"

His quick grin told her she'd hit on a subject that

amused *him*. "You mean like the Hollywood stars who have somebody following them around with a pair of scissors and a blow-dryer?"

"Well, yeah. What's so funny?"

"I'm trying to picture my dad putting up with that, or my mom, for that matter. But there is a salon on the ground floor of the building where we have our offices."

"A building your family owns, I assume."

"Right, but we rent out most of it, and one of the tenants is a top-notch salon. We go in when we need to. No big deal."

"What about your fingernails?"

"Why? Are they dirty?" He lifted both hands and inspected them.

"Just the opposite. They look manicured." She congratulated herself on getting him to let go of the armrests.

"I trim them myself, but that's all I do. The whole family has strong nails and teeth."

When he'd lifted his hands she'd noticed his watch. "Is that a Rolex?"

"No, it's a Blancpain."

"Huh. I've never heard of that, which probably means it's superexpensive. Hundreds, probably." When he didn't respond, she figured she was low. "Thousands?"

"Well, I didn't buy it, but I'd guess it cost a little under eight hundred."

"Dollars?"

"Thousand."

She gasped. *"No."* Then she glanced at him to see whether he was kidding. "You're making that up."

"Nope. It was a birthday present from my folks, so I don't know the exact cost, but there are a limited number of these made, which makes them pricey."

"Pricey? You're wearing the equivalent of a really

nice Brooklyn apartment on your wrist, and you call it *pricey*? I call it outrageous!"

He unbuckled the strap and handed it to her. "If you take a closer look, you'll see why it costs so much. There's a calendar on it, as well as a lunar-phase dial, and the—"

"Keep it away from me." Emma held up both hands. "I don't want to lay a finger on a watch that's worth eight hundred grand."

"Oh, for heaven's sake. Take it. You said you wanted to do research on how the wealthy live. One thing we tend to do is buy limited-edition watches like this."

"Why?" She took the watch, handling it like a live bomb. The strap and metal case were seductively warm.

"Because we value the workmanship and the tradition of watchmaking. At least that's what my dad said when he gave it to me. He expects me to pass it on to one of my kids."

Thinking of him with children sent a little pang of longing zinging through her heart. It was just a little pang, though, because he was so out of her league.

She chose to underline that fact. "I'd hate to be the kid who inherits this watch. Just my luck, I'd leave it in a gym locker or accidentally knock it into the sink when the garbage disposal was running."

"I'll admit I have to be more careful with it than I would with a cheaper watch."

"No kidding. You do realize you could get a Casio, which would do most of this stuff."

"I have a phone that does most of this stuff. But . . . it's a Wallace tradition. We wear really good watches. Roarke has one that's worth about the same or maybe even a little more."

She handed it back to him with great care. "It's very

classy looking, but then it should be for eight hundred large." Her mother had given her a watch for her high school graduation. It had cost around fifty bucks. True, it had gone on the fritz a couple of years after that, but she still had it in her dresser drawer because her mother had given it to her.

"I suppose I've never questioned spending this kind of money on a watch." He fastened the strap around his wrist again.

"That's the sort of thing I need to know for my research, the things a rich—I mean *wealthy* person takes for granted."

He gazed at her. "Let's say you had more money than you could ever spend. What would you do with it?"

"Oh, that's easy. I'd buy my mom an apartment somewhere on Central Park West because she's always talked about how wonderful it would be to live there, alongside people like Barbra Streisand. Then I'd get her a country home in Upstate New York where she could spend her vacations."

"You don't think that would be too extravagant?" He asked the question as if he really wanted to know.

"Of course it would be extravagant, but you said I'd have more money than I'd know what to do with. After I got her all set up, I'd research what charities to support, maybe start a foundation of some kind."

He smiled. "Would you buy a Blancpain watch?"

"Uh, that would be a negative." The wheels of the plane touched down on the runway. "And we're in Chicago."

"That's the best time I've ever had on a plane, Emma. Thank you."

"So should I assume you've never become a member of the mile-high club?"

He stared at her a moment before starting to laugh. "Uh, that would be a negative."

"Because of your fear of flying?"

"No, because of my fear of getting stuck permanently in an airplane bathroom." Still smiling, he studied her. "You would fit, though, if the guy wasn't huge. Are you a member?"

"That would be a negative."

He was definitely teasing her. "Then how are you ever going to write about it if you haven't tried it?"

"I don't have to research *everything*, Aidan. Obviously I have to use creative license for some things. It's not like I'm ever going to have sex with a werewolf, you know."

Something flashed in his eyes, something that looked very much like desire. Then it was gone. "No, I guess you won't ever do that."

She had an epiphany. God, she should have figured it out earlier. Aidan wasn't all that different from Theo, the nineteen-year-old kid who'd e-mailed her. Aidan had read her sex scenes and was convinced she was hot stuff in bed.

If only that were true. She was hardly a virgin, but she'd never experienced the kind of mindless ecstasy she wrote about. She wasn't even positive it existed in the real world. She could tell him that she used her imagination for the sex in the books, too, but he might not believe her. He was a man carried away by a fantasy. A fantasy she'd created.

But he had sense enough to know that they came from completely different worlds, and once the sex was over, whether it lived up to his expectations or not, they'd have nothing much in common. She wouldn't feel at home in his world, and he wouldn't want to scale down his lifestyle to fit into hers.

Correction—he *wouldn't* scale down his lifestyle, as evidenced by the fact they'd flown to Chicago first-class. True, he'd given up the corporate jet, but now he was in Chicago, a city full of luxury options. As she thought about that, she wondered whether he'd made any other changes.

"I understand the media escort was canceled," she said. "Did you book a rental car?"

"A car and driver will meet us at the airport and take us wherever we need to go."

She should have guessed that he wouldn't be driving her around in a subcompact from Hertz. "I forgot to ask about your accommodations while we're here. Were you able to get a room at the hotel?"

He looked wary. "We'll be at the Palmer House instead."

She should have guessed that, too. The Palmer House was historic and would appeal to old money. "The penthouse?"

"It was available."

"I'll just bet it was." She'd heard about it—eleven rooms of luxury—but had never expected to see it in person.

"You can consider it research."

"Don't worry, Aidan. That's exactly what I'll do." No doubt about it, she'd be traveling in the pumpkin coach this weekend. She might as well relax and enjoy the ride.

Chapter 7

Aidan switched on his phone while they were still on the plane and called the car service. While the flight attendant helped Emma with her coat, he gave the driver quick instructions.

Whatever it took, he wanted a single serving of chocolate cake from one of Chicago's best bakeries to be waiting in the town car by the time he and Emma reached it. Yes, he was showing off, and yes, he should cut it out. But he couldn't resist making this happen. He ended the call right as Emma turned around.

"Just checking to make sure the car service is on time," he said.

"They wouldn't dare be late, would they?"

He had to smile. She was beginning to get the picture. The cake would blow her away. "No, but it doesn't hurt to give them a nudge."

Getting off the plane took a while, and Aidan was grateful because the cake wasn't going to be an easy trick. He expected one person to be waiting with a sign at the end of the concourse and another to be running down the cake request. In any event, a chauffeur holding a sign printed with the name WALLACE waited as they left the secure area of O'Hare.

Aidan approached the man, who was a short, compact guy of about forty-five. He wore a navy blazer and no hat, but his most distinguishing feature was a long handlebar mustache.

None of the werewolves Aidan knew sported facial hair. They usually got enough of that when they shifted. Aidan didn't pick up any werewolf vibes from the chauffeur, so apparently Aidan's secretary had gone outside the Were community for this service.

Fortunately, Aidan hadn't felt the presence of any Weres at all since getting off the plane. That meant Theo hadn't somehow found out Emma's flight information, which was a good thing. Maybe they'd be lucky and Theo wouldn't show up all weekend, but Aidan doubted that.

He approached the chauffeur and held out his hand. "I'm Aidan Wallace."

The chauffeur gave him a firm handshake. "Barry Dinsmore. Welcome to Chicago, Mr. Wallace." He glanced over at Emma. "Ma'am, I'll take your carry-on."

"Thanks, but I'd rather keep it." Emma clutched the handle of her rolling computer case as if it contained the secrets of the ages. Aidan had noticed her typing up a story idea on the plane, so in a way, the computer could be more valuable to her than gold.

He hoisted his computer case strap over his shoulder. "Then we're off."

"Wait." Emma stood rooted to the floor in the middle of the stream of passengers. "I have checked baggage."

"Just give Barry your claim-check. Someone will take care of it."

"Someone? But I don't . . ." She looked uncertain.

"It'll be fine, Emma. I promise you'll get your luggage." He flicked a glance in the chauffeur's direction. "You can handle that, right?"

"Absolutely, sir. All I need is the claim-check."

"Okay, although this seems very weird." Emma rummaged through her purse and produced her ticket envelope with the claim-check stapled to it. "You can't miss which one is mine. At least I don't think you can. It's orange, but I've written my name on the luggage tag in case there are two orange suitcases."

"Orange. Got it."

"And it's about so big." She measured out the size with her hands. "Oh, and I have a lime green ribbon tied on the handle to make it even easier to identify."

Aidan tried not to shudder. This was why he'd wanted to take the corporate jet, so they wouldn't be dealing with the horrors of baggage claim and orange suitcases with green ribbons tied on the handle. Emma would no doubt call him a snob for those thoughts, so he kept them to himself.

"I'll remember that, ma'am," the chauffeur said. "First I'll settle you both in the car, and then I'll fetch your luggage. If you'll follow me."

Emma turned to Aidan as they trailed after the chauffeur. "What about you? Don't you have luggage?"

"You don't want to know."

"Probably not, but you might as well tell me. Are you buying a new wardrobe when we get to the hotel?"

"No. I had my clothes delivered to the penthouse last night. They're already hanging in the closet."

"Of course they are." She threw up both hands. "Why didn't I think of that?"

"Give yourself time." Aidan was struggling not to laugh. "You'll get the hang of this."

"No, I won't. I'll never get the hang of how the other half lives. It's crazy."

"Here's the thing, Emma. By traveling with me, you'll be safer than you would be if you traveled by yourself. That's part of the security service. The resources of Wallace Enterprises will create a protective barrier around you while you're in Chicago, where this Theo character lives."

"All this for a nineteen-year-old. If he knew, he'd be so flattered."

"Trust me. He'll know. One of the tactics will be letting him think you're engaged to me."

"Hey! You can't just spring something like that on me, Aidan. I should have something to say about it, don't you think?"

"If we were really engaged, you'd have everything to say about it. But this is a security measure that has nothing to do with reality. All you have to do is go along with me on it."

She walked in silence beside him, her back rigid.

"Emma? Will you roll with this concept or not?"

"You could have warned me. How long have you been planning to handle the weekend this way?"

He hesitated to tell her that he'd come up with the idea before they'd left New York. He'd been trying to figure out how to tell her and had hoped he could do it over cake.

"Not long," he said. "Until just recently, I was still working out the details."

"How recently?"

"This morning on the way to the airport."

She stopped so quickly a man behind her almost ran over her. He muttered curses as he swerved around them. "Are you telling me you're making this up as you go along?"

"No! Look, I haven't had a lot of time to work on the strategy, and I'm refining it as ideas come to me. At first I thought being your media escort would be the perfect cover, but then I realized Theo wouldn't be put off by a media escort. A fiancé, though, is another story."

"As I've said before, Aidan, I don't need all this fire-power. Chances are we won't see Theo at all, but if I'm wrong and he shows up at the autograph table with a lewd suggestion, I'll tell him to get lost. That should take care of it."

Barry turned around with a questioning glance. "Mr. Wallace? Will you and Ms. Gavin be coming with me, then?"

"Yes." Aidan cupped Emma's elbow and guided her toward the exit. Touching her at all sent shivers of awareness through his system, but they needed to get moving. "We'll talk more in the car."

She allowed herself to be hustled along. "We can do that, but I really don't like the fake engagement idea. I realize authors aren't front-page news, but if there's even the slightest chance word could get back to my mother, then—"

"Does she know about the e-mails?"

"No, and I don't want her to. She has a tendency to be overprotective as it is. When I first moved out of her apartment and into my loft, she checked on me twice a day. That's tapered off some, but if she thinks I have some cyberstalker on my trail, she'll camp out in my living room for the duration. I love her to death, but she could make my life a living hell."

Aidan wondered what Betty Gavin would do if she discovered her daughter was about to spend the weekend at the Palmer House with a werewolf. "So that means she doesn't know I tagged along for your Chicago leg of the book tour, either?"

"Are you kidding?"

"Just asking." He broke the connection between them so they could each navigate the revolving door leading outside.

"I didn't tell her I broke up with Doug, either. The combination of that announcement and telling her I need you as a bodyguard on this trip would make her assume I got rid of Doug because you and I are lovers. What a disaster that would be."

"Oh?" That pricked his ego more than a little.

"You know what I mean."

"I'm not sure I do." He handed Barry his computer case, and the chauffeur loaded it and Emma's case into the front seat of the town car.

"I'm just saying that it would be bad enough if she thought we were lovers when we're not. If she hears through the grapevine that we're engaged when we're not—well, I can't even imagine the fallout."

"I can see the problem." And he did. What had seemed like a brilliant plan during the plane ride now looked less than brilliant considering how Emma's mother might react if she accidentally heard about any of this. Aidan understood the tricky nature of family dynamics. The Wallace pack had its share of issues.

Barry held open the back door of the town car and helped Emma inside. Aidan followed her in and noted the interior of the car smelled like chocolate. This trip was becoming more complicated by the minute, so he hoped that at least the cake would be good.

"I can't believe this." Emma stared at the silver tray Barry settled on her lap. In the center sat a large wedge of chocolate cake with dark chocolate frosting—topside up, no less—on a crystal plate. At least it looked like crystal. Considering how the trip had gone so far, she'd be willing to bet it was. An ornate silver fork lay on a linen napkin beside the plate.

"Bon appétit," Barry said as he closed the back door. "I'll be right back with your luggage."

"That won't work." She glanced over at Aidan. "He can't leave the car parked here while he gets the luggage. We'll be ticketed."

"Trust me. We won't be ticketed."

"What do you mean? Of course we will! Or worse yet, we'll be hooked up to a tow truck and . . ." She trailed off as Aidan simply smiled at her. "Did you bribe someone?"

"Not necessary. Barry propped the sign with the Wallace name on it in the front window."

She looked at the front windshield, and sure enough, that placard was leaning against it. "So what, the Wallaces have diplomatic immunity or something?"

"Or something. Aren't you going to eat your cake?"

She gazed at the piece of cake, which had those clever curls of shaved chocolate on the top layer of frosting and one perfect red strawberry nestled in the curls. A strawberry in February.

Her tummy growled. "Yes, I'm going to eat this cake before Barry gets back, so I won't end up with it in my lap when he starts going eighty on the Outer Drive."

"He won't go eighty."

"Sure he will." She picked up the fork and unfolded the napkin in the little strip of her lap that wasn't covered by the tray. "I'm sure nobody will ticket him for speeding, either. I'm surprised there's not a little Wallace family flag suction-cupped to the car."

"There is."

"*No way.* Where?"

"It's on the back fender. I guess you missed seeing it when we got in."

"I most certainly did." Emma picked up the heavy silver tray and handed it to him. "Hold this. I have to see the flag."

Aidan obligingly took the tray while she unbuckled her shoulder harness and turned around so she could get on her knees and peer out the back window. "I'll be damned." She studied the purple flag, which was suitably small and tasteful at about nine square inches. Because there was no breeze, she couldn't see the crest clearly, but it was definitely a family crest.

"What's on it, a pile of gold bullion?"

"Very funny."

"I'm sorry." She looked over at him. "That was snarky, and you don't deserve snarky when you went to all the trouble of getting me that cake."

"Which I'm patiently holding for you. And Barry will be back any minute."

"You're right." She slid back down to her seat and re-fastened the shoulder harness. "Thanks for holding my cake." She took the tray and felt the brush of his fingers against hers. *Zing.* She was aware of him all over again. But she'd have to make do with cake.

She picked up the ornate fork, which looked as if it came out of an antique set of silverware. "Eating in front of you feels very rude."

"Don't worry about it. I'm not a chocoholic."

She sliced down through the moist layers. "Are you implying that I am?"

"You sure reacted like one when I mentioned rich chocolate cake."

"Then I might as well confess. Coffee and chocolate are my two favorite vices." She took the first bite and moaned happily.

"Good?"

"Mmm." She savored the taste and decided it might be the best chocolate cake she'd ever had in her life.

"Rich?"

That made her laugh. "Yes, and moist and decadent, too. It's a crime to eat a dessert like this fast. A person should take her time and draw out the pleasure. I hate to just wolf it down."

He glanced out the window, as if searching the sidewalk for Barry and her suitcase. "Then don't. Even if Barry does eighty, we won't get to the interview for a while."

"Yes, but I'd like to get to the interview without chocolate smeared all over myself."

Aidan made a funny little noise in the back of his throat.

She glanced over at him. "Is anything wrong? Are you hungry?"

"I'm fine."

But he didn't look fine to her. He looked sort of feverish. And the backs of his hands—had they always been that hairy? Maybe she'd been so fixated on the watch she hadn't noticed. He was a manly guy who probably had lots of healthy hair on his chest and his legs. He might even have hair on his back, although she hoped not. That was a turnoff.

As if that mattered. She wasn't going to be seeing his naked back, so whether he had hair growing there was a moot point.

About that time, Barry arrived pulling her orange suitcase. When she'd bought it, she hadn't been worried about whether the suitcase was stylish. Her goal was to own a suitcase that didn't look like every other one circling the belt in baggage claim.

She'd succeeded in that goal. Neon orange with little pink hearts on it, the suitcase could put your eyes out. She hadn't wanted to mention the little pink hearts when she'd described the suitcase to Barry earlier, and after all, the predominant color was orange. *Very orange.*

"Your luggage is here," Aidan said.

"Kind of hard to miss seeing that." She took another big bite of cake. "I'm afraid I left my Louis Vuitton at home."

He turned to her and smiled. Fortunately, his eyes had lost that feverish look. "You don't have any Louis Vuitton."

"No, but I had to say that and see if you were paying attention." As Barry loaded her suitcase in the trunk, she scarfed down some more cake. It was a darned shame to gobble a cake this fine, but she didn't trust herself not to make a mess.

Barry climbed behind the wheel. "All set. Ready to roll back there?"

"I still have cake, Barry. If you can avoid quick lane changes while I'm finishing it, I'd be most appreciative."

"I'll do my best, Ms. Gavin." He pulled away from the curb slowly.

"Barry, are you going to be our driver for the entire weekend?"

"Yes, ma'am, I am."

"Then please call me Emma. I have a feeling we'll be old friends by Sunday."

Barry's smile was reflected in the rearview mirror. "That would be nice. I've only met a couple of live authors before."

"Met any dead ones?"

Barry chuckled. "Good comeback. No, I haven't met any dead ones, but I have a friend down in New Orleans who swears he has."

"I like New Orleans. It's a great town." She looked over at Aidan, thinking to include him in the conversation she'd started with Barry. "Have you been there?" She took another good-sized bite of cake.

"No. Wallace Enterprises contributed quite a bit to the rebuilding effort after Hurricane Katrina, but I've never been there."

"You should go sometime." The chocolate cake was improving her mood by leaps and bounds. "It's sort of spooky, but then I enjoy spooky, as you can imagine, considering the books I write."

"You mean *pretend* spooky."

"Well, yeah, I guess so. It's fun to scare yourself a little with imaginary things." She dropped a glob of chocolate frosting, which landed on her napkin, fortunately. Next time it could land on the front of her turquoise suit jacket, though.

She studied the situation and decided she'd do better if she picked up the plate and held it closer to her mouth. She had about a third of the cake to go, and Barry had promised to drive carefully. She sliced off another chunk.

"Damn it!" Barry swore at the same moment he slammed on the brakes. "Sorry about that, Emma, but this jerk in front of me cut me off!"

"That's unfortunate, Barry." She put the empty plate back on the silver tray. "Because now I'm wearing the cake."

Chapter 8

From the moment Emma had mentioned getting chocolate smeared all over herself, Aidan had wondered whether he'd pay for this ego trip. Now it seemed that he would pay dearly. She'd managed to get both cake and frosting all over the front of her turquoise suit jacket and the white lace camisole underneath. Worse yet, it was smashed into her cleavage.

The fantasy picture of her naked and smeared in chocolate had somewhat come true, but not in a good way. The erotic overtones were all there with no possibility that he'd be able to satisfy the lust they inspired. *Double whammy.*

She glanced down at the mess before looking over at him with a bemused expression. Then she began to laugh.

That made things worse. If she'd ranted and raved about her ruined outfit, or if she'd blamed him for coming up with the stupid cake plan in the first place, he'd have been able to bury his cravings under the weight of her anger. But no, she'd chosen to be a good sport about it, and he was a sucker for a good sport.

Now he wanted to laugh right along with her and *then* lick the chocolate from her cleavage. He might not be a big fan of chocolate. A rare steak was more his idea of a treat. But if he could be allowed to clean that chocolate off her breasts using only his tongue, he'd take that assignment in a heartbeat.

Just his luck, that wouldn't be happening. Still, he had to help her figure this out. Barry was casting worried glances in the rearview mirror and sending out a stream of apologies, despite Emma's amused reaction.

Aidan chose the solution that he would have wanted for himself. "Barry, reprogram your GPS and take us to the nearest Nordstrom."

"Cancel that, Barry." Emma gulped air and sank back onto the seat. "No shopping trips. I have something in my suitcase that will work fine. I just need a plan for changing out of this and into that."

"Gas station?" Barry suggested.

Aidan shook his head. "No."

"Yes, Aidan. A gas station restroom will work fine."

He grimaced. "But it might be cramped and . . ." He gestured dismissively.

"And dirty? It might, but you don't have to go in there, and my sensibilities aren't as delicate as yours. However, before I get out of the car, I should probably wipe some of the cake and frosting off. Otherwise I'm liable to get it on the upholstery, and then it'll spread everywhere."

His libido presented him with a graphic picture of chocolate everywhere on the seat because he'd proceeded to take what he wanted, spreading the chocolate, spreading her legs . . .

"I'm afraid the napkin's compromised, and I don't have any tissues in my purse."

Thankfully, she seemed oblivious to his mental state.

"Do you by chance have a pocket handkerchief that wasn't hand-sewn by Swiss nuns?"

Maybe his sense of humor would save him. He reached into his hip pocket and pulled out a monogrammed handkerchief. "I'm sure the Swiss nuns would approve of using it to aid a damsel in distress."

"As Barry would say, nice comeback." She took the handkerchief. "Thank you. Wow, this is really soft material."

"It's woven from the hair of sacred llamas cared for by extremely devout monks."

She grinned at him. "Okay, okay. I'll lay off the smart remarks. It's just that I'm still thinking about that watch and shaking my head."

He should concentrate on the intricate workings of his watch, Roarke's watch, any damned watch. Something mechanical instead of a warm, willing, moist woman. He didn't know whether she was moist yet, but she would be if he could have a few seconds of her time.

"This gas station looks as if it might be halfway decent," Barry said. "If it's not, we'll go somewhere else."

"It'll be fine. Let's stop." Emma unfolded the handkerchief and glanced at the monogram. "What does the F stand for?"

"Faolan. It's a family name." A family name that meant *wolf.* Instead of giving first names that referenced wolves, the Wallace pack chose to give middle names with that meaning, to make the connection more subtle. There was nothing subtle about his wolf self right now, though. He was ready to howl with frustration, and he could feel hair sprouting on the backs of his hands.

"I like it." She dipped her head and began wiping up some of the chocolate.

Barry pulled the car up to the convenience storefront, located beside the gas pumps. "I'll get your suitcase out of the trunk."

"Great, thanks. You know what I hate about this the most, Aidan?" She picked up a glob of icing from her cleavage and licked it from her finger. "I'm wasting almost a third of this luscious cake."

He had to look away. His chest had begun to itch, and within thirty seconds, he'd have a start on his pelt. "I'll wash out your handkerchief in the bathroom, but it'll take more than a quick rinse to get the chocolate out, I'm afraid."

"No problem." He was trying to focus on something besides her breasts, but when he looked to his right, he was presented with the image of some guy shoving a gas pump nozzle into the tank of his car. Aidan had never thought of that behavior as particularly sexual, but in his present mood it didn't take much to evoke the image of body parts connecting.

Barry opened the door on her side. "Do you want to take the whole suitcase in?"

"That would be easier." She turned to Aidan. "Will you hold the tray for me while I'm in the bathroom?"

"Sure." He took the heavy silver tray gladly. Maybe its weight would hold down his growing erection.

"I'll be right back. We're losing some of that spare time we had before the interview."

"We'll make it, right, Barry?"

"You bet we will, Mr. Wallace."

"You can call me Aidan." He smiled. "We'll probably be old friends by Sunday."

"It's already starting out to be an interesting gig, if you don't mind my saying so." Barry sat sideways in the driver's seat so he could look over into the back.

"Sorry about that sudden stop. It was that or crash into him."

"It's not your fault. It's really mine for ordering the cake delivered." Aidan vowed to be less ego driven and more practical for the rest of the weekend.

"It was a very cool gesture, though. We had to hustle to make it happen, but it turned out well. Except for the last part, of course, when she slapped the plate against herself. That wasn't so good."

"No." But in spite of it all, Aidan cherished the memory of Emma glancing over at him and breaking out into laughter. He'd never forget that.

From inside his suit coat pocket, his phone vibrated. He took it out and looked at the readout. Roarke, who no doubt wanted to know why in the hell Aidan had ignored all his warnings and headed out to Chicago with Emma. He'd deal with Roarke later, maybe during Emma's radio interview.

"Someone from your office in New York express-shipped that flag over," Barry said. "We received it early this morning with instructions to leave it on the car all weekend."

Aidan was so used to the flag that he didn't think about it anymore. "It'll keep you from getting tickets."

Barry nodded. "Apparently so. I've never left a car in the loading zone that long before without getting one. The Wallaces must have some influence."

"We have business connections with the Henderson family."

Barry's eyes rounded. "*The* Henderson family? The one that owns a chunk of the Magnificent Mile and most of Navy Pier?"

"I believe so, yes."

"That explains a whole helluva lot. Pardon my French.

But the Henderson name gets you a lot in this town. No wonder you want that flag on the rear fender."

Aidan decided he might be wise to enlist Barry in the cause. He leaned forward. "There's something you need to know."

"What's that?"

"Although the Wallaces and the Hendersons have a strong business connection, every family has a trouble-maker."

Barry blew out a breath. "You don't have to tell me that. The Dinsmore family has more than one trouble-maker. Is it the Wallaces or the Hendersons with the bad egg?"

"The Hendersons. His name is Theo, and he's nine-teen."

Barry rolled his eyes. "Nineteen. The perfect age to cause problems."

"The thing is, he might try to make contact with Emma this weekend. He's concocted this story that he's a werewolf and therefore she needs to meet him."

"That's the lamest pickup line I've ever heard. Is that what she writes about? Werewolves?"

"Yeah. She doesn't believe in them, of course, but this crazy kid figures if he claims to actually be one, he has an angle. I'll be on the lookout, but it wouldn't hurt for you to be watching, too." Aidan pulled a picture out of an inside pocket of his suit jacket. "This is his high school graduation photo, but I understand he's let his hair grow. It's down to his shoulders now."

Barry gazed at the wallet-sized picture of a gaunt young man with dark hair and eyes. His expression was more of a sneer than a smile. "What do his parents think about him pretending to be a werewolf?"

"That's where it gets tricky," Aidan said. "I'm hoping

to neutralize the problem without either of them finding out what he's up to. They're old family friends of my father's, and he'd rather not embarrass them by exposing their son as a kook and a potential stalker."

"Lots of luck with that." Barry shook his head, which made his handlebar mustache wiggle. "In my experience, it all comes out in the wash. But I'll keep an eye out for this character. Emma's a nice lady. I'd hate to see her being bothered by some nutcase—no offense to your friends and their kid, of course."

"None taken. He *is* a nutcase. And I intend to shut him down."

"You like her, too, don't you?"

Aidan decided the chummy conversation needed to be dialed back a notch. "She's an assignment."

Barry obviously picked up on his tone. "Sure, sure. I understand. And I'll do what I can to help. Well, here she comes, all changed."

Aidan looked toward the convenience store as Emma came toward the car pulling her orange suitcase. Barry hopped out and took it from her.

She still wore her black trench coat, which had miraculously not been baptized by chocolate, but she'd traded her turquoise suit for a snug black turtleneck sweater and gray slacks. Aidan liked this outfit as much as, or better than, the turquoise suit.

It occurred to him that it didn't matter what she wore. No matter what outfit she chose, she'd look like someone he wanted to strip naked and take to bed. That was damned inconvenient.

She smiled as she climbed back into the car. "No big deal. I'm going to take advantage of your pull in this town to get my turquoise suit cleaned so I can wear it when I head for Denver."

"I can make that happen once we get to the hotel."

"I'm sure you can." She fastened her shoulder harness as Barry pulled the car back into traffic. "I don't want to get used to this level of service, but right now it'll come in handy. Want me to hold that tray, now?"

"That's okay. I'll be in charge of it." She'd brought her unique scent into the car with her. As his loins stirred in response, he settled the tray more firmly in his lap. It would serve as a reminder that he had to keep his johnson in check.

"I checked out your flag and your family crest before I got back in the car."

"Okay."

"The creatures on the crest look something like wolves."

"That's because they are." He never had any trouble explaining the family crest because wolves were usually seen as noble animals.

She gazed at him. "Is that one of the reasons you picked up my books? Because your family's crest has wolves on it?"

"In a way." She was closer to the truth than she imagined.

She nodded. "I've always had a thing for wolves, myself. That's why I was drawn to the werewolf concept. Sometimes I wish they did exist, although I'd want them to be like my werewolves and not the way they're portrayed in some books, like ferocious beasts."

"So why did you decide to portray wolves the way you did, instead of going with the ferocious beast concept?"

"I studied wolves in college, back when I thought I might go into wildlife management. They're awesome creatures that mate for life, and so logically werewolves shouldn't be that different. That's if they were real, which they aren't."

"Right." He couldn't ever remember being so tempted to blurt out the truth. But that would be suicide. He was on this book tour to prevent Theo from revealing the existence of werewolves, so he could hardly blow the pack's cover himself.

"Oh, I have your handkerchief." She opened her hand, and it lay in the center of her palm in a soggy gray ball. "I tried to wash it in the sink, like I said, but—"

"I'll take it." He picked up the wet handkerchief and tried to think what he could do with it. If he shoved it back in his pocket—either the hip pocket or the front pocket—it would soon leave a damp spot. Finally he decided to drop it on the floor of the car.

"Don't do that!" She looked horrified.

"Why not?"

"Because it was woven from the hair of sacred llamas cared for by extremely devout monks."

"I made that up."

"I know, but regardless of how it was produced, it probably cost more than half my wardrobe, so you can't simply throw it on the floor of the car."

He gazed at her. "Sure I can."

"That's wasteful."

"Emma, you're going to have to get over yourself, at least for this weekend."

She lifted her chin in an adorably defiant gesture. "What do you mean by that?"

"I mean that we're about to stay in a penthouse that would easily house an entire village in some third-world country. We'll be the only two people in there, but I'll probably turn the heat up to at least seventy-two degrees, thereby contributing to global warming and the depletion of fossil fuels."

"Okay, but—"

"In addition to my unconscionable use of resources to heat those eleven rooms, I intend to take long, hot showers because I love those, especially in the winter."

"Aidan, I'm not—"

"And if there's some sort of Jacuzzi arrangement— which I would expect, but I'm not sure—I'll be filling that tub and using those soothing jets to massage away any tenseness I might have developed in the past few hours." He paused, and a devilish urge made him forget his common sense. "If you hate the idea of all that water for one person, you're welcome to join me."

She flushed. "You and I both know that wouldn't be a smart idea."

"Maybe not psychologically, but when it comes to sharing resources, that's another issue, isn't it?" He shouldn't taunt her because it only made his own frustration level grow, but she was so . . . so *juicy*. He'd known she would tempt him, but he hadn't factored in her overwhelming succulence.

She looked adorably righteous, but that didn't detract from her desirability one iota. "As I've mentioned, I'll be considering this hotel stay part of my research."

"Then you'll want to check out all the amenities. Breakfast in bed, champagne in front of the fireplace, your favorite movies on the flat-screen, a long soak in a bubble bath."

Her eyes narrowed. "You've made your point, Aidan. And I promise not to lecture you about wasting resources again this weekend."

"Good."

"But you may not have as much time as you think to lounge in the Jacuzzi. Have you checked the schedule?"

"I glanced over it."

"Then you might remember that I have signings and interviews through this evening and all day tomorrow and tomorrow night, as well. This is a book tour, not a pleasure trip. Perhaps you'd rather stay at the Palmer House while I take care of my obligations?"

"I think not."

"Then good luck with your resource-wasting plans."

He sighed. She'd bested him. He resented the way she dinged him about his wealth, and he'd tried to tempt her with the possibilities luxury accommodations could provide. Instead of falling for that, she'd reminded him of his duties and insinuated he was nothing more than an idle rich boy.

That wasn't true. He worked hard. But he played hard, too, and he hadn't allowed himself to do that recently. Obviously, he wouldn't be indulging in any playtime with Emma, though, and that was the wisest course of action.

Unfortunately, she wasn't tempted by the possibilities, but he sure as hell was.

Chapter 9

"This is it." Carrying three books, Aidan came toward the signing table. "After this, you're sold out."

A cry of dismay went up from the line.

"I'm sorry," Emma called out. "I can sign bookplates for those of you who weren't able to get the actual book." She put down her pen and flexed her fingers. This kind of success was gratifying, validating, ego boosting, and a whole bunch more adjectives she'd be able to think of if her brain hadn't shut down earlier tonight.

She wouldn't trade this experience for anything, except maybe, at this very moment, a long soak in the Jacuzzi that Aidan had been so happy to dangle in front of her earlier today. She hadn't even seen the inside of the hotel, let alone the eleven-room penthouse he'd described. They'd been on the go all day, hopping from her radio interview to a TV gig at WGN, to a cocktail reception put on by a local library, to this book signing.

The ill-fated chocolate cake was the last thing she remembered eating, although Aidan had brought her food at various points, food she must have eaten at least some

of. She couldn't remember any of it. The cake, though—
that would remain a memory forever.

She wondered whether Aidan had any sort of clue as
to the fantasies that had bloomed in her active imagination the moment she accidentally smashed the cake
onto her chest and thick, creamy frosting had worked its
way between her breasts. That experience would rank
as one of the most sensual of her life. Gooey frosting
sliding against her skin and sending chocolate fumes
upward as it warmed to her body temperature . . . Life
didn't get much better than that.

Only one thing would have improved the sensation—
having a man like Aidan lick it off. In her fantasy world,
Barry would have been somehow taken out of the picture, snatched by aliens or something, so that she and
Aidan could be alone in the backseat of the town car.

Then she could have unfastened her seat belt and
turned to Aidan, who would also be out of his seat belt.
Giving him a searing glance, she'd ask whether he could
help her out. She seemed to have chocolate smeared all
over the place.

"Emma?" Aidan's voice snapped her out of her rev-
erie.

She wondered how long she'd stayed there staring
at the book in front of her, which Aidan had helpfully
opened to the title page. "I'm sorry." She glanced up
at the teenage girl standing in front of her. "How do
you want this autographed?" She snagged her pen and
poised it over the page.

"It's for this guy I know named Theo."

Emma's hand trembled, and she took another look
at the teenager, who resembled all the others traipsing
around the store—dark hair cut short, a black parka
thrown over a snug white T-shirt, and ripped jeans.

Maybe it wasn't the same Theo, but she'd felt Aidan stiffen at hearing the name, too.

Emma decided to get this over quickly. She'd written *To Theo* when the girl started talking again.

"He's a huge fan, and he wants you to write something special in the book. He wanted so bad to be here tonight, but he had to work, so he asked me to come instead."

Emma had a bad feeling about this. "I'll just say, *Thanks for your support.*" Emma started to write but the girl laid a hand on her arm.

"He told me what he wanted in there. Here it is." She handed over a crumpled piece of notebook paper with a message scrawled across it that completely ignored the lines. The message said, *I'd love to meet you.*

"I'm sorry." Emma gazed at the girl. "I can't write that. My time in Chicago is very limited, and writing that would indicate that I planned to—"

The girl laughed. "Oh, I'm sure he doesn't think you'll really meet him. It's just so he can show his friends, you know? It's harmless."

Aidan stepped closer to the table. "I'm sure it is, Miss . . ."

"I'm Terry. Terry Eisenbach."

"I'm sure it's harmless, Terry, but I'd like to talk to you privately for a minute." He rounded the table. "Let's go over by the coffee shop."

"Sure, but I'll get the book, right? I mean, she already wrote *To Theo,* so she can't give it to one of the other people in line, right?"

"You'll get the book," Emma said. She closed it and scooted it to one side as she greeted the next person in line, a young mother holding a sleeping baby.

As Emma autographed the last two books and then several bookplates, she wanted desperately to find out what Aidan was saying to the teenager. Maybe it was a good sign that Theo hadn't come to the store but had sent someone in his place. Maybe all he wanted out of this was an autographed book.

Still, she couldn't write what he'd asked for. That was too creepy. As the last person left with a bookplate in hand, she pulled Theo's book over and opened it to the title page. Hesitating for only a moment, she wrote, *Best wishes, Emma Gavin,* and closed the cover with a snap. That was that.

Aidan returned with Terry, who was sipping on a coffee drink, which Emma figured Aidan had bought. The girl gazed up at him with worship in her dark eyes. Emma could easily understand that look. When Aidan turned on the charm, he was tough to resist.

"Your assistant, Aidan, explained everything to me," Terry said. She spared Emma a quick glance, but she only had eyes for Aidan. "I mean, who would imagine that a message in a book could turn into a legal thing?"

Emma shot Aidan a puzzled glance. He was her assistant now? And what legal thing was Terry talking about?

He nodded wisely. "Anything's possible in this lawsuit-happy climate. I'm not saying that Theo or his family would carry it that far, but Terry agrees that Theo's not the most stable person in the world."

"No, he's not." Terry finally managed to tear her attention away from Aidan. "He might build it up in his mind that you'd actually meet him, and flip out when you didn't. I guess his folks could sue for emotional damage or something. They have the money."

"Oh, really?" Emma glanced at Aidan. "I didn't know Theo came from a ri—I mean, a *wealthy* family."

"Oh, yeah." Terry rolled her eyes. "The Hendersons are loaded. Some people hang out with Theo because he has money, but I don't. I hang out with him because he seems lonely."

"Then he's lucky to have you for a friend." Emma picked up the copy of *Night Shift* and handed it to her. "Thank you for understanding that I couldn't write what Theo asked me to."

"No prob. He won't be happy about it, but at least he has an autographed book, which I took my valuable time to get for him." She lifted her coffee drink and turned back to Aidan. "Thank you *so much* for buying me this. If you need anything else while you're in Chicago, you have my number."

"I appreciate that," Aidan said. "It's good to have contacts in an unfamiliar city."

"I know all the good places for music and dancing." She gave him a coy look. "I'll bet you're a good dancer."

"Actually, I'm a little rusty."

Emma hid a smile. *Rusty, indeed.* He could melt an iceberg with his dance moves.

"I'd be glad to help you get back into it." Terry's expression was hopeful.

"It's a nice thought, but I'll be pretty busy helping Emma get through the book tour. Thanks, anyway."

"Okay, but let me know if you change your mind. With all those long hours, I hope she pays you well."

Emma almost choked.

"She does," Aidan said gravely.

"Guess I'll take off." Terry didn't move.

Emma decided she was supposed to be in charge, so she stood. "We have to leave, too, Aidan. If you'll arrange for the car, I'll say good-bye to the bookstore manager before we leave."

"I'll take care of it." Aidan all but saluted as he walked away.

Terry sighed as she watched him go. "You are so lucky to have him."

"I am. Gay men make the absolute best assistants."

Terry's eyes rounded. "He's *gay*?"

"You couldn't tell?"

"God, no! My gaydar must not be working at all, because I thought he was totally straight!" She shook her head. "Bummer. Well, good luck with the rest of your book tour."

"Thanks." Emma watched to make sure Terry left the area before she began gathering her coat, purse, and the remaining bookplates. As she was wondering whether she should call Aidan to check on his whereabouts, her BlackBerry beeped.

When she read the text message, she laughed.

Is she gone?
Yes.
We R at main door. Need me?

She hesitated only a second while she entertained the idea of *needing* Aidan. She probably did need him, in many ways. But she wouldn't indulge. She texted him back.

No. B rt there.

"Sold out of books, huh?"

She turned. Standing about ten feet away was a tall, angular young man. His shaggy black hair needed a trim, and his jeans and gray sweatshirt looked as if they'd been pulled from the hamper instead of a dresser drawer.

A squiggle of uneasiness settled in her tummy. "Yes,

I'm afraid so." She still had her BlackBerry in one hand. Feeling a little foolish in case she was wrong, she hit Aidan's speed dial letter.

"Guess it doesn't matter." The young man approached. "I met Terry coming out of the store, and she showed me what you wrote. But looks like I get to meet you, anyway."

"So, you're Theo." She prayed that the BlackBerry picked that up. She didn't dare take her eyes off him to check for other people around. It was late, and the bookstore had mostly emptied out. Her peripheral vision told her no one was in the immediate vicinity.

"That's me." He smiled, and his teeth looked very white, and very sharp.

She wondered whether he'd gone so far into the fantasy that he'd filed them into points. She kept telling herself he was only a nineteen-year-old kid, but she hadn't factored in his height, about six-two, or the predatory look in his dark eyes.

He could have been a nice-looking guy if he'd bothered with his appearance, but his careless grooming combined with those wicked-looking teeth sent shivers down her spine.

He stepped closer. "Did you get my e-mails?"

"So *you're* the one who sent those."

"Affirmative, sweet thing."

Her skin crawled, but she kept her tone polite. "I'm glad you like my books. But they're pure fantasy. As we all know, there's no such thing as werewolves." Her laughter sounded about as nervous as she felt.

"Are you sure about that?" He held up a hand, a very hairy hand.

"Amazing what a little spirit gum and fake hair can do, isn't it?" She willed Aidan to show up *now*. She didn't care whether he claimed to be her assistant, her fiancé, or the mayor of Chicago, just so he used his well-sculpted body to put the fear of God into this weird person who was trying to convince her he was a werewolf.

"This isn't fake." Theo held up his other hand, which was also covered with black hair. "Give me another couple of minutes and I—hang on." He sniffed the air. "Gotta go." Moving with astounding agility and grace, he slipped away down one of the aisles.

He'd been gone about two seconds when Aidan arrived, panting. "Missed him. Damn it. Wait here." Without asking her which way Theo had run, he turned away and scanned the various escape routes. Then damned if he didn't sniff the air the same way Theo had, before taking off down the same aisle.

Emma wondered whether she'd fallen down the rabbit hole. The kid had looked somewhat unwashed, but she hadn't been able to actually *smell* him. Maybe Aidan was sniffing because he was coming down with a cold. If so, she needed to keep away from him because catching a cold in the middle of her book tour would be hell.

She did as she was told, though, and waited by the signing table for him to come back.

After about ten minutes, he did, but he didn't look happy. "He got away, probably had a car waiting outside, maybe even Terry's. I can't believe I missed seeing him come into the store."

"I'm sure there are lots of people out on the street, Aidan."

He gazed at her. "I just should have seen him, that's all. It's part of my job, and I wasn't doing it effectively."

She took a deep breath. "Well, he's gone, and that could be the end of it. I hope it is."

"I hope so." Aidan didn't sound convinced. "Give me your coat. We need to get out of here."

"Okay." She allowed him to help her with her coat. After dealing with Theo, she wanted to snuggle against Aidan as he slipped it over her shoulders. "I was planning to say good-bye to the bookstore manager."

"You can send a note." He put his hand at the small of her back and urged her forward. "I'll feel better once we're locked inside the Palmer House."

"So will I. Theo is seriously whacked, Aidan. He's glued fake hair to the backs of his hands, and I don't know if he's filed his teeth, but they look really wicked."

Aidan cursed softly under his breath.

"Do you think we should notify the police?" Emma asked as they hurried through the store. "I didn't want to do that, but the kid may be a danger to himself and others, and . . . well, me."

"I'm not sure what the police could do. At this point he hasn't actually threatened you, and you do, after all, write about werewolves. He could say he was just playing along with the way readers of vampire books show up wearing black capes and fangs."

"You're right." She saw the town car and Barry standing with the back door open for her. *What a welcome sight.* She wanted to run forward and fling herself inside the safety of the car, but she forced herself to walk. "Hello, Barry."

"Hello, Emma." He glanced at Aidan. "Catch him?"

"No, he got away."

"Damn."

"My thoughts, exactly." Aidan climbed in after Emma. "I thought about having sandwiches ready for you, but then I decided you might not want to juggle a hot pastrami on rye in downtown Chicago traffic."

She buckled herself in, but her thoughts were focused on the hot pastrami and rye. "Was that sandwich suggestion a lucky guess or have you been talking to someone who knows me?"

"Uh, Jenny might have mentioned that you liked those. Or it was in that interview I read."

"You must have read that interview with a highlighter." She settled back in the plush leather seat. Her conscience didn't even prick her at the luxury of it. She was safe, and after the encounter with Theo, that seemed more important than class distinctions and squandering resources.

"I've followed your career with great interest."

She turned her head to look at him. "Apparently so. I still don't quite get it, though. I'm not putting down what I do, but usually it appeals to women who love the idea of an alpha male."

He glanced over at her and smiled. "I'll be happy to explain what I like about your books over dinner. I can call the hotel and get them started on a room service order. Do you want the hot pastrami or something else? Steak? Lobster?"

She thought about it and couldn't work up any enthusiasm for a big meal at this hour. It was almost ten, and she had to be up at seven. "The sad thing is that with all the running, I'm not really hungry anymore. Maybe just some cheese and crackers, stuff to nibble on."

"Wine? Champagne?"

Oh, what the hell. She was in the company of a man who was so wealthy he wore an eight-hundred-thousand-dollar watch. "Champagne gives me a headache, but if you'll choose a really good red wine, I'd like that. I won't drink much, but I'm a little tense, and that should relax me."

"You've got it." He punched a number into his Black-Berry and gave someone instructions.

She heard the name of the wine, some high-priced brand she vaguely remembered from a movie. It probably cost several hundred dollars a bottle. She didn't want to know. It would be wonderful, as everything connected to Aidan was wonderful.

When he returned to New York and she flew on to Denver, the party would be over. For now, she was still doing research. At some point she should write down the name of the wine so she could use it in a book.

Aidan put his hand over the mouthpiece of his Black-Berry. "One more question, Emma."

"What's that?"

"They offered to run the water in the Jacuzzi for you. What do you say?"

She ached all over from the constant pressure of being sociable for hours. She was essentially a hermit, but a book tour required her to be *on* much more than she was used to. For a few seconds she thought of all that water, all that electricity needed to heat the water, and how very wasteful a Jacuzzi was compared to a quick shower.

She should really take a quick shower instead. But that wouldn't help her with her research. "I say that sounds great," she said. "But just to be clear, you can't join me."

"Don't worry. I wouldn't dream of it."

He might not, but she would.

Chapter 10

An hour later, Aidan paced the living room of the penthouse while he talked to Roarke. He'd ditched his suit jacket and rolled back the sleeves of his white dress shirt. Emma was deep into her Jacuzzi experience and had her cheese tray and a bottle of Lafite Rothschild in there with her.

He doubted she'd be popping out to hear his conversation. Still, he kept his voice down.

Roarke, who had no such restraints, was yelling into his phone. "You're an idiot!"

"Not according to my test scores."

"Which are nullified by your testicles, apparently. I knew you had solid-brass ones, but this is arrogance taken to the max!"

"Calm down, Roarke."

"Here I thought we had an understanding, and then I check with Dad and find out you're on the damned tour with her, after all! What's wrong with you, bro?"

"When it turned out to be a Henderson, I thought that I'd be the best one to—"

"Fuck it up? That's my analysis of the situation, for what it's worth. You were thinking with the wrong part of your anatomy. You're in the penthouse of the Palmer, aren't you?"

"It's safe." He stared into the flames of the gas fire dancing on the marble hearth. The lit fire was part of the turndown service. "I figured if it's good enough for the President of the United States, then it's got enough security for my purposes."

"Yeah, I'm sure security is the main appeal."

"Absolutely." Aidan glanced around at the sleek penthouse furnishings predominated by a black-and-white color scheme. There weren't enough plants to suit him, but otherwise, it worked. The windows presented a view of city lights and of snow that had just begun to drift down in big, fat flakes.

"Ha. I stayed there once, and the Jacuzzi is all gilt and mirrors. Is she in it yet?"

"Maybe."

"Well, I hope to hell you have the good sense to stay out of there."

"I will." He'd been trying not to think of Emma naked in that Jacuzzi. The maid had lit about twenty candles in the room, and Emma had been entranced. She hadn't been able to change into the hotel robe fast enough.

"You step one foot in there, Aidan, and you know what will happen," he said. "And worse yet, if for some reason you get interested and nothing comes of it, you have that little genetic problem to deal with."

Aidan blew out a breath. "You don't have to remind me. I'm fully aware that I have that problem and you don't, dickhead."

"At least you're only a couple of blocks from the park, in case you start shifting and have to work it off."

Aidan's slight disability was a sore spot, and Roarke knew that, damn him. Aidan was older, but Roarke was free of that particular gene, and he liked to flaunt the fact. "Roarke, let me ask you something."

"No, I have never slept with Britney Spears. She wanted to, but I said no."

"It's not about your sex life, which I find vastly boring. It's about your watch. How much do you think Dad paid for it?"

"Close to a mil, I guess. Why? Jealous?"

"You know a family could get a really nice house or a great condo for the same price as that watch."

Roarke sighed. "That's not the point. Fine craftsmanship is disappearing, but it still exists in some areas, like watchmaking, for example. You could argue that watchmaking is an art form. Your watch and mine are like one of the Renoirs or Picassos the family owns, except we can wear them, which is actually more useful than something that hangs on the wall."

"I suppose." Aidan had been debating the watch question all day, but he felt better now.

"Artisans who make things like intricate watches and intricate blown glass and—"

"Fine wines?" Aidan asked hopefully. He'd just dropped a bundle on the one Emma was drinking in the Jacuzzi, and in case she saw the bill at some point, he wanted to be ready with a justification.

"Absolutely. Fine wines and precision automobiles and sleek yachts. These artisans need patrons, just like in the Renaissance. Without people like Dad and Mom supporting them, the artisans of the world would have to abandon their years of apprenticeship and dig ditches."

"I seriously doubt that."

"Maybe not ditches, but you get the idea. Without

patrons, many amazing creations wouldn't exist. It's our duty to make sure the culture continues in all its facets."

"Thanks. You're the scholar, so I figured you'd be the one to give me the rationale."

Roarke chuckled. "I take it Emma disapproves of your watch."

"We had a discussion about it."

"Discussions are good, bro. That means you're not getting horizontal. Keep it in your pants, okay?"

"That's always been the plan." Aidan didn't appreciate being lectured to by his younger brother, and it was becoming something of a habit with Roarke.

"I don't have to tell you that Dad's nervous about the relationship between the Wallace and the Henderson packs."

"No, you don't."

"Oh, and I'm pretty sure Nadia knows you're in Chicago. You'll need to at least pay a quick social call."

"When am I supposed to do that?"

"Maybe Sunday, before you fly back."

Aidan groaned. "I'll do my best." His attention veered from the phone call as Emma padded out into the living room, carrying a balloon glass full of the Lafite Rothschild in one hand and the half-empty bottle in the other. She was all pink skin and gold ringlets, and she was smiling.

"This is great wine, Aidan," she said.

"Later, Roarke." He disconnected the phone and turned to Emma. "Glad you like it."

"I'm not even going to ask you how much it was."

"Good, because making wine is an art that needs to be supported by those who have the means."

"I guess." She walked over to one of two sofas that faced each other in front of the fireplace. The sleek

Scandinavian frame was covered in black leather. "In any case, I started feeling guilty drinking it all by myself. I'm sure this penthouse must have another wineglass somewhere."

"I would imagine it does."

She held out the bottle. "Then have some with me. I discovered I don't really want to drink alone."

He could imagine what Roarke would say about that plan, but Aidan thought he could handle it. Whatever the maid had added to the water in the Jacuzzi clung to Emma's skin, disguising her scent. "I'll get a glass."

Having wine wasn't the worst idea in the world in another way. He walked into the large dining room and over to a cabinet where several goblet choices hung by their stems. Alcohol tended to mute his genetic problem, so he might actually become less aroused by sharing the wine with her.

Then he came back to find her curled up on the end of the sofa nearest the fireplace, her bare feet tucked under her and the hotel robe representing the only barrier to touching her warm body. His chest began to itch.

But he had the goblet in his hand, and changing his mind now would make him seem indecisive. He shouldn't care what she thought of him, but . . . he cared more than he wanted to admit.

Now he had to decide where to sit. Roarke would advise him to choose the sofa opposite her, which put a brass-and-glass coffee table, plus a couple of heirloom-quality vases, between them. But Aidan figured that would make him seem like a coward, and besides, the wine bottle was on her side of the coffee table.

So he walked over to where she was sitting, eased down onto the smooth leather at the opposite end of the sofa, and reached for the wine bottle. He must have been paying more attention to the slight gap in her robe than to what he was doing because he bumped the wine bottle instead of grabbing it, and it started to go over.

Emma gasped and leaped toward it. She never would have made it in time, but he did. His many Were gifts included reflexes that made his sudden movements a blur, even when captured by the fastest camera shutter in the world. As kids, he and Roarke had tested it. Aidan caught the bottle before a drop of Lafite Rothschild spilled.

Emma took hold of it a split second later. Still clutching it, she stared at him. "I've never seen anybody move that fast."

"I have good reflexes." There was nothing wrong with his eyes, either. Her wild leap from the sofa to catch the bottle had loosened the tie holding her bathrobe closed. He had a perfect view of her creamy breasts. Her nipples, soft and full from the warmth of her bath, were the color of a rosé. He longed for just one taste.

If she hadn't recently immersed herself in a commercially produced bubble bath, he would have been aroused beyond all reason by the temptation of that open robe. He would have taken her right then and there. No power on earth could have stopped him, other than her refusal. She wouldn't have refused. When Aidan was in full command of his sexuality, no woman had ever said no.

But the aroma of flowers did nothing for his libido. He was operating completely on visual stimulation, which didn't stir his sexual needs nearly the way her natural scent would have.

Yet he was stirred. His mouth grew moist, and his cock stiffened.

"Oh. Sorry." She released the bottle and pulled her robe together.

He had a brief glimpse of her soft nipples tightening before she blocked his view with thick terry cloth. Whether her nipples had reacted to the air or his glance, he couldn't say. Her cheeks were pink, but that could be from embarrassment, as well as desire.

"I should have put on clothes instead of the robe." She avoided his gaze as she tightened the sash. "I brought pajamas that cover me from head to toe, but after that wonderful Jacuzzi, I wanted to snuggle into this robe. It's so thick and soft." She looked up. "But it's completely opaque, and I didn't think—I didn't mean to be seductive, Aidan. At least I hope I didn't."

His tailbone ached, and the backs of his hands prickled. He had two choices. Kissing her thoroughly—and not just the quick peck she'd given him on Wednesday night—would temporarily stop the process. If he fooled his body into thinking it would eventually get what it wanted, his shift could be delayed indefinitely. He might even be able to put it off completely. Yet that seemed like such a selfish route to take.

On the other hand, if he didn't kiss her, he would have to leave the penthouse and surrender to the shift somewhere in the middle of Grant Park. He'd be forced to strip down outside in the snow and hide his clothes somewhere they wouldn't get stolen. He didn't like those conditions worth a damn. But he'd brought it on himself. He should just swallow his pride, head for the park, and accept that Roarke was right. He'd been an idiot to think this would work.

Taking off his watch, he laid it on the coffee table. He'd never worried much about it before, but she'd made him more aware of losing it. "I'm going out."

"Out where?"

"For a walk."

Her voice rose in alarm. "Without your watch? Are you planning to go someplace where you'll be mugged?"

"I won't be mugged. I just would rather not take a chance on losing the watch." He wanted to leave without wearing his topcoat, which was one more thing that could be swiped while he was in wolf form, but then she'd get even more suspicious. He opened the foyer closet and took out his topcoat.

"Aidan, you can't leave." She hurried over to him, her bare feet whispering seductively on the carpet. "This is because I flashed you, isn't it? You're afraid you'll do something you'll regret."

He shrugged into his coat. "Or something that would be unfair to you."

"What's that supposed to mean?"

"You said it yourself on the plane today." He chose his words carefully as he buttoned the coat. "We're from different worlds, yet we're inconveniently attracted to each other. If I acted on the impulse I have right now, I'd be doing it with the knowledge I was only . . . using you."

"For sex?"

"Yes." He met her gaze. "For sex. Pure, unadulterated sex. Nothing more."

She swallowed.

"You deserve more than that, Emma. So I'll go for a walk and get myself under control. You'll be safe here, and I won't be long. Maybe an hour or so." He started for the door.

"Wait." She caught his arm. "It's snowing out there."

He glanced down at her hand on his coat sleeve. Such a soft small hand to wield such immense power over him. "No problem," he said. "I like the snow."

"So do I. Let me get dressed and I'll go with you."

He couldn't help but smile. "That would defeat the

purpose. I'm trying to put some distance between us. You need to stay here."

Her grip tightened. "So do you."

He made the mistake of looking into her blue eyes and seeing the hunger there. He gave her as much truth as he dared. "Emma, you don't know me at all."

"I know enough. I know that you're the kind of man who would rather walk off his sexual urges than take advantage of a woman he has no intention of making part of his life."

"It's what any decent—"

"That's where you're wrong. Actually, you're wrong about a lot of things. You say I deserve more than pure, unadulterated sex. In the long run, when I choose a life partner, that's true, but I can't think of anything I'd like better tonight." She gave him a saucy look. "For research purposes, of course."

Lust speared through him, and as he stood there fighting it, his pelt began to grow. "You want to find out how the wealthy do it?"

"Could be."

"We have sex the same as everybody else."

"Somehow I doubt that's true of you." She moved around in front of him and began unbuttoning his coat. "You're much stronger than I am, so you can shake me off and go out that door if that's what you really want."

He clenched his jaw as his teeth began to ache. "It's not about what *I* want. It's about what's best for both of us."

She finished unbuttoning his coat and slid her hands up the front of his shirt. "Maybe unconsciously I wanted to seduce you by wearing only this robe." She gazed up at him as she lightly massaged his chest. "You intrigue the writer in me, Aidan. But you fascinate the woman in me. There's something of the animal in you."

She was on target with that one. He hoped his chest hair hadn't curled up past the open neck of his dress shirt. He had about ten seconds before the buttons would pop from the strain of his growing pelt and the powerful muscles forming beneath it. He had to go *now*.

"I want to undress you, Aidan." She unfastened the first button. "You're so masculine, so—my, you do have a lot of chest hair. So soft, so sexy."

Too late. He'd hesitated, and now he'd never make the lobby in time. He had one option left, and he hoped it would still work for him. "I need to kiss you, Emma." He cupped the back of her head and slid his arm around her waist. "Hold very still."

"Aidan? Your teeth are so white and so—"

He used what little control he had left to lower his head and kiss her gently. *Easy now, light pressure.* He could only tease her mouth with his, because if he kissed her fully, he'd draw blood. His canines were sharp enough.

She was so innocent, so trusting. Dear God, he hoped he hadn't waited too long. If he shifted now, in front of her, she might never get over the shock of it. What if he still craved her after the shift? Would he take her while he was in wolf form? He'd never been in this precarious position before. It was uncharted territory.

But, ah, he wouldn't shift. As she kissed him back and pressed her sweet little body to his, his teeth stopped aching, and his canines began to retract. His tailbone no longer bothered him, either. The insistent pressure he'd felt there had moved forward and now affected his cock. Women were used to that phenomenon. In fact, they seemed to enjoy making it happen.

As his shift gradually reversed, his lust grew stronger. Her natural scent had begun to filter through the fragrant oils from her bath, and he fumbled with the tie of her robe, impatient to remove it and sniff every inch of her naked body.

His topcoat was in the way, and he released her temporarily, still keeping contact with her luscious mouth as he shrugged out of his coat and dropped it to the floor. Freed of that burden, he worked her out of the robe.

Yes. At last he could stroke, touch, fondle. He buried his nose in the side of her neck and breathed in as he ran both hands over her quivering skin. She was smooth, warm, moist . . . *rich.* So rich.

The scent of her drove him to nuzzle her breasts. He'd learned that kisses could disguise his real purpose, which was to breathe in every delicious aroma rising from her body. The more he caressed her, the sweeter she smelled. He trailed kisses down between her breasts as he absorbed every tantalizing fragrance along the way.

Dropping to his knees, he cupped her bottom and kissed her navel, but his goal was the downy patch of blond curls just below, where the musky scent of arousal called to him with a siren's song. When he reached his destination and breathed in her essence, he growled low in his throat.

She trembled, but didn't resist as he sought her out with a swipe of his tongue. She tasted as he'd known she would, like the nectar he'd dreamed of all his life and never found in either wolf or woman. He needed more.

"Come down." Bracketing her waist with both hands, he guided her to her knees, then onto the thick carpet.

Her breath came fast. "Aidan . . . there's a perfectly good bed . . ."

He didn't want a bed. Urging her legs apart, he settled down on the carpet and slid both arms under her hips. Then he took her, burying his nose in her fragrant sweetness and using his tongue to lap, to caress, to arouse in ways that were guided partly by human instinct, partly by the wolf that lay just under the surface.

She responded like the wild thing he'd always suspected she could be. He'd read her books, watched her dance. He'd sensed the sensual creature waiting to be turned loose.

He gave her that freedom. By holding nothing back, by making low urgent sounds deep in his throat, he bid her to writhe in his arms, arch toward his ravenous mouth, and cry out for more. He made her come once, twice, three times before she sagged against the carpet, panting, her body limp and quivering.

The smell of sex filled his nostrils as he suckled her gently, easing her back from the last shattering climax. His shift was in retreat because he'd fooled his body into thinking relief was at hand. If he'd been in wolf form, it would be.

But he'd pleasured her as a man, which meant he had to follow human rules. That meant pretending that he had to avoid pregnancy. Kissing his way back up her moist skin, he gazed into her heavy-lidded eyes. "We need room service."

She frowned.

"Never mind." He feathered a kiss over her lips. "You'll see." Reaching for the robe that had fallen to the carpet, he pulled it over her and got to his feet. A phone sat on a nearby end table.

Picking up the receiver, he punched the button for the front desk. "A box of Trojans, ASAP," he said, and replaced the receiver.

A muffled sound made him turn toward Emma. She had a hand over her mouth, but she was definitely laughing.

Crouching beside her, he tossed aside the robe and lifted her into his arms. "Go ahead and laugh. Some of us still have business to take care of."

"But room service?"

He carried her toward the master bedroom. "That's how the wealthy handle these things. I hope you're rested up, because I have plans for you while we're waiting for those Trojans."

Chapter 11

Emma wasn't going to argue with the man. He'd turned her inside out, and she couldn't believe she had more to give in that department, but he seemed to know his way around a woman's body. No man had ever given her an orgasm on the living-room carpet smack-dab in the middle of a luxury penthouse, let alone *three*.

She was curious as to what he had in mind until room service arrived. Whatever it was, she had a good feeling about it. Aidan was all she'd imagined he would be, and she hadn't even seen the package she hoped he'd deliver to her once he was supplied with condoms.

Settling her in the middle of the king-sized bed, he pulled the covers out from under her in one quick motion so that she was lying on the smooth white sheet. Feeling incredibly satisfied and decadent, she gazed up at the provider of all things orgasmic.

She might be naked, but he was still mostly clothed. She'd managed to get his shirt unbuttoned and pulled out of his slacks, but that was the extent of her efforts.

Still, she had a nice view of his pecs and his muscled

abs when the shirt billowed open. Funny, but when she'd first started unbuttoning his shirt, she'd thought he had more chest hair. Now she could see he had an average amount. She must have been so focused on getting him to stay that she'd misjudged.

There was no chance she'd misjudged the firm length of him pressed up against her when they were kissing, though. No doubt he had some magnificence going on underneath that expensive pair of slacks. She was more than eager to find out what would be modeling one of those Trojans.

"There's another robe in the closet," she said. "You could get out of those clothes and keep the robe handy for when room service arrives."

"I thought I might do that." He stripped off his shirt and threw it on a nearby chair. Then he nudged off his wingtips without untying them.

She barely noticed his shoes because she was too entranced by his biceps. The guy was ripped. No wonder he'd been able to pick her up so easily and carry her in here without breaking a sweat. "You must work out a lot."

"Some." He reached for the buckle of his belt.

She sat up and scooted to the edge of the bed. "Let me."

"All right." He walked to the side of the bed with that loose-hipped, easy stride that turned her into jelly.

"I'm glad I asked." Sitting with one leg on either side of him, she ran her knuckles slowly up and down the material being thrust forward by his erection and was rewarded with the sound of his breath hissing out between his clenched teeth.

"Maybe I should be the one to answer the door when room service arrives," she murmured as she unfastened the buckle on his belt. "You may be indisposed."

"If I am, you will be, too."

"We'll see about that." His belt flexed easily, indicating the dark brown leather was top grade. She could see how a person could get used to handling only the best. She was about to do that once she unwrapped his package.

After his belt hung open, she tuned in to his breathing as she unfastened his slacks. The cadence definitely picked up. So did hers. Because she was a writer and knew the value of suspense, she slowed her movements. Grasping the zipper, she edged it down tooth by tooth. Tension coiled within her, and the body she'd thought was thoroughly sated was no longer in that condition. She wanted him again.

"Emma." His voice was strained.

"I'm building anticipation. It's a plot device."

He made a noise that sounded like—no, it definitely was—a growl.

"Excuse me? Did you just growl?"

He groaned. "I want your hands on me. I want your *mouth* on me, Emma."

"I see." She finished with the zipper and pushed his slacks to the floor.

As he stepped out of them, she admired his black knit boxers that so lovingly cradled his awe-inspiring equipment. She was about to divest him of the boxers, too, but he didn't give her the chance.

Slipping his thumbs under the elastic, he shoved the boxers down, and his glorious cock sprang free.

She drew in a sharp breath. He was even more impressive than she'd imagined. Those Trojans couldn't get here soon enough.

"Dear God, touch me, Emma, before I combust."

She didn't have to be asked twice. With one hand circling his cock and the other cupping his balls, she leaned down and brushed her mouth over the velvet crown of his penis. His shiver inspired her to use her tongue to lick the smooth surface, and he moaned softly.

Another pass with her tongue, and a clear drop of liquid appeared at the very tip. She tasted its salty goodness, and another appeared to take its place. This time she closed her mouth over the rounded dome and applied gentle suction.

He gasped and combed his fingers through her hair to press them against her scalp. Then slowly, gradually, he urged her down, until the tip of his cock nudged the back of her throat. Yet still, her hand encircled the base. She hadn't taken all of him.

Breathing hard, he held her head as he withdrew. Then he went to his knees in front of her. His voice revealed the strain of controlling his needs. "I don't want to hurt you. Not this way, and not when I begin to thrust. But I'm crazy for you, Emma. I'm afraid I'll forget myself and—"

She looked into his golden eyes that glowed with lust. "I'm not afraid."

His thumbs brushed her cheeks. "You should be. You're small. I never expected to be here with you like this, and now that I am, I'm quivering with the need to drive into you. I'm afraid I'll overpower you and take you with no regard for what I'm doing. Don't let me. Make me stop if I lose all reason."

"You won't."

"I can't promise that, Emma. I've never felt quite like this before."

"Never?" Hot excitement bubbled within her at his confession.

"No, never. I'm not sure what's happening to me, but

I want you in a way that . . ." He shook his head. "In a way I can't even explain."

"We'll go slow."

"Maybe I can't."

"Then the first time I'll sit astride you."

"All right." He drew a shaky breath. "That might help."

The doorbell chimed.

"Let me go," she murmured.

"No." He stood and took the robe from the back of a chair. "The trip will do me good. Maybe I'll be more in control when I come back."

"Don't be stubborn. My state of arousal is a whole lot less obvious than yours." She made a grab for the robe. "I'll go."

"No." He held the robe out of reach. Then he put it on, but as he tied it he seemed to realize the problem and pulled on his boxers, too. "I trust this hotel, but if anybody besides the bellman is at the door, I want to be the one answering it, not you wearing a bathrobe and looking as if you've just been . . ."

"Ravished by the Big Bad Wolf?"

He looked startled.

"Just referencing your family crest," she said with a smile. "I think it's cool."

"Oh."

"I hope I didn't offend you by joking about it."

"I don't get offended easily."

"I didn't think so. And for the record, I meant it as a compliment. I don't subscribe to the Little Red Riding Hood view of Big Bad Wolves." She winked at him. "I kinda like them."

"Glad to hear it, little girl." Leering suggestively, he turned and left the bedroom.

Laughing, she hopped off the bed and walked into the bathroom to see whether she looked as ravished as she felt. Sure enough, anyone who saw her would know exactly what she'd been up to. Her tousled hair and the flush that covered her entire body would give her away.

She combed her fingers through her tangled hair and then ran her hands over her breasts and down her body. Every nerve ending was alive and singing with joy. She hadn't had sex like this in ... well, ever.

"Emma, where did you go?" Aidan called from the bedroom.

"In here."

He walked into the bathroom holding the box of condoms. When he saw her standing in front of the gilt-framed mirror, he paused. "You're so beautiful." Shoving the box into the pocket of the robe, he came up behind her and reached around to cup her breasts.

She leaned back against him and wiggled a little so the robe parted. His chest hair felt so soft and silky, almost like the pelt of an animal. "You make me feel that way."

"You should always feel that way. Your breasts are perfect." He brushed his thumbs over her nipples. "I love watching them tighten when I do this."

Her pulse quickened. "It's really something, watching you touch me."

"Touching you. Arousing you." He buried his nose in her neck. "The more you're aroused, the better you smell."

"Then I must smell really good right now." She'd become damp and achy as he played with her nipples and fit his pelvis against her bottom. She felt the insistent press of his cock as it strained against the knit material of his boxers.

"You smell incredible." He nipped the side of her neck gently as he slid one hand down between her legs. "Especially here." Dipping his fingers into her wetness, he brought them back up to his nose and breathed in.

She rested her hands on the counter and closed her eyes. "Again, Aidan."

The air moved as he took a step back. "Lean over." The command came softly, but there was no doubt it was a command.

She did as she was told, bracing her hands against the counter and leaning forward. He caressed her from behind, probing and stroking with his fingers until she was panting with pleasure. She was close, so close.

Then he stopped, slipping his fingers free.

She cried out in frustration. "Aidan, please . . ."

He made a sound low in his throat. Something hit the floor, a paper crinkled, and then he was back, pumping with his fingers, bringing her the release she craved. Her climax burst upon her, bringing with it wave upon wave of exquisite pleasure. She was drenched and wide-open when she heard his soft growl of need.

Clutching her hips firmly in his big hands, he took her from behind with a swiftness that made her gasp. She tensed against the expected pain, but none came. As he plunged into her over and over, she lifted her hips in silent invitation. Fierce joy surged through her at knowing that her wet vagina welcomed him, all of him.

He stretched her more than any man had, and she gloried in the sensation of his thick length enclosed within her. The intense friction and the elemental joining of his body with hers awakened her womb as nothing had before. He'd given her climaxes, but not like this. The blood roared in her ears as her orgasm built with a slow and steady power timed to the rhythm of his thrusts.

Another growl rose from deep within his chest as he increased the pace. His thighs slapped hers, and if he hadn't steadied her with his strong grip, she would have toppled under the repeated impact of his body.

Ah, but the pleasure. The pleasure rolled toward her, coming faster and faster, until *yes, yes, YES.* With a high, keening cry, she came. He shoved home once more, and his bellow of satisfaction echoed against the walls of the room.

His big body trembled against hers as he let out a long, slow sigh. His words were hoarse and filled with anxiety. "Dear God. If I've hurt you . . ."

If she'd had the breath, she would have laughed. She gulped for air and finally managed to say, "You didn't."

He was silent for a moment. "Would you tell me if I had?"

"Yes." Opening her eyes, she lifted her head so that she could see him reflected in the gilt-framed mirror. "We look like actors in an X-rated movie."

"Don't think I haven't been enjoying the view. Still am."

She smiled at him. It was quite the pose. There she was, gripping the counter and bent over to allow this beautiful man access. Her breasts bobbed with any small movement, and his sculpted chest heaved as he recovered from their adventure. Both of them glistened with sweat.

She'd never forget this image as long as she lived. "I loved every second," she murmured.

"Me, too." Slowly he withdrew and wrapped his arm around her waist to help her up. "But now we're going to bed."

"That could be fun for a change."

He met her gaze in the mirror. "Not so much. We'll be in separate beds, in separate bedrooms."

"Aidan! You can't be serious."

"I'm totally serious. I've seen what this book-tour schedule does to you. You need sleep." He leaned down and nuzzled behind her ear. "I have a feeling you'll conk out the minute I'm gone."

"No, I won't." She sounded spoiled and pouty, but she couldn't help it. "I'll lie awake all night, wishing you were there beside me. Let's share the king bed in the master bedroom."

"If we did that, you'd never get any sleep." He nipped at her skin.

"Sure I would. We'll just cuddle."

"We'd do a lot more than cuddle."

"Maybe, but then you'd sleep and I'd sleep. Then, if we woke up, we could do more than cuddle again, and then go back to sleep. See, lots of sleeping going on."

"I usually don't sleep much." With his mouth on the curve of her shoulder, he breathed in deeply. "And with you in my bed, I can guarantee I'd be awake all night."

"You're just saying that because you're being over-protective of my sleep time. All guys sleep after having sex. I don't believe that you wouldn't."

"Believe it. Good night, Emma." Nipping at her shoulder once more, he left the bathroom.

"Wait! You can't just leave like that." Her legs were still rubbery, but she hurried after him as best she could. "I insist you come back here, Aidan Wallace!"

He moved fast for a big man. By the time she reached the door of the bedroom, he was no longer there. He wasn't in the living room, either.

"All right, Aidan!" she called out. "I'm going to

search the entire ginormous suite until I find you, and then I'm going to use my feminine wiles on you until you agree that we should share that big bed! You're being silly about this."

Before starting her search, though, she went back to the bedroom to make sure he wasn't there playing a trick on her. She looked behind the door and then in the closet. He wasn't there.

On her way back through the living room, she picked up the robe that had been left lying there. The curtains were drawn back to show off the spectacular view of skyscrapers at night, and in spite of being so far up, she still didn't feel comfy running around naked in front of open windows. Somebody in an adjacent office building could be working late.

She laughed at her paranoia as she tightened the belt on the robe. *That someone* working late would have to be equipped with some high-powered binoculars to see anything. Sometimes her imagination ran out of control. Having Theo show up tonight had spooked her a little bit, too.

Maybe that was another reason she wanted Aidan to stay in her bed tonight. His was a very comforting presence to have in case Theo inspired any nightmares. Walking through the spacious penthouse, she taunted Aidan with remarks about what a chicken he was. At some point she added in clucking noises.

Finally, she arrived at a bedroom door that was locked. She rapped on it. "Aidan, are you in there?"

"Yes." He was chuckling, though, just as she'd thought he might.

Games were okay. Games were good, in fact. "I was thinking of ordering up dessert from room service and asking if they'd include a can of whipped cream."

"Sorry, but I'm not into sweets."

"Well, I am. I was thinking you might enjoy having me suck whipped cream off your—"

"Go to bed, Emma."

"Go to hell, Aidan." She said it sweetly, but she was genuinely miffed at him as she stomped off to her own room. Throwing off the robe, she crawled naked into bed and fell asleep without remembering to turn out the light.

Chapter 12

Aidan had caught Emma's scent long before she'd rapped on the door of the bedroom he'd designated as his from the outset. When her scent threatened to affect him, he'd switched to breathing through his mouth and even then, not too deeply. Even a faint whiff of her could tip the delicate balance he was struggling to maintain.

So far, he hadn't become aroused enough to initiate his shift, but it wouldn't take much of a seduction effort on her part before he'd be right back where he'd been during that tense moment in the foyer when he'd nearly shifted right in front of her. If he allowed her to arouse him again, he'd have the same damned choice—sex with her or a cold run through the park in wolf form.

Because he'd chosen this bedroom originally, his clothes hung in the closet. Once he'd locked himself in here, he'd pulled on sweats and a T-shirt. That would be enough to get him through the hotel lobby, but he'd rather not go through all that.

Fortunately she'd left quickly. Had she stayed even a minute longer, he might have flung open the door and pulled her inside, because he didn't relish romping through Grant Park tonight. The risk of discovery was huge.

Apparently he'd made a gross miscalculation as to the effect she'd have on him. Usually sex with a woman—or a female werewolf for that matter—left him satisfied, at least enough to put sex out of his mind for several hours and sometimes for days or even weeks. Not with Emma. Within moments of that first shattering orgasm, his craving for her had returned.

Because it had come on him so quickly, he'd doubted a second round would have been enough. He might have needed to have sex with her three times, or even four. That wasn't fair to her, not with the obligations she had the next day.

He had only himself to blame for the problem. He'd foolishly surrendered to an overwhelming need to take her in semiwolf fashion, something he'd been warned not to attempt with a human female or suffer the consequences. Although neither of them had been on all fours, the position had been close enough to subtly blend his wolf instincts with his human male sex drive.

It was a powerful and dangerous combination, one he'd learned of during the private sex-education classes every young werewolf had to attend upon reaching sexual maturity. According to the instructor, a werewolf could exercise reasonable control over his or her carnal desires by keeping a strict separation between animal copulation and human sex.

That was easy for Aidan when he was in werewolf form. He and his she-wolf partner had one choice and one choice only. Ah, but when he was a man ... choices abounded. And he was a highly sexed male who loved variety. Still, there were many interesting positions, so he'd been careful to avoid taking a woman from behind and use all the others—until tonight.

Now he understood why his instructor had been so clear on this point. Weres belonged with Weres, and the packs spread across North America would be safer if it stayed that way. Human females had always been classified as an occasional indulgence, one that carried the added danger of exposing the entire Were population.

Thank God he and Emma hadn't gone the full-wolf route with Aidan mounting her while she was on her hands and knees. Even lacking the intention of binding her to him as a mate, he might have strengthened the bond between them to a level that would be almost impossible to break.

But all was not lost. He still might be able to override this lapse in judgment.

He wasn't quite clear the best way to do that. Logic told him he shouldn't have any more sexual contact with Emma, but she wouldn't understand why, and he wouldn't be able to tell her. Maybe if they had sex, but only in the missionary position, she'd once again fit into the category of an occasional indulgence, one he could give up when that became necessary.

She wasn't in that category now. Thinking of giving her up depressed the hell out of him. She was smart, funny, and sassy. He'd bit his lip to keep from laughing out loud when she'd pertly told him to go to hell.

But her intelligence and sense of humor weren't the most compelling reasons he wanted Emma Gavin. The reason was far more basic than that—her scent drove him insane. It had from the first, and after experiencing full-body sex with her and breathing in all her enticing aromas, he was hooked.

He needed advice, but he wasn't about to call Roarke. Either he'd wake his brother or interrupt him in the middle of a hot date. Either way, Roarke wouldn't be in the mood to discuss Aidan's options, especially considering Roarke completely disapproved of this bodyguard project.

Aidan lay back on one of the two double beds in the room. Sometimes he could think better in wolf form, and by doing that, he'd guarantee he wouldn't lose the battle and head into Emma's room.

As much as he hated shifting against his will when he was aroused, he didn't mind it at all when he commanded it to happen. Shifting on command provided its own kind of release, and maybe in wolf form he'd find wisdom. He sure as hell could use some wisdom.

The door was locked, and the penthouse was quiet. If he had to guess, he'd say Emma had crawled into bed and fallen asleep immediately. She'd had a tiring day and several good orgasms at the end of it. In his experience with human females, that contributed to a good night's sleep.

He quickly removed his clothes and stretched out on the bed. Then he turned to gaze at the fat snowflakes falling lazily past his window. Shifting was an art form that was, in the mature werewolf, supposed to be entirely voluntary. Aidan had always resented the genetic defect that caused his involuntary shifts, but he was proud of his ability to shift on command.

The process required something akin to self-hypnosis, and the snowflakes provided the necessary focus for his attention. As he concentrated on their easy descent, the shift began. Because he wasn't resisting it, as he had when he was with Emma, the sensations caused pleasure rather than pain. Within seconds his rich brown, silver-tipped pelt covered his body, and his teeth grew sharp and whiter.

Rolling to his side, he gave room for his tail to grow until it became a sensitive extension of his body. His hands and feet became large paws, and the muscles and sinews of his arms and legs transformed until he became an animal capable of leaping a six-foot wall in a single bound.

But there would be no dramatic leaping and running tonight. Instead he paced the room and stretched, adjusting to his wolf body and pausing to shake himself from head to tail. He cherished this wolf form when he could choose it instead of having it thrust upon him in a potentially dangerous situation.

As a wolf, he connected to the forest, to the heavens, to the moon. In the city, he couldn't see any of those things, and certainly not in this hotel room. Yet he padded over to the window and looked out because the outdoors was his element. The window glass reflected a majestic wolf with silver-tipped fur and deep-set golden eyes.

As he stood watching the snow fall onto the street below, he sensed another of his kind nearby, perhaps on the street below. Instantly his whole body tensed. In his wolf state he could communicate with other Weres, but only through the exchange of thoughts.

He tossed the first volley. *Who goes there? Friend or foe?*

A friend to Weres. A foe to all who would enslave us.

Shit. Theo. *What in hell are you doing here?*

Demonstrating my tracking skills. Didn't want you to get too comfortable up there in the penthouse with Emma.

Aidan sighed. *Get this straight, Theo. Your little game is over. You're endangering us all, and it will stop now.*

I'm not the only one endangering us. Does she know what you are?

No. And she won't.

Liar. You'll reveal yourself because you want her.

That's the act of a traitor. If that accusation inflamed Theo, so be it. Aidan wanted to draw him out, challenge him, subdue him.

Are you calling me a traitor?

You're taking chances like one.

Care to come down and settle this now?

Nice try. I'm staying here.

Coward.

Guardian.

Silence greeted that statement. Then came the response. *Because you want her. You're guarding her for yourself.*

Aidan left the window and paced the bedroom as he deliberately shut down his Were senses. But Theo's accusation echoed in his head, despite the fact he could no longer hear those thoughts rising from the street below. *You're guarding her for yourself.* That couldn't be. He would mate with Nadia or someone of equal stature in the Were community.

Emma represented, as his sex-education instructor had said, a temporary indulgence. Once Aidan had pledged himself to Nadia or some other werewolf princess, he would have no other. That was the werewolf code, and he would abide by it.

A yearning to see Emma filled him, but if he changed back to human form, that yearning would translate into physical desire. He moved to the door, his paws silent on the thick carpet. Turning the lock took several swipes of his large paw, but eventually it gave way.

He scratched at the door until it swung open. He hesitated. Going to her now was reckless, but he needed to see her, needed to know she was okay. Surely she'd be sound asleep after an exhausting day.

Lights glowed in the living room because no one had turned them off. The gas flames still danced on the hearth because he and Emma had been too engrossed in each other to douse the fire. As a wolf, he could remember what he'd done with Emma while in the form of a man, but the memory didn't fill him with lust. He no longer desired her, but he would protect her with his life.

Quietly he moved into the bedroom. Lamps on either side of the massive bed were on, casting their light over Emma, sprawled diagonally across the big bed. Her blond hair fanned out over the pillow she cradled in both arms.

She was partially covered by the sheet and a section of the black-and-white comforter. Then, whimpering in her sleep, she turned onto her back, dislodging the sheet and exposing both breasts.

To Aidan's dismay, his scrotum tightened and his penis thickened. In his entire life of moving between the worlds of human and Were, he'd never felt sexual desire for a woman while in wolf form. It seemed he'd altered something basic in his physiology when he'd taken possession of Emma tonight in that primitive way.

But he was not ruled by that change. With one last glance at her creamy breasts, he turned away. As he started out of the bedroom, her scream caused him to whirl and face her. Had Theo managed to break in?

No. She screamed again, the covers clutched to her

throat as she sat up in bed and stared in terror at the
thing that had frightened her.

Him.

Shit. He bolted from the room and dashed into his
bedroom. Panting, he nudged the door closed and flung
himself against it in case she followed him. Then he
closed his eyes and focused every fiber of his being on
changing back.

She'd stopped screaming, which meant she'd called
the front desk. It would take them time to get here. He
had maybe two minutes, maybe three. *Do it, Wallace!*

Shifting under pressure was never a fun idea. Far better to take his time and ease into the new body, sort of
like slipping into a warm Jacuzzi. Shifting fast was like
leaping into a boiling cauldron, but he could do it.

He clenched his teeth against the shock, but in less
than a minute, he was back to being a man, a man who
could pull on sweats and a T-shirt and answer the door
when hotel security arrived.

Two uniformed men, one chubby and one skinny,
peered past him. "Is there a chance you have a dog in
here, sir?" asked the skinny one. "We had a report of a
dog—actually the lady on the phone said it was a wolf,
which would be entirely against hotel regulations. We
figured it had to be a large dog, but you would need to
clear the presence of such a dog with the management."

Aidan opened the door. "You're welcome to look
around, but there's no dog."

"It was a wolf." Emma stood in the living room
wrapped in the hotel robe. "I woke up from a sound
sleep, and there was a wolf in my bedroom."

Aidan glanced at her. "Emma, I think you must have
had a nightmare."

"I did not! There was a wolf in my room. I saw it with my own two eyes. A huge wolf with silver-tipped fur. Search the place. It's probably hiding somewhere."

Aidan hated what he had to do, but there was no choice. "By all means conduct a search, gentlemen, but I guarantee you won't find anything. Miss Gavin writes books about werewolves, and she has a very active imagination."

For the first time doubt flickered in Emma's blue eyes. "But I saw it, Aidan. It was *there,* looking at me."

"I'm sure you thought you did." He went to her and gathered her close, careful not to make it a sexual gesture. She wouldn't be in the mood, but he seemed to always be in the mood.

"It seemed so real."

"I know how that is." He rubbed her arm in a companionable way. "You're sound asleep and something wakes you up, like the heat going on. You're pulled right out of your dream, and for a moment, you see something that isn't really there. It's happened to me several times."

"I wasn't dreaming about wolves. At least I don't think I was."

"But it makes logical sense that you might. You're in a strange place and a strange bed. You've had an emotional day, which included confronting an idiot who's trying to make you believe he actually *is* a werewolf."

She slumped against him. "I suppose you're right, but Aidan, I've never been so frightened in my life. I thought it was truly a *wolf.*"

"Well, it wasn't." *It was a werewolf, aka me.*

"Couldn't find anything, ma'am." The chubby security guard came back into the living room. "Ed's making sure nothing's in any of the other rooms, but we checked everywhere. Opened all the closets, looked under everything, checked in the shower. Looks like just the two of you are here."

"I'm so sorry," Emma said. "I hate that you went to all this trouble for a silly nightmare."

The security guard smiled. "Don't think a thing about it. Part of the job." He glanced over at his partner. "All clear, Ed?"

"All clear, Ken. But if you have any more problems, ma'am, give us a call. We're up all night anyway, and checking for wolves in the penthouse is a lot more interesting than anything on late-night TV."

"I feel pretty foolish," Emma said. "Someday I'll probably be able to laugh about this and make it into a good story, but right now it's just embarrassing."

"Ah, this is nothing," the guard named Ken said. "You wouldn't believe the things we get called for. We had a magician whose bunnies and doves all got loose. Took us three hours to corral them."

Keeping a supportive arm around Emma, Aidan shook hands with both men. "Thanks for your time."

"No problem," Ken said. "Lock up behind us."

"I will." Giving Emma a squeeze, he crossed to the door and threw the dead bolt.

"Aidan, I feel like such an idiot."

"Don't." He was the one who felt like an idiot for scaring her to death and making her doubt what she'd seen. "You've been under a lot of pressure."

"I guess." She gave him a pleading look. "But I really don't want to go back in there by myself."

He'd figured this was coming, and the next few hours would be torture. But he deserved to be tortured after frightening her like that. "I'll stay with you."

"Thank you, Aidan."

"But we're not having sex."

"Don't worry. I'm too spooked to do that, anyway."

Well, that's one of us. He turned off the fireplace and the lights in the living room before following her into the master bedroom. The scent of her drew him like a moth to a flame. But he would resist. With luck, his heavy burden of guilt would keep his johnson deflated for the next few hours.

Chapter 13

Emma slept the rest of the night curled against Aidan's strong body. At his request, she'd put on her pajamas, and he'd left on his sweats and T-shirt. She couldn't remember sleeping more soundly in her life.

When she woke up, it was with a sense of something missing. Gray light filtered through the crack between the drapes, and as she came fully awake, she realized what was missing, or rather *who*. Aidan had left the bed.

The spot where he'd been was still warm, and she rolled to that section and sniffed the pillow. She still couldn't identify the brand of his subtle aftershave, although it had a hint of musk. Maybe today she'd ask him the name of it.

In the meantime, she had to get cracking if she expected to make the drive-time radio interview at eight fifteen. She climbed out of bed and headed for the master bath. Water was running somewhere in the suite, but Aidan had left the master bath to her.

Just as well. One peek at him in the shower and she'd jettison her morning appointments. That thought

brought her to a dead stop in the middle of the bedroom. *Good Lord.* Would she really behave that unpro-
fessionally because she wanted to have sex with Aidan?

Probably. And that was unnerving as hell. She'd
worked too hard to get to this point in her writing career to jeopardize it for sex with a man, any man, but
especially this one. Aidan had made it clear that they
could *hook up*, as he'd phrased it, but never have a more
long-term commitment than that.

Had she allowed one fabulous night of sex with a talented lover to sidetrack her completely? If so, shame on
her. She'd do well to get her priorities straight.

Striding purposefully into the bathroom, she pulled
off her pajamas and turned on the shower. She moved
through her routine quickly and efficiently, determined to
focus on what was important—namely, promoting *Night
Shift.*

She couldn't blame Aidan for her lack of dedication,
though. He'd resisted her all along. The man had been
prepared to walk for an hour in Chicago's freezing cold
rather than take her to bed. She'd asked him to stay.

Apparently she couldn't handle the heat, though, so
she'd best keep out of the kitchen. If one night with him
had affected her so strongly, she'd be wise not to repeat
that behavior tonight. Time for some old-fashioned
self-control.

When she returned to the bedroom after showering,
washing her hair, and using the blow-dryer, she noticed
a tray on the dressing table. It held an insulated carafe
of what smelled like coffee, a cup and saucer, a small
pitcher of cream, and a piece of chocolate cake that
looked almost identical to the one she'd smashed into
her turquoise suit yesterday.

No eggs, no fruit, no bran muffin. Nothing that would

have been good for her, which was exactly the way she liked her food first thing in the morning. Some men might have taken it upon themselves to provide her with what she *should* be eating, but Aidan had chosen what she wanted, instead.

Damn him, anyway. Why did he have to be the perfect man? Other than his extreme wealth, of course. But without that wealth, she wouldn't be enjoying top-notch room service in the penthouse of a very expensive hotel. His money was part of him, and she hadn't exactly been suffering as she'd enjoyed the luxuries he'd provided so far.

Still wearing the hotel robe so there would be no chance of messing up her outfit with chocolate cake this morning, she sat at the dressing table and poured herself a cup of coffee. She could devote ten minutes to this indulgence, which should inject enough caffeine into her system to get her through the radio show.

"Can I get you anything else?"

She turned to find him leaning in the bedroom doorway dressed in slacks and another snow-white dress shirt open at the collar. Her wayward glance went to his belt, and warmth settled between her thighs as she remembered unfastening it, remembered the heft and feel of his cock, remembered how he'd tasted. Oh, he could get her something else, all right, but it would be worse for her than chocolate cake for breakfast.

She toasted him with the coffee cup. "You're aces for having this brought up. Thanks for not assuming I needed protein before my big day."

"I've been paying attention." He looked relaxed leaning there with his hands shoved in the pockets of his slacks, but lines of tension bracketed his mouth.

"Listen, Aidan, about last night, I—"

"The wolf thing? No problem."

"No, not the wolf thing." She looked into his caramel-colored eyes. Funny, but his eyes were the same color as the eyes of the wolf she'd imagined standing beside her bed in the middle of the night. *Whoa.* Had doing it doggy-style made her dream about him as a wolf?

He sighed. "We should probably talk about that, but I don't want to make you late. On the other hand, it isn't the type of discussion I want to have in front of Barry."

"Let me go first." She knew for certain he was about to tell her they wouldn't be having sex anymore. She wanted to be the one who said that. It was a matter of pride.

"All right."

"We can't have sex anymore. It's too distracting, and I need to concentrate on my book tour."

He looked decidedly relieved. "I understand."

Of course you do, you rat fink. If I hadn't called it off, you would have. How dare you give me the best sex of my life and then decide we should be abstinent for the rest of the weekend?

But she didn't say any of that. Instead she smiled at him over her coffee cup, even though that smile took all the willpower she had. "It was fun, though. Thanks for a good time." She knew it was a smartass comment, but he'd been ready to dump her, so she felt justified.

He rolled his eyes. "That sounds like something you'd write on a public-bathroom wall."

The eye roll irritated her more than it should have. On some level she acknowledged that he looked way too good leaning in the doorway, and she still wanted him, which wasn't a good idea. "But you'd never see it if I did, because you avoid public bathrooms."

"Damn it, Emma!" He pushed himself away from the doorframe. "I'm sick of your remarks about my money."

"Maybe I'm sick of being reminded every five seconds that you're richer than God! Oh, excuse me, that would be *wealthier* than God. My mistake."

"Are we fighting?"

"Yes. And it's about time. Think of it as class warfare."

"You're not exactly poor, Ms. Bestseller." He pointed a finger at her. "You can afford a loft apartment in the Village, and that's not cheap."

She lifted her chin. "I like living in Manhattan. I'm closer to my publisher."

"I doubt that's the only reason. I think you like the prestige of that loft. And you may ride the subway, but that turquoise suit has a designer label on it."

"What are you doing snooping through my suitcase?"

"You said you wanted it cleaned. I came to get it while you were in the shower."

"Oh. Thanks." She sounded ungracious, but it was tough to be grateful when he was withdrawing access to the one thing that intrigued her the most—his sexy self.

"Because of my name on the hotel registration, you'll have that suit cleaned and hanging in your closet by this afternoon."

"I appreciate that, Aidan."

"I'm sure you do. It's a pricey outfit. Dolce and Gabbana, if I remember right."

She should have figured he'd have an eye for labels. "How do you know I didn't get it at Goodwill?"

"Did you?"

"Well, no, but some of my clothes come from there."

"Anything you brought on this trip?"

"That's beside the point."

He sighed and glanced up at the ceiling. "You're right. We're arguing about nothing."

She couldn't stand it any longer. Although she'd acknowledged her reasons for staying away from him, he had his own reasons for staying away from her, and not knowing those reasons was driving her crazy.

Taking a deep breath, she faced him. "I need to be clear about something. If I don't get an answer now, it will bug me forever."

He looked wary. "About what?"

"Yesterday you implied that we couldn't expect to have a relationship. I leaped on that and started complaining about your money, but I never gave you a chance to explain. Why couldn't we have a relationship, Aidan?" She hated the longing in her voice when she said that, but she couldn't take it back.

He gazed at her for several long seconds, as if considering his answer. "You'll probably think this is medieval."

"Try me."

"The truth is, I'm expected to marry someone connected to a family with power and wealth equal to the Wallaces'."

Her jaw dropped. "Seriously?"

"Yes. I owe my family a great deal, and I intend to do what's expected of me."

"What about love?"

"That's a modern concept, and it's fine for the masses, but—"

"*The masses?* Are you listening to yourself? You sound like some prince from a royal family!"

He nodded. "In a way, I am. Love of family, loyalty to family are more important than my individual preferences."

"I can't imagine." She stared at him, unable to comprehend that kind of self-sacrifice. She would never have believed it if he hadn't told her himself. "I adore my mother, but if she attempted to choose the man I marry, I would shut her down so fast."

"And there's the difference between us." His chest heaved. "You need to get ready, and I need to make a few calls. I'll meet you by the front door in fifteen minutes."

"I'll be there." She drank her coffee quickly while she ate the cake much faster than she would have liked. Then she finished getting ready, all the while trying to assimilate what Aidan had told her. To think of a twenty-first-century man caving to that kind of manipulation boggled her mind.

He was a person, not a chess piece. This was America, for crying out loud, the land of the free. He should be free to marry anyone he chose. But he seemed to have accepted his obligation without question. No matter how she turned the concept around in her mind, she couldn't make it fit with the strong, confident man she'd come to know.

She wondered whether he was afraid of losing his inheritance and all that the Wallace fortune provided in the way of bennies. He did enjoy his perks. Still, from what she'd observed of his character so far, he was a man of honor. She doubted a loss of income would make him do something he didn't think was right. For whatever reason, he believed in this custom of allowing his family to dictate his marital future.

In the meantime, she suspected he'd sown his share of wild oats. He enjoyed sex with a gusto that suggested plenty of experience with the endeavor. In that case, why didn't he want to sow a few more with her this weekend?

He didn't, though. She'd have bet her next royalty check that he'd come into her bedroom with the express purpose of calling a halt to their fun and games. She'd barely beat him to the punch.

The more she thought about that decision on his part, the happier she became. He'd decided to back off for the same reason she had. The sex had been too intense for both of them. While she was afraid of losing focus on her career, he was afraid of becoming so attached to her that he wouldn't be able to honor his duty to his family.

Greatly cheered by that conclusion, she located her purse and her satchel containing her book-signing materials before walking out into the living room exactly at the fifteen-minute mark he'd set.

He paced in front of the unlit fireplace, his Black-Berry to his ear. The remnants of his breakfast sat on a tray on the coffee table.

Curious, she took inventory. He'd had coffee, too, but from the looks of the plate, he'd had steak and eggs instead of chocolate cake. Made sense. He was a big guy who would need to support all those gorgeous muscles with the right kind of fuel.

She didn't mean to eavesdrop on his conversation, but short of retreating to the bedroom again, she couldn't very well help it. Oh, hell, she might as well admit she'd been straining to hear what he was saying from the minute she'd realized he was on the phone.

Years ago, she'd accepted the fact that writers were notorious eavesdroppers. She got some of her best story ideas that way. Add to that her natural curiosity about anything to do with Aidan, and she became the human equivalent of a wiretap.

"Sure, Nadia. We'll be at the bookstore about one this afternoon. I'd love to see you. We should have time for coffee during Emma's signing. See you then." He disconnected the call and turned to Emma. "Ready?"

"Yes." She fought the urge to ask him who Nadia was.

He gestured with the BlackBerry. "Somebody I've known ever since I was a kid. She's going to drop by the signing."

"Great." And she knew, just *knew* that Nadia was a potential candidate for this arranged-marriage deal. He'd known her since he was a kid, which meant the two families were close. Emma read the tabloids, and she was aware that wealthy families socialized with other wealthy families, even if they lived in cities as far apart as New York and Chicago.

Instantly Emma hated this Nadia person who was colluding with Aidan's family to imprison him in a loveless marriage. True, he was going along with it docilely, but apparently, he'd been brainwashed from a young age. The whole concept seemed just wrong.

Wrong as it was, though, it was none of her business. Having one really steamy night of sex with a man didn't give her the right to meddle in his personal life. This situation wasn't a plot point in one of her books. She couldn't simply rewrite the script to suit her worldview.

Yet she obsessed about the unfairness of it all during odd moments when she didn't have to concentrate on something else, like one of her two radio interviews or her morning TV appearance. Aidan accompanied her to all of them and stayed in the background. They didn't talk much in the car, either. After the easy banter they'd shared on the plane and their sexual abandon with each other in the suite, their silences were awkward.

Emma didn't know what to do about that. The day's schedule marched steadily toward the one o'clock bookstore event, to which Aidan had so graciously invited Nadia *whatever*. Maybe her last name was Rockefeller or DuPont.

Emma secretly hoped Nadia would turn out to be a dull and colorless woman who could hardly wait to get her hands on a specimen the likes of Aidan. That would further justify Emma's indignation, to think of Aidan shackled to someone who would bore him to tears during their first week of married life.

At the bookstore, Emma snagged another coffee drink to keep her courage up for the reading session ahead. She dreaded the reading portion of the event far more than the autograph session. Signing books and talking to readers was gratifying, even if it wore her out. But listening to herself read her own words aloud was pure torture because she never got over the urge to edit her work, even after it was finished.

Still, she was expected to read, so she did. It wasn't that she never knuckled under to satisfy others. But she wasn't into self-sacrifice, which Aidan seemed to be. Ordering his entire life to further his family's ambitions made no sense to her. As one o'clock drew near, the prospect of reading before an audience took on extra significance because Nadia would be there, Nadia the albatross around Aidan's neck.

Emma tried to imagine that Nadia wasn't thrilled about the arrangement, either, but any woman would take one look at Aidan and think to herself, *I want some of that.* Emma certainly had.

As the time for the reading approached, Aidan stood to one side of the rows of chairs and talked with the bookstore manager. Emma pretended to scan the passage she would soon be reading while watching him from the corner of her eye. Yep, he was certifiably gorgeous. Nadia couldn't possibly be upset about her fate.

With five minutes to go, the chairs had filled and newcomers were forced to stand. Emma was gratified by the turnout, which was a constant source of amazement to her. When she wrote a book alone in her loft, she had a difficult time imagining all these people reading it. But they did, and for that she was very grateful.

Aidan hadn't made a move toward any of the women who'd taken a seat, so Emma didn't think Nadia had arrived yet. Then he turned, as if sensing the arrival of someone. It was the oddest thing, as if he knew she was coming before she even arrived.

Emma felt a pang of something that just might have been jealousy. Maybe he had a bond with this childhood friend that was so strong he felt her before he saw her. Emma couldn't expect to compete with that.

Or that. When Nadia rounded a bookshelf and started toward Aidan, Emma groaned softly in dismay. The woman was stunning. She moved like a runway model, and she had the figure of one, too. Tall and fashionably slim, she was dressed in an elegant silver jacket and skirt that provided an eye-catching contrast to her long black hair. Gray eyes and thick lashes gave her an exotic look that any man would find intriguing.

As Aidan gave her a hug, Emma felt as if someone had dunked her heart in ice water. These two obviously belonged to an exclusive club, one to which Emma would never be invited. Aidan wouldn't dread spending his life with this glorious creature. They were made for each other.

Emma should count herself lucky that she'd been able to spend one night in Aidan's arms. Now that Nadia had shown up, Aidan might very well forget that Emma existed. She had to laugh at herself, thinking this morning that she'd had a decision to make as to whether she'd have more sex with Aidan. It had never been up to her.

Chapter 14

When Nadia arrived, Aidan didn't sense more than one werewolf in the area, so her brother Theo hadn't tagged along. *Good.* He needed to talk with Nadia alone and find out what she knew about her younger sibling's mental state. Having her come to the bookstore served a dual purpose, though. It would also remind him of his responsibilities to the pack.

One glance at Emma told him that she got the picture, which was another reason he'd wanted Nadia to attend the signing. He'd made so many mistakes regarding Emma, and he'd never be able to atone for all of them. But he could start setting the record straight now.

He deserved her anger and resentment, both of which he saw etched on her beautiful face. Having those emotions directed at him sliced into his heart, but he would bear it. The more she disliked him, the better off she'd be.

He smiled at Nadia. "You're looking great."

"So are you." Her gaze was friendly, but there wasn't a flicker of passion in those gray eyes.

"Let's get some coffee."

"Okay, but I want a book before I leave, and I want her to sign it."

"Then let's buy one before we get the coffee. She might sell out." Aidan led the way through the rows of bookshelves and snagged a copy of Emma's book on the way to the cashier's counter.

After paying for it, he handed it to Nadia. "A small thank-you for coming down here."

"I was happy to. I'd heard you were in town, and I was hoping we'd get a chance to catch up."

"Then let's get some coffee and do that."

Within minutes they were seated across from each other at a small bistro table, steaming lattes in front of them. From Aidan's chair he could glance sideways and look between a row of bookshelves to the spot where Emma stood reading from her book. She'd chosen a forest green knit dress today, and he'd decided it was his favorite.

"She's very pretty," Nadia said.

"Who?" He faced Nadia and tried to look innocent.

"You know who."

"I've been hired to keep an eye on her."

"So you said." Nadia looked amused.

"Anyway, thanks for showing up on short notice. I hope I didn't screw up your work schedule."

"Nah, I needed the break. I'm in the middle of designing my fall collection, and I was sick to death of hunching over the drawing board trying to think of a coat style that hasn't been done to death. This is nice." Nadia cupped both hands around her latte. "So, what's going on between you and Emma Gavin?"

"Next question."

"Oh, so you don't want to talk about it." She took a sip of her latte. "That's not very sporting of you."

Aidan blew out a breath. "I misjudged there. Too much heat between us. This morning I gave her the talk about my family's expectations."

Nadia's gray eyes warmed with sympathy. "I know what that's like. I've given that speech to a few guys. I suppose she thought you were nuts to go along with such a thing."

"Yeah, she did. Let me ask you something." Although no one was sitting close enough to hear the conversation, he lowered his voice out of habit. "Have you ever resented the idea that you'd eventually have to marry for the good of the pack?"

"Not yet."

"Meaning?"

Nadia kept her voice low, too. "It means I've never found anyone, man or Were, who was worth the pain of challenging the system." She took another drink of her latte. "Since you're asking that, I'm wondering if you have."

Aidan quickly shook his head. "Nope. Just an idle question."

"You've never struck me as the kind of guy who asks idle questions. Coming on the heels of you giving Emma that speech this morning, I have to wonder if she means more than you're willing to admit."

"She can't mean anything to me. She's human."

Nadia leaned closer to him. "It's not as if Weres have never mated with humans, Aidan."

"I don't know any personally."

She sat back. "I do. I guess you've never met my uncle Lenny."

"No."

"He fell hard for a Las Vegas showgirl, and now Aunt Trixi is part of the family. Last year she taught me and my cousin Judy how to twirl tassels with our nipples. In opposite directions."

Aidan laughed. If he were the least bit interested in Nadia, that tassel-twirling comment would be a turn-on. Instead he just thought it was funny. "Now there's a marketable skill if I ever heard one."

"Yeah, it was fun." She glanced at his latte. "You're not drinking that."

He'd completely forgotten it was there. He shoved it aside. "Did your aunt continue to dance in Vegas?"

"No, of course not. She moved here. She and Uncle Lenny have a house on the estate up in the Dells."

He lowered his voice again. "Virtually under house arrest, I suppose."

"I think she was at first, but now she's allowed to visit her family in California and stuff like that."

Aidan tried to imagine Emma voluntarily giving up her writing and allowing her existence to be monitored by the Were community. It would never happen, not in a million years.

"So much depends on the person involved and whether they're adaptable," Nadia said.

"Right." He shook his head. "Let's get off that depressing subject. There's something else we need to talk about."

She sighed. "My obnoxious little brother."

"He's fixated on Emma."

"I know. He has all her books, and he boasts about how they're friends."

"They're not."

"Of course they're not. Theo's delusional. He moved into the city this summer, and he spends way too much time alone in his little apartment. I hate to say it, but I think he's got some revolutionary ideas going on."

"I was afraid of that."

"He's mentioned several times that Emma understands us and would want us to be free of what he calls 'stupid restrictions.'"

Aidan groaned. "Oh, yeah. Let's go back to the days of being hunted with torches. That would be lots of fun."

"I've tried to tell my dad that we need to do something about Theo, but whenever I suggest that he could bring us down, my dad says all young alphas are high-spirited. Then he accuses me of being in competition with Theo because one of us will be in charge someday." She shivered. "Having Theo in charge is one scary thought."

"Obviously Theo needs an alpha male to set him straight. And soon, before he drags Emma into this and causes everybody a big problem."

"My father should be the one to handle him, but I guarantee he's not going to. I would if I could, but I can't buck my dad on this."

"Then it looks like it'll have to be me."

Emma looked up when she finished reading the passage from *Night Shift*. Aidan and Nadia still sat in the coffee shop, their heads close together as they carried on what was obviously an intense conversation. *Aidan and Nadia.* One name was the mirror image of the other. Their parents must have planned it that way.

She felt like a naive fool. From the beginning, she'd known Aidan was out of her league. He'd never pretended otherwise. She'd told him that some recreational sex would be just hunky-dory.

Except it wasn't so hunky-dory now that she understood how fleeting that experience had been. No man had ever excited her as Aidan did. What if she never found another guy who triggered that kind of uninhibited response? Was she doomed to settle for second best?

"Miss Gavin?" A bookstore employee touched her on the elbow. "Are you ready to autograph books, now?"

"Oh!" A line had formed in front of the table, and because Emma also stood in front of the table, she was face-to-face with the first person in line, a grandmotherly woman dressed in purple sweats.

Emma smiled at her. "Hi, there."

"Hi, yourself, sweetie. You looked so sad just now. I hope everything's okay."

"Everything's wonderful. If you'll excuse me, I'll just move around to the other side of the table so I can sit down and autograph your book for you."

"Take your time. My name's Sylvia. Say, I'm *so* excited about the party tonight. I didn't make it last year, but I'll be there this time. I'm coming in costume."

"The party." Emma had totally lost track of what she was supposed to be doing after the book event. Seeing Nadia had torpedoed her thoughts. Then she remembered. "Oh, the *party.*" She had one more radio interview this afternoon. Then from seven to ten tonight, she'd be the guest of honor at the monthly meeting of the Werewolves and Wine Club, which convened in a private room above a bar in downtown Chicago not far from the Palmer House. The members were all avid readers of anything werewolf related, and she was a popular author with the group.

She'd attended once before, and most everyone came in some sort of werewolf costume. Emma appreciated their enthusiasm, but she'd decided prior to her first visit to the club that she wouldn't do the costume thing. Her decision had been the same this year, too.

"I'll look forward to seeing you there, Sylvia." She slid the autographed book back across the table.

"What are you wearing?"

"A black dress."

Sylvia looked surprised. "No fur of any kind?"

"I want to make sure everyone knows who I am."

"Oh, right. That makes perfect sense." The woman reached over and patted Emma's hand. "See you there. And for the record, I love the way you write sex scenes."

"Thank you." Emma hoped she'd remember Sylvia by the time the party rolled around. But then again, maybe she wouldn't recognize her in a werewolf suit.

Nearly an hour later, all the books were gone and Emma had signed several bookplates for those who weren't able to buy a book. She'd chatted with the bookstore manager and expressed her gratitude. *Time to wrap things up*. As she signed one last bookplate for a latecomer, she became aware of Aidan and Nadia standing off to one side of the autograph table.

Nadia held a book in her hand. Well, that was classy of her, to buy a book even if she hadn't arrived specifically for that purpose. Emma knew full well Nadia had come to see Aidan.

The two of them walked over to the table after the last autograph seeker left.

Aidan spoke first. "Emma Gavin, I'd like you to meet Nadia Henderson."

Emma blinked. Theo's last name was Henderson, but surely that was a coincidence. She held out her hand. "I'm happy to meet you, Nadia."

"Same here. I hope you don't mind signing one more book." She laid a copy of *Night Shift* on the table.

"Not at all. Thanks for buying it." Emma was determined to be gracious to this woman who seemingly had everything—looks, money, and a future with Aidan Wallace. Jealousy was a terrible emotion, and Emma wanted to be rid of it. She wanted to be, but she wasn't. She longed to leap across the table and close her hands around Nadia's lovely throat.

Instead she wrote, *Enjoy the fantasy. Best wishes, Emma Gavin,* in this cursed woman's book. She wondered whether Nadia had slept with Aidan. Oh, hell, who was she kidding? Of course they'd had sex. Two people who looked as though they had and were pledged to marry someday? They'd certainly taken a test-spin and kicked the tires of their future marital ride.

Smiling so much her cheeks ached, Emma closed the cover of the book and nudged it back toward Nadia. "Too bad we can't go out for a drink or something, but I have a radio interview in thirty minutes."

"Of course! I need to be going, anyway. Work calls."

Despite herself, Emma was curious. "I don't think Aidan mentioned what you do."

"I design organic clothing."

"Oh. That's terrific!" Well, that was the topper. Besides looks, money, and access to the world's most eligible bachelor, Nadia ran a green business. Emma was in favor of green businesses. In another life, she might have bought clothes from Nadia Henderson. But she would go stark naked before she'd buy a single stitch from the woman who would bear Aidan's children.

Yes, she was being petty and unfair, but she'd had a lot of caffeine, not enough sleep, and rock-star sex with a man who would never touch her again. A girl couldn't be blamed for being a little irritable under those circumstances.

"So"—Emma stood and gathered her things—"we need to take off, Aidan."

He nodded and pulled out his BlackBerry. "Let's go. I'll make sure Barry's waiting in front."

"I'll just walk out with you." Nadia fell into step beside Emma. "The bus stops only about half a block from the front entrance."

Emma glanced over at her in shock. "You took a bus here?"

"Sure. Why not?"

Because you're loaded. "I just thought you'd probably have a driver, like Aidan."

"I can see the point of a driver for something like your book tour because you have to move quickly from place to place."

"No, I mean Aidan always has a driver, even in New York."

"Oh." Nadia smiled. "I guess he hasn't seen the light. Most of my family's the same way, but I keep telling them that chauffeur thing is so last century. We need to make more conscious choices about our mode of transport."

"Yes, we do." Emma hated to find herself agreeing with Nadia about anything, but taking public transportation was one of her favorite causes. She glanced over at Nadia's silver suit. "Is that suit organic?" She seriously doubted it.

"Yes. I realize that's hard to believe with the metallic sheen of the fabric, but I've patented a special process to create that effect without using any toxic dyes. My mission is to make organic at least as stylish as haute couture."

"Impressive." Despite herself, Emma *was* impressed. It appeared that Aidan would end up with a wife who was intelligent and eco-conscious, in addition to being a knockout. No doubt they would be very happy together. Emma wanted to weep at the injustice of it all.

Barry had pulled up outside in a no-parking zone, but the Wallace flag flew from the rear bumper, so Emma knew the town car was golden. She turned to Nadia and held out her hand. "It's been a pleasure. I wish you and Aidan all the luck in the world, although you won't need it, I'm sure."

"Thank you." Nadia's grip was firm. "Just so you know, he thinks you're very special."

A lump formed in Emma's throat. "I think he's special, too."

Nadia held her hand for a moment longer. "Take care of yourself, Emma Gavin."

"I will." She turned and climbed into the car as Barry held the door open for her.

"Give me a second, Barry," Aidan said. "I need to double-check a couple of things with Nadia. You can go ahead and start the car."

"You've got it." Leaving the back door open for Aidan, Barry walked around and slid in behind the wheel of the town car.

"I still can't get used to hanging out in illegal parking spaces, Barry," Emma said.

"Me, either. But apparently the Wallaces have a connection with the Hendersons, and the Hendersons are big medicine in Chicago. That flag on the back is all we need for the royal treatment."

"That woman Aidan's talking to is Nadia Henderson."

"Is it, really? I wondered. I've seen pictures of her and thought it might be her. Too bad about her brother, though."

A cold chill slid down Emma's spine. No, the last

name wasn't some weird coincidence. She kept her tone casual. "You mean Theo?"

"That's the one. Aidan told me we needed to watch out for him. What the hey. Every family has at least one bad egg."

"Yes, I suppose they do." And Aidan had known all about this bad seed from the beginning. No wonder he'd wanted to handle this problem personally. Emma reached in the pocket of her dress and pulled out the card Nadia had given her. Then she crumpled it into a ball and deliberately tossed it on the floor of the town car.

Littering wasn't something she normally did, but she felt like breaking a few rules, getting a little rowdy. Without knowing it, she'd been a pawn in a game played by the very wealthy. And she was no longer willing to play, at least not by their rules.

Chapter 15

Aidan wasn't surprised that Emma didn't make conversation on the way to the radio station or during the drive back to the hotel. He couldn't expect to be her favorite person after he'd asked Nadia to the book event and forced Emma to confront the harsh reality of his situation. His heart ached for her, and also for himself if he was honest, although he loathed the concept of self-pity.

For a moment there in the coffee shop, when Nadia had mentioned her uncle Lenny, he'd wondered whether he'd been foolish to reject Emma so completely. But once he'd heard the full story and had figured out that Emma would never go for the same deal as Nadia's aunt Trixi, he'd fallen into despair.

He never should have agreed to have sex with Emma, but he'd been weak and she'd been . . . irresistible. She still was, and he wasn't convinced he'd ever get over her. Roarke had been right all along. Aidan should have sent someone else to handle this assignment.

Too late for regrets, though. He had to see this mess through to the end and protect Emma from whatever gonzo plan Theo had dreamed up. In the process, he'd shut Theo down. Theo might have been a troublemaker, but he was also a pack animal who obeyed pack rules. When a bigger and stronger alpha subdued him, he'd be forced to give up his revolutionary plans, at least while that alpha lived. Aidan expected to live a very long time, and he would be reminding Theo of his presence on a regular basis.

In the meantime, he and Emma needed to eat something before they headed out to the next event. He'd noted with some concern that it was a werewolf costume party. He hoped to hell Theo hadn't heard about it.

As they neared the hotel, Aidan turned to Emma. "Would you rather stop for something to eat or order room service?"

"Room service is fine." Her tone was prim.

Her prim tone and room service for dinner both suited him. Sitting across from her in stony silence in a restaurant wouldn't be a barrel of laughs.

When they reached the hotel, Emma got out of the car, thanked Barry, and informed him they'd walk to the party, so he was free until the next morning.

As Aidan followed Emma out, Barry glanced at him, obviously wanting confirmation for that plan of action.

"That won't work, Emma." Aidan sensed a fight coming and hoped he was wrong. "I'm not opposed to a walk, but for security purposes we need to take the car."

She turned to him. "Be honest with me for once, Aidan. How much security do we really need to deal with a spoiled rich boy? Or is all this elaborate *security* primarily designed to protect your girlfriend's family name?"

Aidan sighed. "So you made the connection."

"Actually, no, I didn't. Chicago's a huge city, and I was

sure it was some strange coincidence that Nadia and Theo had the same last name. While you were talking to Nadia on the curb this afternoon, Barry mentioned something to me about the Henderson's problem child, and then it all clicked."

Aidan glanced at Barry, who looked stricken. "It's okay," Aidan said. "I didn't tell you to keep it quiet. It's never been a secret."

"But it was news to me!" Emma crossed her arms and glared at him. "I would have appreciated knowing this factoid when you knew it, Aidan. I'm assuming you found out the night you traced Theo's e-mail and decided you had to come along on this jaunt."

"Yes."

"So instead of being all about protecting me, this is all about protecting the Henderson family—who will someday be your in-laws—from public embarrassment."

"No. My top priority is your protection. It always has been."

"Considering the fact that you hid your connection to Theo's family, I'm not sure I can believe you."

"I didn't *hide* it. I just didn't mention it."

"Same thing."

"No, it's not. If I'd been determined to hide it, I wouldn't have said anything to Barry. And I damned sure wouldn't have invited Nadia to your book event."

"Does she know her brother is the reason you came to Chicago?"

"She does now."

Emma threw up her hands. "Situation solved. That's one savvy woman. She'll get her brother by the ear and make sure he behaves himself. She has a lot more to lose if he becomes tabloid fodder than you do."

"He won't listen to her." Aidan couldn't very well

explain pack hierarchy, but Nadia, clever and accomplished as she might have been, couldn't confront Theo against her father's wishes. He was the pack alpha, and Nadia had to obey him.

"He has parents, then." Emma's breath made clouds in the cold air. "Nadia can call in her parents. Hell, *you* can call in the parents! Why hasn't anyone done that? Why are we all tiptoeing around the problem with this kid?"

Aidan scrubbed a hand through his hair. He would rather not have this argument within hearing distance of the hotel doorman, but he and Emma needed to come to some sort of understanding. "His parents don't believe there's anything wrong with Theo, other than youthful high spirits."

"I've known families like that," Barry said. He seemed eager to be a peacemaker. "The kid is hell on wheels, and the parents don't want to see it. They keep thinking their son or daughter will grow out of it. Sometimes they do. Sometimes they don't."

Emma glanced at Barry. Then she studied the sidewalk and tapped her foot. Finally she looked at Aidan. "Okay, we'll take the car."

"Good."

Her expression contained sympathy. Not a lot, but some. "You placed yourself in an awkward position by coming to Chicago with me, didn't you?"

"To say the least."

"Bet you wish you'd sent somebody else."

"Devoutly."

A hint of a smile touched her mouth. "Well, I'm glad you're here."

"You are?" He was stunned. "Why?"

Her smile broadened. "Research."

*   *   *

Emma shared a light dinner with Aidan in the penthouse. They agreed that the long dining table felt too formal, so they ate in the living room in front of the gas fire. As if by mutual consent, they talked about everything except Theo. They discussed the interviews she'd done, the turnout at the bookstore, even the weather.

She could see no point in dragging out the subject of Theo again. There wasn't anything more to say, anyway. She wouldn't say she felt sorry for Aidan, exactly. He was the engineer of his own complicated scheme and deserved whatever grief came of this weekend. But still, he'd bitten off way more than anyone could possibly chew. He'd signed on to handle what might be an impossible task—protecting her from his future brother-in-law while keeping the problem from becoming public. Apparently, he couldn't expect support from his future mother-in-law or father-in-law. His future wife was supportive but unable to control her brother.

On top of all that, he was wildly attracted to Emma, and she, to him. She'd made things worse by talking him into going to bed with her. Although she couldn't bring herself to regret that experience, it hadn't been a great idea for either of their sakes.

But Aidan could have stopped her cold with the complete dossier on Theo, one containing info on Aidan's connection to the Henderson family. Had she understood why sex between them was such a bad idea, she would have made a greater effort to back away from the gorgeous Aidan Wallace.

What was done was done, though. She'd had her romp in the hay with one of the wealthiest bachelors in the country. Her heart might be nicked, but it wasn't broken.

Besides, as she'd claimed in all honesty, she would file this weekend—the good, the bad, and the incredibly dysfunctional—under the heading of research. No experience in a writer's life was ever wasted. At least that was the way she consoled herself when life didn't turn out as happily ever after as the endings to her books.

After finishing up her dinner, she excused herself and went into the master bedroom to get ready for the party.

"Should I change?" Aidan called after her.

She paused in the doorway and turned back to him. "Not unless you have a werewolf costume hanging in your closet."

"That would be a negative."

"Then go as you are. That'll be more than fine."

"Good. Then I'll see if the Bulls are on TV." He picked up the remote. "Are you wearing a costume?"

"No. I'll be wearing the proverbial little black dress."

"Just curious, but why wouldn't you want to go along with the costume idea? I'm sure you could buy something at a shop in New York."

"Yes, but I'd look like a five-foot-three blond woman in a furry suit. It would be an insult to the magnificent werewolves in my books. Those wolves have presence."

Aidan nodded. "They do. I like the way you've described them, like actual wolves, only bigger and more majestic. It's a nice image."

"They're very much like the wolf in my dream, the one I was sure walked into my bedroom last night."

"Nightmares can be scary."

"I was a little scared at first." She rested her hand on the doorframe. "But now I wish I could see that wolf again. He could have walked right out of one of my books."

"You're sure it was a male?"

"Definitely a male. Big head, powerful shoulders. And there's a look in the eye of a true alpha. He had it."

"A look in the eye? How do you know that if werewolves don't exist?"

She smiled. "All alpha males have that look, as if they know exactly what needs to be done and are prepared to do it. You get that look sometimes, Aidan."

"No kidding."

"I wouldn't kid about something like that. It's very attractive." She met his gaze and saw the very look she'd just described—focused, intense, hot.

One glance was all it took to create the same sizzling awareness between them that had caused so much trouble last night. She knew without a doubt that if either of them made a move toward the other, they'd be on the floor tearing at each other's clothes.

She slapped the doorframe. "I need to get ready." Then she turned, walked into the bedroom, and closed the door behind her. She locked it for good measure.

Even a lock wouldn't stop a true alpha, but it might slow him down and make him reconsider whether what he wanted was what he should have. Aidan had a powerful sex drive, and for whatever reason, he was drawn to her.

Exciting as it was to be wanted that fiercely, Emma wasn't willing to pay the price of surrendering. One night with Aidan had given her a benchmark for what she wanted in a man. A second night could convince her she had no hope of finding it. Except with a man she couldn't have.

"One thing about this costume party," Aidan said as they rode the few blocks to the bar where it would be held. "If Theo caught wind of it, he's liable to show up."

"And do what? There'll be fifty or sixty people there, at least, maybe more. Yes, it was creepy when he suddenly appeared in the bookstore wearing fake fur on his hands and some kind of fake teeth, but that was partly because nobody was around."

"All I'm saying is stay close. Let me know if you're going to the bathroom, stuff like that."

"Which brings up another point I've been mulling over. What's Theo's goal?"

Aidan had some ideas about that, but he couldn't share them with Emma. "I don't know for sure."

"I mean, he can't think he'll actually convince me he's a werewolf, so what's he really after?"

Aidan figured he had to come up with something, and the more innocuous, the better. He didn't want to scare her unnecessarily. "Maybe just the chance to have a conversation he can brag about to his friends."

"I would be happy to have a conversation with him. It's the part where he claims to be a werewolf that bothers me. You don't suppose he's mentally unbalanced, do you?"

"No."

She peered over at him in the darkened backseat of the car. "So the werewolf thing is just an attention getter?"

"Something like that."

"I hope he's not there, Aidan. I think I'd recognize him, but in case I don't and you spot him, let me know."

"If he's there, I'll know."

"How? He could be in full costume, so you can't even see his face."

I'll smell him. But he couldn't very well say that, either. "I'm trained to pick up vibes. Part of being in the security business is being able to pick out the bad actors in a crowd. Theo isn't exactly subtle."

"True." She took a deep breath. "We're here."

Aidan glanced out the window of the town car. A large neon sign advertised ANDY'S ALE HOUSE in orange letters. The main bar was on the ground floor, but he could see lights on the second floor, where the party was in full swing.

Barry swerved to the curb, put the car in park, and came around to open the door for them.

"We shouldn't be long, Barry." Aidan climbed out and offered his hand to Emma.

She gave Aidan a sympathetic glance. "I'm afraid we can't just make an appearance and leave. We'll need to stay a couple of hours."

Aidan sighed. "Okay. See you a little after nine, Barry." Two hours in a crowded, noisy space would be hell on his ears, but he'd deal with it.

"I'll be here." Barry returned to the driver's seat.

Emma hugged her coat around her and gazed up at the second floor of the bar. "I'm afraid this won't be anything like the place you took me on Wednesday night."

"You mean Jessie's?"

"Yes. I love the atmosphere there."

"I do, too." He longed to say they'd go again when she came back from her tour, but he knew they wouldn't. The heated glance that had passed between them after dinner tonight told him that he couldn't afford to spend any more evenings with Emma. He wanted her too much.

One glance and he'd felt the beginnings of a shift. Had she stayed a moment longer, she would have heard his low growl of frustration. While she'd been in the bedroom getting ready for the party, he'd sat on the couch pretending to watch a basketball game while waiting for that shift to reverse. He was thankful that it had.

"We should go in," Emma said.

"Before we do, let me say something." He realized that out here on the street was a kind of safety zone, where they could talk without anyone hearing them, and yet he wouldn't be tempted to pull her into his arms.

She turned to him. "I'm listening."

He took a moment to enjoy how great she looked standing there in her black trench coat, a snazzy little red evening purse on a chain over her shoulder. Her blond hair curled around her raised collar and her blue eyes . . . ah, how he loved gazing into those eyes, whether they were filled with laughter or lust.

"Aidan? You wanted to say something?"

"Uh, yes. Sorry." He gathered his thoughts, which had scattered when he looked into her eyes. "I want to apologize for not giving you all the information about Theo immediately. You had the right to know that he belongs to a prominent Chicago family and that the Wallaces have ties to that family."

"But if you'd told me, chances are I never would have allowed you to come along."

"That wasn't the reason for not telling you, though. My father wanted me to handle this as quietly as possible so there wouldn't be any ill will between the two families. Having you in the loop wouldn't have furthered that cause. I accepted that rationale."

"Of course you did. He's your father, and besides, you work for him. I was angry at first, but I get it now."

"The thing is I should have told you, anyway. I should have trusted you with the information."

"Not necessarily. You don't know me all that well. How could you be sure how I'd react?"

"I suppose you're right." But he knew her better than she thought he did. After spending three months watching her behavior in many different situations, he knew she was trustworthy.

"In any case, rest easy on that point, Aidan. I don't blame you anymore, and I promise to have only good memories of you."

"Same here." He fought the urge to pull her close, but that's why he was standing out on the sidewalk saying this instead of waiting until they were back in the penthouse.

She clasped her hands together. "So, apology accepted. Ready to face the crowd?"

"In a minute. There's something else."

"Okay."

"When we get back to the penthouse, I'm going straight to my bedroom, and I'm asking you to go straight to yours. If we linger at all, I—we can't linger, Emma. I'm not that strong."

Her gaze softened. "Me, either."

"So you're okay with that plan?"

"No, but I'll do it. We have to be smart about . . . we just have to be smart."

"Yes, we do. Emma, I wish—"

"Don't say another word, Aidan. You'll only make things worse. Let's go in." She started toward the entrance of the bar.

With a sigh he followed her. She was right. He needed to shut the hell up before he said something they'd both regret.

Chapter 16

"Emma, it's me, Sylvia. From the book signing."

Emma peered through the eyeholes of the ugliest plastic werewolf mask in the world. "Hey, Sylvia! I never would have recognized you."

"I know! Isn't this a great mask?"

"It's scary, all right." The werewolf's lips were pulled back in a snarl worthy of the creepiest horror movie.

"I improvised the rest. I think it works, don't you?" Sylvia gestured to her baggy gray sweat suit and fuzzy gray slippers.

"Absolutely." Emma took another gulp of her wine.

"Want to hear me howl?"

"Uh, well, I—"

"Owwwwooooooo!"

"Nice howl." Emma drank more wine.

"This is the best party. I've been groped twice."

"Groped? By whom?"

"I don't know! That's the fun part of a masked ball, you know. This isn't exactly a ball, but we're all in disguise, so it's the same idea. A little pinch here, a little nudge there. It's all in good fun."

"I'm glad you're enjoying it." This was Emma's idea of hell. She liked to look into people's faces when she talked to them. That was how she gauged reactions to the conversation. Everyone here, with the exception of Aidan and the waiters, had dressed up as a werewolf. Emma stood in a sea of fur, trying to get her bearings.

The crowd milled around her, jostling her sometimes, stopping to chat other times. She'd initiated a few exchanges herself by commenting on the costumes.

The Werewolves and Wine Club members had been nice enough. Many of them had made a point of coming over to say how much they enjoyed her books. A few had brought copies from home for her to sign, which she did happily. These were hard-core fans, and she knew they talked her up at bookstores and on the Internet.

But she couldn't shake the feeling that they didn't really need her here. She'd created the world, but they'd made it their own, and now she was extraneous. They didn't mind her being here, but they viewed her as essentially an outsider. If she'd been one of them, she would have come in costume.

Throughout the evening, she'd studied the people in attendance, in case one of them turned out to be Theo. She'd seen him only briefly in the bookstore, but she remembered he was tall, well over six feet, and lanky. She'd kept track of one guy who fit that description, but when he approached her, his voice had sounded nothing like Theo's. She was sure she'd recognize that voice again if she heard it.

Aidan had stayed within sight, and she found comfort in watching him interact with the costumed guests. He knew how to work a room, and she suspected he was working this one to make sure Theo didn't slip in unnoticed. She wondered what Aidan would do if Theo did show up. Would he take him outside and put the fear of God into him with a little physical intimidation? She didn't doubt it. As much as she'd protested that she didn't need or want a bodyguard for this trip, she was grateful to have Aidan at this party, sifting through the crowd. He drank only mineral water, and she appreciated that, too.

He was working on her behalf. Sure, he was working for his family, too, but he'd said her safety was his primary concern, and he was an honorable man. She believed him.

She also wanted him with a fierce longing that no amount of wine could mute. No doubt, other women in the room wanted him, too. He looked like a *GQ* model with his hand-tailored suit and his white silk shirt open at the neck. Emma smiled as she thought of Sylvia, who wouldn't be above pinching Aidan's butt as she glided by.

The noise level grew, and Emma cast a surreptitious glance at her watch. Twenty minutes to go before Barry would arrive to save them. Yet once he did, they would go straight back to the hotel and separate for the night. At least here she could admire Aidan from afar.

As if he sensed her gaze on him, his head came up, and he looked straight at her. She smiled and hoisted her glass in his direction, toasting his party skills. He smiled back at her, but then someone demanded his attention and he turned away again.

"He's a cutie-pie."

Emma looked for the person who'd made that comment and found Sylvia standing beside her with her mask pushed to the top of her head. She held a plate of finger food in one hand and a glass of white wine in the other.

"He is that," Emma agreed.

"Nice buns."

"Intelligent, too."

"He has intelligent buns? Does that make him a smart-ass?"

Emma laughed. "You're too quick for me, Sylvia."

"Nah, I'm just an old lady. But I've seen the way you look at him, and the way he looks at you. You two would make beautiful babies together."

"Sorry to burst your bubble, Sylvia, but Aidan and I aren't a couple."

"Really?" Sylvia glanced from Aidan to Emma. "You look like you are, always keeping track of each other. I thought you must be together. I was hearing wedding bells."

"Won't be happening."

"Then I guess I can tell you that I did a stealth-pinch move on him."

Emma grinned. "I can pretty much guess what that is."

"I'm sure you can. I sidle over, pretending I'm listening in on the conversation, and then—*bam!*—I pinch and leave. But I could barely do the stealth pinch on him. He has a very firm butt."

"I know."

"Oh, really?" Sylvia widened her eyes as if shocked by the news. "How would you know that, missy?"

"I'll never tell."

Sylvia set her plate down on a nearby table and waggled her finger at Emma. "Men like that don't come along every day. I should know. My Ned was one of a kind. We were married for fifty-two years. I'm still mad at him for leaving me."

"He left you?"

Sylvia shrugged. "He had to. He died."

"Oh, Sylvia, I'm sorry. That must have been very hard."

"It was. I felt really punk for a couple of years. But life goes on. I picked up one of your books and after reading it, I said to myself, *Sylvia, there are still men out there to pinch!* So I'm back in the game." She picked up her plate again. "I'm off to get more food. Thanks for keeping me young, Emma."

In the general category of compliments, Emma thought that was an outstanding one. Maybe this party hadn't been such a lost cause, after all. And she'd been able to Aidan-watch for a solid two hours.

About that time he walked over and stood beside her. "How are you holding up?"

"Not too bad. You?"

"I've been pinched a time or two."

Emma smiled to herself. "I'm not surprised." She studied the crowd. "I never did see him. I don't think he came tonight."

"He didn't."

"You sound very sure of that."

Aidan set his glass of mineral water on the table next to them. "That's because I am very sure of that. He didn't show, which is good. Maybe he gave up after last night's fiasco. He has a book, thanks to his friend Terry."

"Maybe Nadia talked to him and convinced him to back off."

"Maybe."

Someone jostled Emma, and she grabbed her purse

as it started to slide down her shoulder. "It's really crowded in here. The party hasn't been as arduous as I expected, but I'm ready to leave."

Aidan shot a look at his cuffs and checked his watch. "Barry should be down there in about five minutes."

She couldn't resist teasing him. "I saw how you did that maneuver. You like checking your limited-edition watch, don't you?"

He glanced over at her and smiled. "It's elegant. I appreciate elegance."

Her good mood evaporated. "Like Nadia," she said without thinking.

"I'll admit Nadia is elegant," he said. "But so are you."

"Me? I'm short and stubby."

"Stubby? Hardly."

"Maybe stubby is too harsh, and I guess I'm sort of cute, but nobody—and I mean *nobody*—has ever accused me of being elegant."

He touched her cheek, his fingers very warm. "Then consider yourself accused."

Although he removed his hand almost immediately, Emma felt the imprint of his fingers as they said their good-byes, retrieved their coats, and walked back down the stairs to the street, where Barry waited.

Elegant. He was just being nice, of course. They were close to the end of this adventure, so he could afford to be nice. In a few minutes, they'd go up to the penthouse and into their isolation units, or at least that's the way she'd begun to think of their separate bedrooms.

The car ride was quick and silent. Emma concluded that both of them were thinking about the night ahead and their vow not to have anything to do with each other. She forgot that they needed to give Barry instructions about picking her up for the flight to Denver in the morning.

Aidan, ever the efficient one, didn't forget. "Emma's flight leaves at ten twenty," he said. "So if you'll pick her up at eight, that should give her enough time to clear security."

"You're not going to the airport with me?" Somehow she'd expected him to.

"If Theo didn't show up tonight, I don't think he'll cause a problem in the morning. He's nineteen. Typically they aren't morning people."

"So we're home free."

"Looks like it. Now, I'll be happy to go to the airport with you if you want me to, but my flight back to New York doesn't leave until one, so—"

"No, no. I'll go to the airport on my own. No worries." She felt abandoned, which was stupid. She'd traveled alone for several years, and Aidan was undoubtedly right about Theo. If he hadn't made a move at this point, he wasn't likely to do so.

Aidan used his key to get them on the right elevator and then into the penthouse. She'd thought of digging hers out to prove that she could get her own self into the room without having a man to do it, but the gesture seemed kind of silly, so she didn't bother.

Once they were inside the confines of the penthouse, she intended to follow the rules. But if she couldn't have Aidan, she might need some chocolate cake to compensate.

"I'm going to my room," she said, "but I'm in the mood for some dessert."

He paused and looked at her.

"That's not code for sex, Aidan. I'm talking about actual dessert." She crossed to the phone sitting on a small table in the living room. "I'm going to order up some of that chocolate cake I had for breakfast this morning. Do you want anything?"

Once again his expression revealed exactly what was going through his mind.

"I didn't mean it that way. Go to bed, Aidan. We'll get through this."

"Yeah." Grimacing, he turned and headed toward his bedroom. "Just put the tip on the bill."

"Thanks for everything!" she called out to him. That was lame, but she didn't think she'd see him again, and she was grateful for all that his wealth and status had provided this weekend. The sex had been good, too, but she wouldn't say she was *grateful*. Only needy girls were grateful for sex. She was appreciative, though. She hoped he'd take her global statement as encompassing . . . well, all of it.

"You're welcome," he said without turning around. Then he walked into his bedroom, closed the door, and turned the lock. There was no mistaking that sound, a definite metallic click that meant he was locking her out.

What the hell? Did he think she would be so overcome with lust that she'd barge into his room, even after he'd made it clear they wouldn't have sex tonight?

She abandoned her phone call. Striding down the short hallway, she rapped on the door. "Aidan, that's plain insulting!"

His reply was muffled by the door. "What is?"

"Locking your door, that's what! I promise you that I'm not going to encroach on the territory you've clearly defined. Now if you want to suggest that *I* lock *my* door, that's a different matter. I can't speak for your self-control. But I damned sure can speak for mine, and you don't need a freaking lock to keep me on my side of this door."

By the end of the speech, she was breathing hard from indignation. Or mostly from indignation. She was also breathing hard because he was on the other side of that door, probably taking off his clothes, maybe putting on sweats and a T-shirt again, maybe not . . .

"You're right." His voice was very close to the door. A soft metallic sound indicated that the door was no longer locked.

She stood by the door, contemplating whether she should suggest that maybe, if they both understood that this would be the very *last time*, they could indulge in a little more recreational sex. Just for tonight. Because after that, they'd never see each other again. Except for book signings, although she wondered whether he'd skip those. He probably would, all things considered.

"Go away, Emma."

"How did you know I'm still here?"

"I know."

"Well, I'm leaving. But I just want to say that—"

"Don't say it."

She hated being interrupted in the middle of a thought. "What's wrong with telling you I appreciate the time we've had together?"

"Hey, you're the one who told me that saying anything more would only make things worse."

She sighed. "So you're really serious about this abstinence plan?"

"Deadly serious."

"Then I'm leaving." She walked a few feet away and paused to see if he'd open the door.

"You're still there," he said.

"You must rock out on hearing tests. Okay, I'm really leaving, now."

"Good."

She stomped into the living room, making as much noise as possible so that he'd know she was truly moving away from his door. Apparently cake was going to be her only option tonight.

After ordering both the cake and a pot of coffee with a pitcher of cream, she walked into her bedroom and took off her heels. Good thing Aidan hadn't confronted her on the shoe issue, because these strappy black patent beauties were Gucci.

After all the times she'd dinged him for his expensive tastes, she felt a little guilty about the shoes. Footwear was one of her indulgences because she'd never found an ecofriendly shoe that a girl could take dancing.

Sitting on the bed, she massaged her feet. She loved wearing the shoes . . . for about an hour. Sometime during the second hour, her love always waned, and she was as eager to get out of the shoes as she had been to put them on.

Barefoot, she decided to haul out her suitcase and start packing while she waited for the cake and coffee to arrive. She'd simply pretend that she was alone in this penthouse, and that there was no ripped man hiding behind door number two. She was used to being alone on these book tours.

But it was one thing to start out alone and continue on alone. Starting out with Aidan for company and then continuing on alone wasn't going to be a lot of fun. They'd been together constantly ever since they'd met at the airport, and she felt somewhat . . . attached.

Her feeling of attachment could be related to the great sex they'd had, although she believed it went beyond that. She liked talking to him, liked teasing him, even liked arguing with him. They just . . . clicked.

Intellectually, physically, and emotionally, she and

Aidan matched up. From his reaction to her, she'd be willing to bet he felt the same way. But he didn't dare say so because he had this archaic family obligation. She still had trouble with that. *Talk about lack of personal choice!*

The arrival of her late-night treat interrupted her packing, and she went to answer the door. Aidan would have been proud of the way she checked the peephole first. The uniformed bellman delivering her tray was the same one who'd brought dinner a few hours earlier, so she opened the door.

But just to be absolutely safe, she peered into the hallway. Nobody else there.

"Where would you like the tray, ma'am?" the bellman asked. "Over by the fire? It's a nice night for a fire."

"So it is." She'd intended to follow Aidan's advice and close herself in her room, but she would never be in this penthouse again, so why not enjoy cake and coffee in front of the fire? "That would be terrific." She walked over and flicked the switch to turn on the flames.

The bellman arranged the tray on the coffee table and handed her the check to sign. She added a generous tip and gave it back. "Thank you. This hits the spot." At least it hit *one* spot: the chocolate craving part of her. That would have to suffice.

"Have a nice evening." The bellman smiled and left. The door locked behind him with a soft click.

Emma sat on the sofa and fixed up her coffee exactly the way she liked it. Denver would be soon enough to begin cutting back on cream and chocolate. Tonight she needed both.

Her coffee on the end table and her cake in her lap, she stared into the dancing flames and told herself to enjoy the experience because she wouldn't have a fireplace in her next hotel room. Then she took a big bite of cake. Maybe she wouldn't cut back on chocolate in Denver, after all. She'd be feeling deprived enough without denying herself that bit of comfort.

The cake was gone way too soon, and sitting in front of the fire by herself wasn't nearly as much fun as she'd hoped it would be. She set the empty plate and coffee cup on the tray before standing and stretching. After turning off the fire, she carried the tray into her bedroom. She could finish off the coffee while she packed.

When she decided to shut the bedroom door, she told herself it wasn't because she was putting more barriers between her and Aidan. Closing the door made the bedroom feel cozier. Too bad every time she looked at the big bed, she remembered curling up in Aidan's arms last night.

Her turquoise suit hung in the closet in a plastic bag, and when she checked it, all the chocolate was gone. She unhooked it from the rod and pulled off the plastic so she could pack the suit in preparation for her next event in Denver, on Monday.

As she folded it, she heard her bedroom doorknob turn, and her pulse kicked up a notch. So Aidan had given in, after all. Working to hide a smile of triumph, she faced the door. But as the door opened, adrenaline shot through her. The person coming into her room wasn't Aidan.

She opened her mouth to scream, but nothing came out. Theo, dressed in an old black sweatshirt and sweatpants, closed the door behind him and twisted the lock. Then he faced her looking smug. "Hello, Emma."

At last she found her voice. "How did you get in?" She was proud of herself for the calm way she said it despite the painful thudding of her heart.

"I have your key." He reached into the pocket of his black sweats and held it up.

"That can't be mine. Mine's—"

"Not anymore."

Then she remembered someone had jostled her at the party. She'd had to clutch her purse to keep it from falling off her shoulder. "You were at the party."

"No. I hired the finest pickpocket in the greater Chicago area."

As the panic slowly cleared from her brain, she realized that, although he stood between her and the door, once she called for help, Aidan would be between Theo and escape.

"I don't know if you've thought this through very well. Once I start yelling, you'll have nowhere to run."

"I know, but I'm willing to take that chance. I'm hoping you won't start yelling until you've heard what I have to say." His gaze was earnest. "This is critical, and you're the kind of person who will understand the issues."

Lord help her, she was eternally curious about people, and he'd just appealed to that curiosity. She'd start yelling in a minute. With Aidan's sharp hearing, he'd respond quickly. "What issues?"

"I can tell from the way you write about werewolves that you really get them."

"Theo, if you're about to claim that you're a werewolf, then this conversation is over. There's not enough spirit gum and fake hair in the world to convince me that you're . . ." She paused as he raised a hand and fur began growing on it.

Blinking, she looked again. "Okay, that's a trick. I don't know how you're doing it, and it's very impressive, but I want you to stop. It's creepy, Theo. It's not a turn-on for me, if that's what you're hoping."

"You say that now, but just wait." He nudged off his shoes.

Damned if hair wasn't growing on his feet, too. "Stop that, Theo! Eww!"

"Believe me, yet?" His voice had deepened into something resembling a growl.

"Good God! What are you doing to yourself?" She stared in horrified fascination as the seams of his sweat suit ripped open. This wasn't happening. She couldn't be seeing what she thought she was seeing.

And yet . . . Theo was gone. Standing in his place, with bits of black fabric clinging to its black fur, was a large wolf. It took a menacing step toward her.

She screamed, and in the same instant her bedroom door splintered as a large form hurtled through it. Now a second wolf, larger and more powerful than the first, stood by the shattered door. The golden-eyed creature from Emma's nightmare had arrived.

Chapter 17

Aidan had stuffed towels under the crack in his bedroom door to block out Emma's scent once he'd realized that she was intent on hanging out in the living room and he'd be able to smell her easily there. That had been his first mistake, muting his ability to smell.

Then he'd made a second mistake. Desperate for a distraction, he'd called Roarke, knowing his brother would provide an extra incentive to keep him in his own room. Roarke hadn't disappointed. His disapproval of Aidan's methods for neutralizing the threat from Theo registered about nine on the Richter scale.

"So you're telling me that last night, *after* shifting, you waltzed into her bedroom to check on her? You couldn't have thought to do that *before* you dressed in your fur overcoat?"

"You know I can think better after a shift."

"That's debatable, buddy boy. A thinking wolf wouldn't have tiptoed in to peek down at Sleeping Beauty, knowing that she might—oh, I dunno—*wake up* and said wolf's ass would be grass. That's the sign of a wolf who's a few bones shy of a full rack of ribs, if you know what I mean."

Aidan closed his eyes and let his brother rave on. Roarke was his lifeline to sanity, his anchor, so he wouldn't go out that door. Emma was willing to spend the night in his arms. She'd said as much not long ago. And now she was eating cake, the same cake he'd fantasized rubbing all over her firm little body just so he could lick it off.

"Do you want me to fly over there tonight?" Roarke sounded eager to get into the middle of this rodeo. "I could take the corporate jet and be there in no time. We could double-team Theo, and with me there, you won't be as tempted to boink the lovely Emma."

"No, I don't want you to fly over." Aidan smiled. Roarke would grab any excuse to climb into that corporate jet. Then he'd talk the pilot into letting him have the controls. He was licensed for single-engine aircraft, and Aidan predicted he'd be piloting the Learjet before too much longer.

"I think I should," Roarke said. "From the sound of things, you don't have this situation under control."

"Theo didn't make a move tonight, so he may have gone to ground. This penthouse is as safe as Fort Knox, so no worries for now. I'll see if I can smoke him out tomorrow morning. Once Emma leaves, I'll be free to handle this any way I choose. I—hold on." He walked over to the door and sniffed. Even through the towels he'd stuffed under the door to block Emma's scent, he picked up a musty odor, like that of a werewolf shifting . . . *Shit!*

Dropping the phone, he pulled away the towels and flung open the door.

He commanded his shift as he moved and ignored

the ripping of seams. His T-shirt and sweats lay in pieces along his route. Straining toward the shift, he heard Emma scream. He entered the final phase right as he launched himself through the central panel of the door. He was counting on it being hollow. Fortunately, it was.

One quick glance told him Emma was okay, at least physically. Her eyes were wide with shock. He had no idea how he'd explain this. The nightmare excuse wasn't going to cut it this time.

But Theo was his first concern. They didn't have to fight if Theo acknowledged Aidan's superiority. Avoiding a fight would be a good thing, considering that Emma was there to witness it and they were surrounded by expensive furniture. The ruined door could be the extent of the damage if Theo would cooperate.

The black wolf spun around to face him.

Aidan held Theo's gaze as they circled each other. *Give it up, Theo. You're outgunned.*

That's what you think, old man. Bring it. I can take you any day of the week. Theo snarled and flattened his ears to his head.

Aidan didn't discount the young werewolf's age and agility. Chances were he'd been in a fight more recently than Aidan, who no longer felt the need to battle for dominance. He'd proved himself when he was younger, and the pack members knew he was in line to take over when his father stepped down, so the challenges had been few and far between recently.

Now he wished he'd sparred more with his brother, just to stay sharp. But he would handle Theo. The kid was risking the future of packs everywhere, and he had to be stopped. Tonight.

Aidan kept his attention firmly on the black wolf.

Your choice, Theo. This can be easy, or it can be hard. I'd advise you to make it easy on yourself.

You're stalling.

I'm giving you a way out.

Theo growled low in his throat. *Fuck you, Aidan.*

So be it. Aidan moved in a split second ahead of Theo's charge and lunged for the black wolf's throat.

Emma's scream registered but didn't deter him. He knocked Theo to the ground while sinking his teeth into the soft skin beneath his jugular. A quarter inch more and he'd take the young wolf's life. That was guaranteed to ruin everyone's evening.

So he eased up, which allowed Theo to twist away and turn, closing his teeth over Aidan's hind leg. Ignoring the pain, Aidan pulled his leg free. Being hamstrung by this young pup wasn't his idea of a good time. And now he was bleeding all over the carpet. Housekeeping was going to hate that.

No more Mr. Nice Guy. He lunged for Theo's throat again, and this time he held on and issued his ultimatum. *Give up unless you want your carotid artery severed.*

You won't kill me. I'm a Henderson.

The kid had a point, damn it.

I'll claim self-defense.

From the corner of his eye, Aidan saw Emma approaching. She had the hotel hair dryer raised as if she was about to bring it down on somebody's head. Whether it was his or Theo's, he couldn't be sure.

He'd take his chances. *Don't look now, but Emma's about to bean you with a hair dryer.*

No way.

'Fraid so. So your option is to surrender to me or I'll hold you down so she can knock you senseless. Which story would you rather have circulating?

Shit. I surrender to you.
Werewolf's honor?
You got it, big guy.

Aidan relaxed his grip and let Theo wiggle out from under him. Emma must have still considered him a threat, because she smacked him a good one on the head with the hair dryer. He went down for the count.

The moment he was unconscious, he began shifting back to human form. Emma seemed transfixed by the sight. She stood there rigidly, her hand over her mouth.

Aidan padded into the master bath and nudged the door closed with his paw. By the time he came out wearing a towel, Emma had thrown her comforter over Theo while she continued to stare at him.

She glanced up when Aidan emerged from the bathroom. He met her gaze without flinching. In some ways he was relieved that she finally knew. But damage control was going to be a bitch.

She swallowed. "So it was you last night."

"Yes."

"Not a figment of my imagination. Not a nightmare."

"No."

"You asshole!" She hurled the hair dryer at him, and the cord snaked out behind it.

He ducked, and the dryer smacked against the wall before dropping with a thud to the carpet. The plug had caught him on the arm as it went by. He'd have a welt there soon.

"Coming into your bedroom as a wolf was a tactical error," he said.

She opened her mouth as if to say something and then closed it again. Finally she shook her head. "Forgive me. You're talking about tactical errors and I'm still trying to—to get my head around . . ."

"I know." Instinctively he moved toward her.

She held up her hand like a traffic cop. "Keep your distance, Aidan. I don't know who you are or what you are, and until I get my bearings, picture a large bubble of protection around me, okay?"

"Okay." He took a deep breath. "Just for the record, this is a whole new experience for me, too. I've never revealed myself to a human before."

"So you're not . . . human."

"I'm mostly human. But I can shift into wolf form, so that means that I—"

"I know a little something about werewolves, Aidan. I've been writing about them for six years. I just never expected to meet one." She glanced down at Theo's prone form. "Or two."

"We should probably see if we can revive him."

She glanced at his leg. "And stop your bleeding. You're making an unholy mess. Is that real blood?"

"Yes, it's real blood! I'm not an alien, for Christ's sake. You write about this stuff. You should know."

"I make it all up!"

"Well, you happen to be correct about most things. I'm a man in this form, and I bleed like a man, but I'll heal faster because of the shift." And he was making quite the mess. In the excitement of the moment, he'd forgotten that Theo had created a sizable gash in his calf when the kid had tried to cripple him. No doubt about it, Theo would have followed through if he'd hit Aidan's Achilles tendon. Good thing that hadn't happened.

"Get some washcloths from the bathroom," Emma said. "You can hold one on your leg and I'll sponge Theo's face. That might wake him up. Oh, and bring the tie from my bathrobe. I left it hanging on the back of the bathroom door."

"What's the tie for?"

"Theo, of course. When he's conscious, he could be a lot of trouble. We'd better tie him up before we revive him."

"We don't have to tie him."

She frowned. "I'd rather be safe than sorry. I don't want the two of you getting in another fight, either as men or beasts. Once is plenty for me."

"There won't be another fight."

"How can you be so sure? He's whacked, Aidan. Not that you aren't, too, but you're whacked and seminormal. He's thoroughly whacked."

He decided to ignore her *whacked and seminormal* comment for the time being. "Think about what you've written, Emma. Werewolves are pack animals. Once an alpha has subdued another pack member, he returns to his subservient position. You had that very situation in *Shifty Business.*"

"You mean I was right about that? Cool!"

"You were right about a lot of things." He wondered how and when he should tell her that she'd been under investigation because of being so right. "On top of that, once Theo discovers he was knocked unconscious by a woman wielding a hair dryer, he won't be any trouble at all. He'll never want the rest of the pack to know about that. We have blackmail material that will last a long time."

"*We*? What do you mean, *we*? Come tomorrow morning, I'm outta here." Her voice was full of bravado, probably false bravado.

He wanted to avoid this discussion until they'd both calmed down. "We'll talk about that later."

"What do you mean by that?" Her voice rose in pitch.

"Let's take care of Theo and figure out the best way to get him home. Then we'll discuss the options."

"There's only one option. I'm leaving for Denver in the morning to continue my book tour." Her chin lifted in defiance.

In truth, he wasn't sure how to handle this. Security had been breached, and precautions must be taken. He couldn't just let her fly off to Denver by herself. Not after she'd witnessed something like this.

"I'll get the washcloths." He went into the bathroom.

She followed him. "Look, Aidan, I don't care how rich you are or how much real estate you own. I don't care if every single Wallace is a werewolf."

Thinking discretion was the better part of valor, he pulled white washcloths from the towel rack and stuck two under the faucet.

"I'm a free citizen of the United States of America," she continued bravely, "and I'm going to Denver in the morning."

He squeezed out the washcloths. "These should work for Theo."

She took the washcloths and tossed them on the counter. "I mean it, Aidan. Don't mess with my book tour. It's important to my career."

"I know." He took a dry washcloth and pressed it against the wound in his leg.

She was standing close to him, close enough that her scent had begun working on him again. In the heat of battle, he blocked out any irrelevant sensory impressions, but afterward, there was always the urge to release tension in some way. A run through the woods worked. Sex worked.

"Here, let me do that." She crouched down beside him. Apparently she no longer felt the need for the bubble of protection she'd claimed earlier.

"I've got it. Go see about Theo." He didn't dare look

at her. From this position he could see down the front of her little black dress.

"You're a real bossy-pants, Aidan, do you know that?"

"Just go check on him, please."

"All right." With a sigh she rose, grabbed a washcloth from the counter, and walked into the bedroom.

He watched her go, his attention captured by the way her firm little backside moving seductively under the stretchy black material of her cocktail dress. His tail-bone began to ache.

She called to him from the bedroom. "He's gone!"

Tossing the washcloth in the sink, Aidan left the bathroom. Sure enough, Theo was no longer lying unconscious on the floor.

Aidan wasn't all that surprised. If he'd been in Theo's place, he would have cut out the minute he regained consciousness. But the kid couldn't have made it down the elevator and through the lobby naked.

Then Aidan figured it out. "Looks like he took the top sheet from your bed and wrapped himself in that so he could ride the elevator to the lobby."

Her eyes widened. "And then what? He couldn't hail a cab wearing a sheet. No cabdriver is going to take a chance on picking up what looks like a loony."

"I'm sure once he made it out to the sidewalk, he found a dark alley and shifted back to wolf form. He's running now and praying nobody ever finds out how thoroughly he was humiliated tonight."

Emma walked over to the bedroom window and pulled back the curtain. "I don't have a lot of sympathy for him after the way he's behaved, but I still hate to think of him alone out there in the cold, especially when he's hurt. I popped him good with that hair dryer, and he had some gashes on his throat, too."

"He's a wolf, Emma. This is how a wolf reacts to humiliation. That was my goal, to humiliate and intimidate him. I wanted his complete surrender, and I got it."

She shivered. "That seems harsh."

"He was prepared to reveal himself to a human and break pack law. He had to be dealt with."

She gazed at him. "But he succeeded, didn't he? He did reveal himself to me. And so did you."

"Yes."

She continued to stare at him, and judging from her expression, she was beginning to realize the magnitude of the problem. "Well."

This would be the time to offer some comforting platitude, like *It'll all work out.* But he was too honest to give her false hope. He wasn't sure how it would work out.

Her attention moved to his leg. "You're still bleeding. Let's at least solve that issue. Go on back in the bathroom, and let me see if I can get it to stop."

"All right." Tending to his wound seemed like the sensible thing to do, so he followed her suggestion, or rather, her order. He understood why she, too, might be getting a little bossy.

Her previous worldview had been shattered, and in sorting through the wreckage, she was trying to regain some measure of control. He could allow her to dictate how his wound should be tended, but he couldn't let her decide how the next few days would go, or maybe even the next few weeks or months.

He wondered whether she realized that her life had changed forever and it was never changing back.

Chapter 18

Emma was beginning to get the picture, and it was an unsettling one. Now that the initial shock had worn off and she could think, she'd started piecing things together. Apparently, she'd stumbled upon a group of beings who didn't want their presence known.

Or more precisely, they'd stumbled upon her. All she'd intended to do was promote her book. She hadn't invited real werewolves to show up. But they had, and now she possessed knowledge that the werewolves didn't want other humans to find out.

If not for Aidan, she'd fear for her life. The simple way to plug the hole would be to eliminate her. Problem solved. But Aidan wielded power among werewolves. She'd seen that demonstrated with Theo. Aidan wouldn't let anything happen to her. She was counting on that.

So the first order of business was taking care of her protector's leg. She also wanted information, lots of information. The more she knew about this strange new world, the less she'd have to fear from it. At least that was the theory.

Back in the bathroom, she dampened a washcloth and knelt down so she could dab his wound. "I want to clean it up a little before I apply pressure. Do you suppose you need a tetanus shot?"

"No."

"Rabies?"

"Werewolves are incredibly resistant to any kind of disease."

She made a mental note of that. "Why?"

"We're a very old species. We've built up immunity to most of the diseases known to either man or beast."

"Makes sense." She pressed the damp washcloth against the jagged tear in his skin, skin that looked and felt like that of a man but could transform into the hide of a wolf. Despite being in a very precarious spot, she was fascinated at the prospect of interacting with a creature she'd thought lived only in her imagination.

"I'll bet modern science would love to tap into that immune system." She said it without thinking, but the heavy silence that greeted her comment conveyed volumes. "But of course that's impossible," she said quickly, "because then they'd know you existed." *Be smart, Emma. Even Aidan might not be able to protect you if you keep making remarks like that.*

"In the old days, werewolves were hunted almost to extinction," Aidan said. "We're not eager to go back to those times."

"I'm sure not. Aidan, you can trust me. I'm not going to put you or the others at risk."

"That's easy to say, Emma. Harder to do."

Her sense of uneasiness grew, but she was reluctant to ask the hard questions for fear she'd get some hard answers. She liked her life the way it was. She didn't want it to change.

"The bleeding's slowing down some." She held a dry washcloth against his leg and braced her other hand on the far side of his calf to apply some pressure to the wound. "I'm beginning to understand what the arranged marriage is about. You're like the prince of the Wallace family, and Nadia is the princess of the Henderson family."

"We generally use the word *pack* instead of *family*."

"Even when you're in human form?" She found herself becoming more aware of his human form. He'd fastened a towel around his waist, but other than that, he was naked.

"Obviously not around other humans. But pack loyalty is important, even when we're in human form. Although we spend the majority of our lives as humans, our wolf instincts remain strong."

The thrill of facing the unknown coursed through her. She might as well admit that she'd chosen to write about werewolves because she found them erotic. And now, here was an actual werewolf, right here in the bathroom with her. An almost naked werewolf.

Her body responded with a rush of moisture. But he was wounded. He needed rest and relaxation, not a roll in her king-sized bed.

If she couldn't satisfy her craving for him, she could at least satisfy her curiosity. "When you shift from a human to a werewolf, what does that feel like?"

"It depends on how long I have to go through the process. Ideally, I can anticipate having to shift and allow plenty of time. Tonight that wasn't the case, so tomorrow I'm going to be a little sore."

"And you can shift at will, no matter what the moon phase is?" Could he shift now, while she was holding on to his leg? But she wouldn't ask that of him. This wasn't a parlor trick.

"The moon's no longer a factor for us. It was centuries ago, but we've learned quite a bit about how the physiology works, and we're no longer dependent on the moon."

So he was capable of shifting at any time. That was both exciting and intimidating. "When I created my werewolves, I wanted them to shift whenever they chose to. The story wouldn't move very fast if they only shifted every twenty-eight days."

"I remember how impressed I was when I read your first book and saw that you'd set it up that way."

She couldn't believe they were calmly discussing the reality of shape-shifting. Last night she'd had sex with a werewolf. Doggy-style. That took on new meaning, now. Erotic meaning. "What mind-body control you must have." She realized that she'd begun stroking his leg and stopped immediately.

"Most of the time, I have control." His breath hissed out between his teeth, and he pulled his leg from her grasp. "That's enough. I'm fine."

"Did I hurt you?"

"No." He edged toward the bathroom door. I'm just—you don't have to—maybe I should get dressed."

"Aidan, you look as if you're in pain. What's wrong?"

"Nothing. I'll go to my room and grab some clothes."

She scrambled to her feet and followed him. "Use the hotel robe instead. You need to bandage your leg. I'll call room service and have some first aid supplies sent up."

He whirled. "Don't follow me, Emma!"

"Aidan?" She looked closer. His chest hair was thicker now than it had been a minute ago. Her pulse jumped. "Are you . . . shifting?"

"Yes, damn it, I am. This doesn't happen to all werewolves. Just me. It's a genetic defect. If I become aroused and frustrated, I start to shift."

She glanced at the towel around his waist and noted the tenting effect. Knowing what lay beneath that terry cloth created a corresponding ache in her womb. "But if you have sex?"

"Satisfaction reverses the process. But considering the evening's events, sex isn't what either of us needs right now."

She swallowed. God, but he excited her. "Speak for yourself. Considering the evening's events, a little sexual release sounds like a wonderful idea to me."

"It will only complicate things more."

"Or simplify them. Your choice, of course, but if you'd rather reverse the process with my help, I'll be in my bedroom. Naked."

She turned and walked back through the doorway, stepping over the shattered remains of what was once a door. Then she paused and glanced back at him. "This time you won't have to break down a door to get to me."

Her scent telegraphed her readiness and gave him a trail to follow. Every wolf instinct drove him forward, but reason held him back. He still had no plan. In the morning he'd have to alert the pack that security had been breached—his fault, mostly. Then he'd have to lay out a procedure for handling that breach.

He needed to think, to plan, to strategize. Both Emma's future and his depended on how he handled this situation. Losing himself in the wonders of her body wouldn't help him figure that out, and it might cloud his mind.

Check that. It would definitely cloud his mind. When confronted with the powerful aphrodisiac that was Emma's essence, he struggled to remember his own name. The more he allowed himself to succumb to that heady feeling, the more complicated the problem became.

But her scent . . . How could he ignore that siren call? Lifting his head, he sniffed the air. The rustle of clothing would have told him, as well, but his nose gave him the first indication that she was undressing, just as she'd promised.

His balls tightened, and his cock grew hard. He knew the moment she slipped off her panties because her scent swirled around her and drifted through that open door, inviting him inside, inviting him to take her.

Once she'd announced her willingness, both in words and the seductive sway of her body as she'd left the room, his shift had begun to reverse. If he turned away from her and denied himself, the shift would resume. He'd spend precious moments trying to subdue his sexual urges and retain his human shape, moments he could ill afford to lose.

Was bedding her the most efficient use of his time and energy, then? He considered that with a self-mocking smile. But the thought had merit.

Once he'd satisfied this craving, he'd be free to tackle the problems at hand. He'd be able to focus, whereas now—now his brain was filled with the red haze of lust.

She'd asked him to take her, requested the release for herself. She'd suffered a shock, and he was the cause of that shock. Easing her tension was the least he could do, under the circumstances. Granting her wish would be a kindness. And he was a kind being. *Oh, yes. Very kind.* He smiled again, amused at his ability to rationalize what he'd known all along he would do.

He pictured her lying in that big bed, her golden hair fanned across the pillow, her creamy thighs spread in welcome. Come morning, he'd have to abandon all thoughts of sinking into her warmth. But it was not morning yet.

With a low growl, he ripped the towel from his waist and strode into the bedroom. She'd left a small lamp on the dressing table turned on. The room was cast in shadow, and shadows were his element.

"Hello, Aidan."

"Hello, Emma." He gazed at her lying on the bed almost exactly as he'd imagined. Resting one knee on the mattress, he leaned down to claim her mouth. He'd taken her in wolf fashion the night before, but he would be more careful this time. He'd possess her the way a man possessed a woman. That might keep the bonds from becoming too strong.

Slowly he stroked her breasts as he continued to kiss her lips, angling his head, using his tongue, nibbling and tasting, finding traces of chocolate, of coffee, and most of all, of hot desire. She tunneled her fingers through his hair and gripped the back of his head, rising to meet his kisses.

He gave thanks that he had command of a man's body, as well as the form of a wolf. Without a man's body, he wouldn't be able to savor this prelude, this dance of mouths that taunted them both with what was to come. He wouldn't have hands with which to fondle, fingers to rub and squeeze.

Sometimes, when his wolf nature was dominant, he became impatient with foreplay. Tonight he cherished Emma's sighs of pleasure as he played upon her voluptuous body.

When her nipples grew tight and her breasts lifted into his caress, he swept his hand downward over her flat stomach to her soft curls and onward to the heat that had brought him here. As he touched her there, sliding his fingers inside her wet channel, the urge to join with her became a driving force, an ache so strong that his pelvis jerked in reaction.

Her moan of need echoed his own. Her rapid breathing and restless hips told him it was time.

She wrenched her mouth free of his. "Condoms." She gulped for air. "Bedside table."

He kissed her again as anticipation unfurled within him. He hadn't considered this consequence of the night's events, but now that Emma knew what he was, he was free to experience sex without a latex barrier. "There's no need for condoms."

"But—"

"I couldn't tell you before." He dropped kisses on her cheeks, her throat, her breasts. "I can't make you pregnant."

"Whoa, big boy." She cupped his face in both hands. Breathing hard, she nevertheless delivered her message. "That sounds like a line of bull." She took another quick breath. "We used one last night."

"You thought I was human last night."

"You're very much like a human right now."

"But not the same."

Her words were filled with the strain of curbing her excitement. "So you can't make babies?"

"Not unless we're mated."

"Mated?"

"In the werewolf sense, for life."

She looked doubtful.

"Trust me."

"That's what they all say."

"In my case, it's true. You can trust me." He moved between her thighs and probed gently with the tip of his cock. "Will you trust me, Emma?"

She met his gaze, her kiss-swollen lips parted as she took rapid, shallow breaths. "Yes. Yes, I will."

For a brief moment, he was humbled by her surrender. Then the demands of his body sent him surging forward, thrusting deep, burying his quivering cock in her wet warmth.

Murmuring her name, he withdrew and drove in again. Once again the sensation of gliding into her with nothing between them but their own slick moisture made him gasp in delight. The glorious friction prompted him to pump again.

He groaned. Sliding his hands under her bottom, he cupped her satin skin and pushed in as far as he could go until they were locked in tight. "Emma, this is . . ."

Her eyes bright and her cheeks flushed, she lifted her hips to create an even tighter bond. "Great."

"Yes."

She mirrored him, cupping his buttocks in her warm hands, pressing her fingers into him. "I can feel you quiver. I can feel the shape of your cock."

"I can feel when you contract around me." He rotated his hips gently. "Like that."

She whimpered. "Again."

He moved in the opposite direction and watched excitement grow in her expressive eyes. Easing back, he slid forward again.

"Mmm. More."

He didn't need to be asked. The intense pleasure of thrusting into her pushed him onward. He moved faster now, greedy for the increasingly erotic sensation of skin against skin. The juicy aroma of sex filled the air and the *slap slap slap* of bodies melded with the *creak* of the bed and the *thump* of the headboard against the wall.

As she tightened around his cock, he watched her

eyes darken. His wolf senses would know when she neared her climax, but he craved the sound of her voice.

"Talk to me, Emma." He pumped steadily as her body quivered beneath his. "Are you coming?"

"Soon." She gasped and clutched him tighter.

"I can see it in your eyes. I can feel you rising, reaching . . . ah, Emma . . . come for me . . ."

"There . . . harder . . . right . . . *there.*" Crying out, she lifted her hips as her spasms milked him, coaxing him to surrender to the climax that he'd fought to keep at bay until now. With a groan he drove into her once, twice, and shuddered as the pulsing of his cock rode the ripples of her orgasm.

As his body quieted, he settled against her, careful not to give her his full weight, but longing to touch every inch of skin he could reach. Tomorrow he would face the wrath of his pack, but tonight he'd been given a gift— full-out sex with Emma. He would never have had that if she hadn't learned what he was.

Tonight, his heart was filled with gratitude and something more, something that should frighten him. But he was too happy. Tomorrow perhaps he'd be frightened by his growing connection to her. But not tonight. Burying his nose against her neck, he breathed in with one thought: she was *his.*

Chapter 19

For the second morning in a row, Emma woke up alone in her bed while the spot next to her was still warm. But she had a feeling this morning would be nothing like any morning she'd ever experienced in her life. True, Aidan had been a werewolf yesterday, but she hadn't known it. Today she did.

She smelled coffee. A quick lift of her head to check out the dressing table confirmed that the coffee was in the living room, along with Aidan. She could hear his voice. He was probably on the phone again. Was he talking to Nadia?

A hot stab of jealousy made her realize how possessive she'd become. And that was foolish because Aidan's life had been planned from birth. Besides, she had more immediate problems than whether Aidan would eventually marry Nadia and produce little werewolves.

What were they like, the little ones? Could they shift from birth or did they develop the ability later? In the world of her books, werewolves looked like human children until puberty. The onset of sexual maturity gave them the ability to shift, and they went through an awkward phase while they learned to manage their wolf status.

If she'd guessed right, then teenage werewolves had it way worse than teenage humans. Besides raging hormones and zits, they had to deal with hair and fangs. She wondered how Aidan had managed, considering his genetic defect. Puberty must have been torture for him.

The curtains were still drawn over the window, and the light was dim in the bedroom. She had no sense of what time it was. Rolling to her side, she peered at the bedside table clock.

Shit! She leaped out of bed and looked frantically for the hotel robe she'd been using. It lay over a chair in the corner, and she ran to grab it and shove her arms into the sleeves. She'd never make it to O'Hare in time for her flight, so she'd have to rebook.

Fortunately, her first event in Denver wasn't until Monday morning, but still. She should have set her alarm on her phone or asked for a wake-up call. This was embarrassing and unprofessional.

Before she dealt with it, though, she could use some coffee. On her way out to the living room to find it, she realized that Aidan hadn't bothered to wake her up, either. Maybe he'd forgotten the time of her flight, but she doubted that was the case.

Come to think of it, he'd never fully responded when she'd made her impassioned speech about going to Denver regardless of the werewolf issue. But she *was* going to Denver. He would just have to trust her to keep her mouth shut about what she'd seen here last night.

The living room looked cozy and domestic, with the fire going and a room service tray on the coffee table. Aidan paced over by the windows, his BlackBerry to his ear. His sweats this morning were black, as was his NYU sweatshirt. He looked massive and slightly dangerous dressed all in black.

As he paced, he glanced outside and frowned. "Yeah, socked in, which helps."

She couldn't imagine how much he could see out the windows, which were iced over. But maybe he had X-ray vision, too. In any case, the question of flights had just been answered. She hadn't missed her plane if O'Hare was shut down.

Aidan listened to the person on the other end for a few seconds. "I understand. I'll monitor her twenty-four-seven. You have my word, Dad."

Her jaw dropped. He might have given his word to his father, but she sure as hell hadn't!

He turned slowly toward her, the BlackBerry still to his ear. He showed no surprise at finding her there, but then he wouldn't. His sense of smell and his hearing were those of a wolf. "I'll keep you posted. She won't be a problem. Take care, Dad. Bye." He disconnected the call and gazed at her.

"What the hell was that all about?"

"Think of it as the werewolf version of Homeland Security. You'll continue to be under constant surveillance, except now you'll be aware of it."

She stared at him as the significance of his statement sank in. "You've been watching me?" She spoke quietly, but inside she was seething. "How long has that been going on?"

"About three months. Your books were so accurate that the pack figured you had a werewolf informant. I've been trying to catch you communicating with him or her, but of course, you didn't have an informant, which meant there was nothing to find."

"So when you came to my book event in Manhattan and generously gave me a ride and bought me a drink in your exclusive club, you were on assignment?"

He nodded. "Essentially."

"You son of a bitch."

"Yes."

He looked so calm and in control that she longed to pick up something, anything, and throw it at him. But that would only prove how out of control she was. "You pretended to like my books, pretended to like *me,* but all along you were spying?"

"I didn't *pretend* to like your books. I think they're great. Come to think of it, if I hadn't raved about your books to my family, none of this would have happened, so you can blame me for being a fan or blame yourself for being a great writer. But assigning blame won't get us anywhere."

Oh, but she wanted to blame him for *something.* "You had sex with me! Was that part of your assignment, too?"

"No, that was a mistake."

"A *mistake*?" Now she really wanted to hurt him, except he was some superbeing, and she didn't know a single martial arts trick.

"Sometimes mistakes turn out to be wonderful."

Oh. Some of her fury melted.

"But that doesn't mean I should have allowed that to happen. Roarke, in particular, warned me that I'd get into trouble if I spent too much time with you. He was right."

She thought back over their two nights together and took some satisfaction in knowing she'd caused Mr. All That to step over the line. But if he was a lying sack of cow chips, then he might have lied about something very important.

She folded her arms. "Aidan, so help me; you need to tell the truth on this one. Could I be pregnant?" She took a deep breath. "With puppies?"

His mouth twitched. At first she couldn't tell whether he was trying not to laugh or trying not to yell at her. When he snorted, she figured it was the first.

Scrubbing a hand over his face, he looked down at the carpet for a moment before glancing back at her. His golden eyes danced with humor. "No, Emma, you're not pregnant. And even if you were, you'd have a beautiful baby, not a puppy. A werewolf grows up looking like every other child. Shifting comes with sexual maturity."

"So I was right about that!" Her elation temporarily made her forget that she hated him.

"Yes, you got that right, too."

"And you're sure I couldn't be pregnant? Because in the human world, it would be a distinct possibility, and last night you felt very . . . human." The memory turned her on a little, which was inconvenient because she really wanted to hate him, and holding on to hate while desire tried to work its way in was tough.

"It's a biological fact for Weres. Once we've chosen a mate for life, then, and only then, will conception take place. Until that time, we're sterile. Obviously no woman is going to simply believe that I'm sterile and disease free unless I explain that I'm a werewolf. But you already knew, so we were able to have sex without a condom."

"Okay, moving on." Lingering over this topic could derail her anger completely, and she needed her anger. It made her feel more powerful. "You said you've been watching me for three months."

"Approximately, give or take a few days."

"How many privacy laws did you break doing that,

wolf boy?" She wondered whether she could get a rise out of him.

His gaze didn't flicker. "Most of them. We try to work within the law when we can, but in the case of pack security, we do what is necessary."

"What did you use? Hidden cameras? Bugs? Tails?"

"All of the above. We installed cameras and recorders in your loft. I've monitored your phone calls and followed you whenever you went out. You've been my only assignment for three months, Emma. I kept very close track of you."

"Did you put cameras in my bedroom?" She thought about the few nights Doug had stayed over.

"No. I vetoed that."

"Why? You were invading every other area of my life—why not spy on my sex life, such as it was?"

He hesitated, as if wanting to say more. Finally, he made a dismissive motion with his hand. "We didn't need that information. Doug isn't a werewolf."

"For all I know, he could be! I mean, you are, and Theo is, and your father is, and—Wait just a doggone minute— your werewolf father is old friends with my publisher. For all I know, Roger Claymore is a werewolf!"

"No."

"You're sure?"

"Positive. And neither is Doug."

"How do you know? Couldn't he be from a visiting pack or something?"

"I can pick up a Were's scent immediately. It's nothing like a human's."

Something about that comment didn't make sense, and then she figured out what it was. "Then why didn't you come out when Theo arrived in the suite? You must have smelled him."

Aidan flushed slightly. "I—I had stuffed towels under my door."

"Why in heaven's name would you do something like that?"

"To block your scent."

"To block my . . ." Understanding slowly dawned. "It affects you that much?"

"Yes."

She didn't want to feel sympathy for him, but she couldn't seem to help it. He'd been trying to do the right thing for his pack, and he was just too darned attracted to her, poor werewolf. Talk about self-defeating behavior.

She took a deep breath. "Well, I'm about to make things easier for you, Aidan. I heard the promise you made your father, but you would have been wise to consult me, first."

His head came up and his gaze met hers. "Don't fight me on this."

"I don't intent to fight you. I intend to ignore you. First I'll pack my things. Then I'll call a cab and leave the hotel. If you try to stop me, I'll call 911. Or I'll start screaming. Whatever it takes, but I won't be put under house arrest."

Aidan sighed. "I was afraid of this."

"And it should come as no surprise if you've been spying on me for three months. You know how I cherish my personal freedom. You can't possibly think I'd put up with having you constantly in my business."

"There are compelling reasons for it, and we need to talk about those." He took a step toward her. "You have every reason to be upset, but—"

"Upset? That's a wimpy word. I'm *furious* about the way you and your precious *pack* have messed with me.

I'm determined to get as far away from you as possible. You're threatening my way of life, Aidan, and I won't have it."

"And you're threatening ours! Emma, don't be foolish."

She lifted her chin. "Foolish by your definition, I suppose."

"Foolish by any definition, damn it! There are members of my pack who are talking about having you killed."

That got her attention. In the back of her mind she'd wondered how worried they'd be about a human knowing their secret. She decided they must be pretty damned worried.

"Killed," she said, as if discussing the weather, although her knees were shaking. She wondered whether they'd come after her in human form or as a wolf pack. "As in murdered."

"They would see it as an act of self-defense."

"But I've done nothing! Theo started it!" She cringed. Now she sounded like a six-year-old.

Apparently terror had a way of turning a person into a frightened child. The writer part of her noticed that. She hadn't written terror all that well before, but she'd be able to write it now, assuming she lived.

"You and I both know this was Theo's deal, but now he's back home claiming I'm the traitor who became your lover and revealed myself to you. He's the pack savior who charged up here to take me down, but you sneaked up behind him and knocked him unconscious with a hammer."

"A hammer? Where would I get a hammer?"

"I didn't say it was a very good story. I guess he couldn't admit he'd been felled by a hotel hair dryer."

Emma's brain was spinning. "Let me get this straight. He's back home and making up lies about what happened."

"Yes."

"But you told me that in a pack situation the defeated wolf slinks away in total humiliation. What happened to that scenario?"

Aidan shrugged. "Kids today."

It would be funny, except they were talking about life and death, here. *Her* life and death.

"Yeah, but surely nobody believes his bogus story."

"Unfortunately, his father does. And his father is the Henderson pack alpha, so that's a problem. My father and Leland have already exchanged harsh words."

"Are we talking about a werewolf war?"

"I don't think so. I hope not. Emma, will you sit down so we can talk about this?"

The threat of being murdered by a pack of werewolves did diminish the appeal of making a grand exit from the hotel. She blew out a breath. "I need coffee."

"Have a seat. I'll get it."

Feeling suddenly cold, she plopped down on the sofa next to the fireplace. "Lots of cream."

"I know."

"I suppose you would. You probably know the names of my friends, where my mother lives—oh, God, my mother. She'll be glued to the weather reports because she knows I'm supposed to fly out of Chicago today. I have to call her. Come to think of it, I'm surprised she hasn't tried to call me."

"I turned off your phone."

"What?" Leaping from the sofa, she started for the bedroom. "We're fixing that situation right now."

"Don't, Emma. Leave it until we've talked."

She whirled to face him. "Look, Your Alphaness, I understand that I'm in a precarious position. I get that your protection might be the only thing keeping me from a bitter end, but I would appreciate it if you'd use the word *please* instead of just barking orders." Then she realized what she'd just said and began to laugh. "*Barking.* That's funny. Barking orders." She got the giggles so bad that she doubled over.

"Werewolves don't bark."

She glanced up to find him regarding her with stern disapproval, which made her laugh all the more. "Good to know. I'll make a note of that for my research."

"Please do." He set her cup and saucer on the coffee table.

"There! You said *please.* That proves you can do it."

"Don't patronize me." He straightened and fixed her with a glare from those golden eyes. "And don't think this is easy for me, either. As of last night, my life became tied to yours for some indefinite amount of time. I've already devoted three months to this project, and I thought it would be over this weekend and I could get back to my normal routine."

Intrigued by that statement, she returned to the sofa. "And what is that, exactly?"

"It doesn't matter. I was only making the point that you aren't the only person being inconvenienced."

"Your normal routine matters to me. The more I know about how a real werewolf lives, the better my books will be."

He stared at her. "You know, I don't think you get it, after all. There's no guarantee you'll be able to keep writing those books. Or any books, for that matter."

Her stomach pitched. Fear of death was one thing. Being told that she wouldn't be able to write—that would be a living death, which was way worse. "That's unacceptable," she said. "I have to write."

The fierceness left his expression as he regarded her with sympathy. "After watching you for weeks, I know that, too," he said softly. "I think it's time you sit down so we can talk."

Chapter 20

Aidan wasn't about to make any promises he couldn't keep, but when he saw the desperation in Emma's blue eyes at the thought of losing her beloved writing, he vowed to do everything in his power to preserve that part of her life. Yet he knew the books were one of his father's biggest concerns. If Emma continued to write and publish them, knowing what she knew, she might slip and reveal the Weres' secret.

Obviously sobered by the threat of losing her writing career, Emma had returned to the sofa instead of going in search of her BlackBerry. She picked up her coffee and took a sip, but her gaze was unfocused. He could tell she was thinking hard, trying to find a way out of this box she found herself in.

"We should have something to eat," he said. "I'll order chocolate cake if you insist, but I'd love to see you take in something more substantial than that."

"Oatmeal would be great," she said. "It's what my mother used to fix me on winter mornings as a kid, and it's my other comfort food besides chocolate."

He refrained from gagging at the thought of that gooey stuff. He'd been forced to eat it out of courtesy once when a woman he'd been seeing made it for breakfast. "Oatmeal it is." He walked over to the phone.

"If they can bring it with some soft butter, golden raisins, and brown sugar, I can make it taste the same as it did when I was eight years old. Oh, and lots more cream, please. I think we need more coffee, too."

"Done." He picked up the phone, ordered her oatmeal with all the fixings and the steak-and-egg platter for himself.

"And hot chocolate with whipped cream," she called to him right before he hung up the phone.

"Hang on a sec," he said to the person taking the order. He turned to Emma. "I thought you wanted coffee."

"I want that, too. But if they could fix the hot chocolate with real whipped cream, and shake on a little bit of cinnamon—not too much—and some chocolate sprinkles, that would be excellent."

He gave the order and came over to sit across from her on the other sofa. They had some decisions to make, and putting the coffee table between them would help him keep on track. "I take it hot chocolate with whipped cream and that other stuff—"

"Cinnamon and chocolate sprinkles."

"Is that comfort food, too?"

"Absolutely. It goes with the oatmeal. Why are you making a face?"

"Because I'm trying to imagine drinking that sugary thing along with all the sweet stuff you're putting on the oatmeal. It sounds god-awful."

"You don't have a sweet tooth."

"No, I have a meat tooth."

"Ha, ha. Is that werewolf humor?"

He thought about that. "I don't think there is such a thing."

"Really? You all take yourselves that seriously?"

"Absolutely."

"So when you're all sitting around the bonfire, nobody tells a joke that starts out, *These three werewolves walked into a bar*?"

"Nope." But the concept made him smile. Maybe he and his pack could lighten up. Someone like Emma hanging around could be a good thing, although Emma herself wouldn't be hanging around. He'd already determined that she'd hate being confined to the estate the way Nadia's aunt had been for the first few years of her marriage to Nadia's uncle.

"I've been thinking about the problem," she said. "And I think the answer is having me sign a contract promising never to divulge the existence of werewolves." She beamed at him. "You must have legal eagles at your beck and call. Have one of them draw up an airtight contract, and I'll be happy to sign it."

"Nice try." He drained his coffee cup and set it back in the saucer. "But people break contracts all the time."

"I don't!"

"That's admirable, but a contract is worthless to us. Contracts only work when the person who signs it is worried about being sued. If you break the contract, we can't sue you. You'd have exposed us, and our whole world would collapse into chaos."

She cradled her coffee cup and stared into it. "I see your point. I'm like a live hand grenade."

"Pretty much. My dad has the corporate jet on standby. He's instructed me to bring you to the estate the minute the weather clears."

"What estate?"

"It's in Upstate New York. It's my—well, the Wallace family home. Someday I'll inherit it."

Her eyes lit up. "Are we talking about a mansion full of werewolves?"

"That's one way to put it, yes."

"Cool. I'm not saying that I'll agree to hang out there forever or anything, but I'd love to see it."

He was having trouble keeping up. "I thought you were determined to continue with your book tour?"

"Well, I am." Her expression became resolute. "Yes, that's what I need to do. Finish the book tour." She sighed. "But going to that estate—can you imagine how that would be for a person who's spent years creating a fictitious world that she suddenly discovers is real?"

Aidan was no fool. He'd figured out early on that the book tour was a duty more than a pleasure. He saw an opening and took it. "What if I could arrange to keep all the stores on your tour happy without you having to physically be there?"

"I don't think that's possible."

He noticed that she hadn't turned him down flat, though. "I'm not saying it would be the same as if you actually visited the stores, but the weather is bad. Denver isn't going to be much better, and after that you're booked into Seattle, which has snow predicted for next weekend. You won't hit any good weather until LA and Phoenix."

"Winter book tours are problematic."

"So let me arrange for a virtual tour. I'll have large monitors delivered to any store that doesn't have one, and you can do a live author chat at the same time you would have been there for the event."

"What about the autograph session?"

Once again, she hadn't said no, so he ran with it,

spending Wallace money with every word out of his mouth. "We'll get a list of the names from each store. You can autograph the books off-site, and we'll express-ship them to be distributed."

"That's a pricey option. Who's going to pay for it?"

"Wallace Enterprises."

"Then how about throwing in free coffee drinks to all those who buy a book?"

"We could do that."

"And an appearance by the cover model of *Night Shift*?"

In one stroke, she'd upped the cost by several thousand dollars. He wondered how much she'd actually end up costing him. On all counts. "Who would know? You see only his torso."

"And a bit of his long black hair. Trust me; the readers know who he is. Hire him to show up at the bookstores, and I doubt they'll even miss me. What do you say?"

"If I get this guy, you'll give up the book tour and come to the estate instead?"

"I'll seriously consider it. But not to stay longer than a few days. And my mother has to know where I am at all times."

"You mean geographically or in general terms?"

"I mean she has to know where to find me."

Aidan shook his head. "Sorry. It's very secluded. We don't make the location public knowledge."

"What? Are you planning to blindfold me after I get in the car?"

"No, but we take a lot of back roads. You wouldn't be able to retrace your steps."

"You're making this sound way too spooky, and I'm telling you right now that I don't like scaring my mother."

Aidan hadn't pegged Betty Gavin as a woman who scared easily, so he figured this was another bid on Emma's part to gain some control. "How about telling her you're at the Wallace family home in Upstate New York? Wouldn't that be good enough?"

"She's going to want an address, and if I give her this song and dance about an exclusive estate no one's allowed to know about, she'll worry that you're kidnapping me and she'll never see me again. I'm her only kid. She's very protective."

"I don't doubt it, but—"

A rap at the door indicated their breakfast had arrived.

Emma stood. "I'll get it."

"Let me." Aidan moved swiftly to intercept her.

"Aidan, cool it. I'm not going to run out the door wearing a bathrobe."

"I know you won't." He stepped in front of her. "But the Henderson pack member standing guard in the hall doesn't. If you appear at the door, he might try to tackle you, which could play hell with the delivery of our breakfast."

Her eyes widened. "There's a werewolf guarding the door?"

"Yes, but anyone looking would see a six-five, two-hundred-fifty-pound bodybuilder." He left Emma to consider the presence of a guard at the door while he ushered the server in with their breakfast.

The server arranged everything quickly and seemed eager to leave. Aidan didn't blame him, considering the hulking presence outside the door. According to Howard Wallace's information about the guard, he was the Hendersons' enforcer, a powerful werewolf who owed the pack his life and would kill for them. Literally.

Aidan had closed the door behind the server when his BlackBerry chimed with his dad's ring. "That's my father. I need to get it. Go ahead and eat." He crossed to the coffee table and picked up his phone.

"Don't worry. I will. But ask him about the address thing. He's a parent. I'm sure he'll understand."

Aidan doubted it. The Wallaces had been guarding their location for a hundred years. They'd bought the abandoned and largely forgotten property through an intermediary. The pack had renovated it themselves slowly and quietly to maintain secrecy.

In the early years, they'd disguised the road by using a system of ropes and pulleys to raise and lower fallen trees. Aidan's dad had replaced that awkward system in the fifties when he built a rushing, seemingly treacherous creek across the road using theme-park technology.

All Wallace vehicles were equipped with a button that slowed the water to a trickle. A touch of a second button opened the dam upstream, and the creek flowed again. Howard had created a modern-day version of a medieval moat.

Aidan answered his call. "Hi, Dad."

"Is Emma's phone turned off?"

"Yes. I turned it off this morning. I thought—"

"I get that. I get that." Howard sounded impatient. "But it seems her mother is a persistent woman. When Emma didn't pick up her messages, her mother tried the hotel where Emma was supposed to be staying, and then she pestered the hell out of the airlines, and finally she called Roger Claymore, who was at his place in the Hamptons and not happy to have his Sunday morning interrupted."

"And Roger called you."

"Bingo. And I'm calling you. Roger told us to take care of it, and I promised him I would."

Aidan looked at Emma. She'd cradled the mug of hot chocolate in both hands and taken her first sip. There was whipped cream on her upper lip. Aidan's lust had been resting from the exertions of the night before, but now it yawned and stretched.

Turning away from the seductive picture of Emma savoring her hot chocolate, he paced a few feet away and lowered his voice. "Should I let her call?"

"I think you have to. That woman isn't going to rest until she hears her daughter's voice."

"Yeah, but I can't just let Emma say whatever she feels like saying. The call has to be scripted."

"So script it."

"But then it'll sound like a hostage situation."

"We have to take that chance. Emma needs to call. I assured Roger that Emma is fine and we have the situation well in hand, but he's not completely convinced that's the case. And I have to admit, neither am I."

"I'll handle it."

"Ask him about the address!" Emma called out.

"What did she just say? Something about an address?"

"Never mind, Dad. Everything's under control. Bye." He massaged the bridge of his nose and took a deep breath before turning back to Emma.

"I tried not to eavesdrop, but I'm pretty sure I heard the words *hostage situation.*"

For a woman uttering that sentence, she looked reasonably calm. Maybe the hot chocolate had worked some sort of magic because the mug was empty. Emma had also started in on the disgusting mess she'd created with the oatmeal and its array of embellishments.

She looked almost happy. But then, she hadn't heard that her mother was ready to call out the National Guard to find her.

Aidan searched his overworked brain for the best way to broach the subject. "I don't want you to get upset about this, but—"

"Hold it right there. Nothing good ever comes after a sentence that starts like that. Did you get permission for me to give my mother the address of your estate?"

"No. In fact, there's no address, and the place isn't on any map. The only way for anyone to know where it is would be to actually go there. And before you even suggest it, I'm telling you right now that your mother isn't going there."

"I know that." She sat primly on the sofa, the bowl of oatmeal in her lap. "But if I don't give her a better idea of where this mysterious estate is, she'll demand to know why I'm being so secretive, and that's not good, either, is it?"

"No." He sat on the sofa opposite hers and put his BlackBerry on the coffee table. "It's time to call your mother, though."

"I've been saying that."

Aidan wondered whether he was losing his mind, but he could come up with only one scenario that might satisfy Betty Gavin. "Are you willing to alter the truth a little when you call her?"

"Are you asking me to lie to my mother?"

"Yes." He braced himself for an explosion.

"No problem."

His jaw dropped.

"Don't look so surprised, Aidan. You think I want her to be on the werewolf hit list because she knows too much? The trick will be to give her the kind of info that will keep her from snooping around on her own."

"Well, she already has some information. When you didn't pick up your messages, she tried to contact you through the hotel where you were originally booked."

Emma flopped back on the sofa with a groan. The oatmeal quivered in the bowl but didn't spill out.

"Better not get that oatmeal on anything. I've heard NASA uses that stuff to make repairs on the space shuttle."

"Don't try to change the subject. How do you know this about my mother?"

"Because when you weren't registered at the hotel, she called the airlines, and when she discovered your flight had been canceled, she called Roger Claymore to find out where the hell you were."

"And Roger called your father, who called you."

"Exactly."

Emma sat forward and put her bowl on the tray. "I've suddenly lost my appetite. How am I going to explain"— she swept a hand around the penthouse suite—"*this*?"

"I have an idea."

"Then give it to me because I got zip."

"First, you explain that you broke up with Doug."

"Yeah." She eyed him warily.

"And then you tell her I've swept you off your feet."

"Aidan, I don't think—"

"Let me finish." He was warming to this story, strange as it had seemed in the beginning. "Then you say that, because I'm richer than God, I've arranged for a virtual book tour so that you and I can jet off to a lover's hideaway. You can't tell her where because I'm keeping it a secret even from you, as a special surprise, but it could be tropical."

Emma buried her face in her hands and groaned again. "This is so bad."

"Why? Isn't it the sort of romantic adventure a mother would want for her daughter?"

"Yes." She combed her fingers through her tousled hair and gazed up at him. "It's precisely what a mother would want for her daughter. She's never been crazy about Doug."

That makes two of us. "So she'll buy it, right?"

"Oh, she'll buy it, and she'll start imagining how fantastic the wedding will be, and how my whole life will change now that I've found Prince Charming, and how *her* life will change. That dream of an apartment on Central Park West will seem a lot closer, now. And then— *bam!*—it'll all come crashing down because we'll break up."

"I see your point."

"I'm setting her up only to knock her down later. I hate that."

Aidan stared at his breakfast, which was quickly congealing into something cold and inedible. He didn't feel much like eating, anyway. "I don't know what else to do, Emma." He lifted his head to glance across the coffee table. "I'm afraid anything less will have her asking all kinds of questions, just like you said she would."

"It's actually a brilliant plan," she said softly. "And if I consider the alternative—that my mother will start investigating my whereabouts and get herself into deep trouble with the werewolf world—I don't have much choice. I'd rather deal with her disappointment than be afraid for her life."

Aidan nodded. "That's the logical way to look at it."

"I still hate it."

"I know." The worst part was he did know. After all

those weeks of keeping track of her, he understood how deeply she loved her mom. Deliberately causing her pain would be tough. But as Emma had rightly figured out, it was the lesser of two evils.

"For what it's worth," Aidan said. "I hate it, too."

She held his gaze. "Thanks. That helps."

Chapter 21

After Emma retrieved her phone and returned to her place on the sofa to make the call, Aidan came over to sit beside her. She appreciated that. In many ways Aidan was a very nice guy—um—werewolf.

She took a deep breath, filling her senses with the musky aroma that was Aidan. Perhaps it wasn't some expensive aftershave she inhaled. The scent that drew her could be a blend made up of his natural element— deep woods and moist earth, combined with the primitive essence of a powerful male wolf.

She still had trouble melding the two entities—the man beside her and the golden-eyed wolf that hurtled into her bedroom last night. In her books, where she'd been somewhat removed from the concept, it had seemed perfectly plausible. Faced with the reality, she discovered that the chasm between man and beast was too wide for her mind to make the leap.

That worked to the pack's advantage, she supposed. Most people would assume they'd imagined seeing a large wolf in a populated area where no wolves had roamed for centuries. If someone happened to witness an actual transformation, they'd assume they'd had too much to drink or needed new glasses. A casual sighting would be passed off as a trick of light or somebody pulling a prank.

Emma couldn't hide behind those excuses, but she wanted everyone else to, especially her mother. Betty Gavin answered on the second ring.

"Emma, my God, where *are* you?"

"Mom, I'm so sorry to worry you. I'm at the Palmer House in Chicago with Aidan Wallace."

"The Palmer House? With Aidan?"

Aidan slid his arm around her shoulders, and for the space of this phone call, Emma decided to pretend that what she was about to tell her mother was true. If a fiction writer couldn't weave her own fantasies, then who could?

"I didn't want to tell you right before I left because I didn't know how everything would go, but Aidan took me out for a drink and dancing after the signing Wednesday night. We had a terrific time, and I broke up with Doug the next morning."

"Wow, *Emma*. And Aidan is there with you now?"

"Yes." She snuggled into his warmth, and he cooperated by holding her close. "He invited himself along on my book tour and then changed my hotel reservations, which is why you couldn't find me where I was supposed to be. We're in the penthouse, and he's spoiling me rotten."

"A whirlwind romance! I love it! So is he continuing on with you to the other cities on your tour?"

"Not exactly." Emma battled her guilt at deceiving her trusting mother by remembering that deception was the only way to keep Betty safe. "Because the weather's turning out to be a problem anyway, Aidan's setting up a virtual tour, which I can do from anywhere there's an Internet connection."

"I think that's very smart, Emma. I never did like the idea of all that flying around when the weather's bound to be miserable. Good for Aidan. I can see already that he's looking out for you. Are you both coming back to New York, then? Because I'd love to have you both over for dinner. Nothing fancy, probably not what Aidan's used to, but I—"

"Maybe soon, Mom." Emma's heart squeezed as she thought of the approaching letdown. "But Aidan and I want to spend some time alone, so he's arranged a tropical getaway for us."

"Ooh, I like that! So classy. Where?"

Aidan's arm tightened around her. He was close enough to hear both sides of the conversation and had to know how her mother's enthusiasm cut her to the quick.

"He won't tell me! It's a surprise, so I'll just have to let you know when I get back."

"Can't you call me from there?"

"I could, Mom, but I'll be . . . sort of busy."

Her mother laughed. "Of course, of course. Never mind me. Call me when you get a chance, but I don't want to be the bothersome mother who needs her daughter to check in twice a day. Just . . . have fun."

Emma's throat tightened. "I will, Mom. I love you."

"I love you, too, honey. And I'm so happy for you."

"Bye, Mom. I'll be in touch."

"Bye, sweetie."

Emma disconnected the call and buried her face against Aidan's shoulder. "That was awful, just awful."

"You handled it beautifully." He stroked her hair.

"It wasn't hard. She would never in a million years

suspect that I would lie to her about something like this. She's always wanted a special man in my life, somebody she considered good enough for me. Now she thinks I have one, but I don't, and I just *hate* that I lied to her about it."

He wrapped her in his arms and kissed the top of her head. "Don't forget why you're doing this. You're protecting her."

Battling tears, she sat up so she could look at him. "You know what? I wish you'd never read one of my books. And if you had to read one, I wish you'd decided it was stupid and tossed it in the nearest Dumpster."

"Emma, by writing about werewolves, you were going to attract a Were's attention sooner or later. Isn't it better that I'm the one who made the first contact, instead of some nutcase like Theo?"

"So you're saying I would have been sucked into the werewolf world eventually, simply by writing the books I do?"

He combed her hair back from her face as if she were a little child he needed to comfort. "I think so, yes."

"That makes no sense. A bunch of people write about werewolves. Are all of them being monitored?"

"Depends on whether their werewolf characters are anything close to the truth. In one story I picked up, the Weres had wolf faces and hairy humanoid bodies, so they were ugly as sin. Plus they ran around killing and eating people." He made a face. "Disgusting."

He was so clearly offended that she couldn't help but smile. "So that book went in the Dumpster?"

"First I ripped it in half, and then I threw it in the fireplace, where it burned to a satisfying crisp."

"I see. Remind me never to present you with a bad book."

He laughed. "That might be the only time I've done that. Usually I just toss them if they're bad."

"You've read a lot of werewolf books, then?"

"Quite a few. It's a hobby of mine. Anyway, you can imagine how happy I was when your werewolves turned out to be responsible citizens and loyal pack members." He gazed at her. "In other words, your Weres have dignity. I appreciate that take on the subject."

She shrugged. "It was my fantasy of how they would be if they did exist."

"And we do."

"I know you do, Aidan. But I have to say that sitting here on the sofa with you, when you're so *human,* I can't imagine that you can suddenly turn into a wolf." She studied his face. "When I look into your eyes, I see a man."

"Are you absolutely sure about that?"

"Yes. All I see is . . ." Her voice trailed off as something in his eyes began to change.

The difference was subtle at first, a slight altering of the pupils. Then his focus sharpened, and a primitive light began to shine in those golden depths.

Her breath caught.

"The wolf is always there, Emma."

As she responded to the intensity in his eyes, her pulse quickened and sexual awareness danced along her nerve endings. "Always?"

"Yes."

"Even during—" She swallowed. "During sex?"

"Especially then. When you become aroused, your scent drives me crazy." He paused and his glance flicked over her. "It's driving me crazy now."

She shouldn't be surprised that he could sense the hot desire simmering just under the surface, ready to spill over at any moment. Whatever he was, man or wolf, she wanted him. "Are you going to . . . shift?"

"I will soon if I stay here with you. I should leave—take a walk . . ." He hesitated. "Unless—well, unless you're willing to help me stop it."

A familiar ache began low in her belly. "By having sex?"

"Yes, but considering how my family has interfered with your life and forced you to lie to your mother, I wouldn't blame you for denying me."

He had a point, but she craved what he offered. By denying him she'd deny herself. "I'm not into revenge."

"Maybe not, but what about self-preservation? You know I'm committed to Nadia."

"Have you had sex with her?"

"No."

That single word meant more to her than she'd ever let him know. "Why not? She's lovely."

"She doesn't excite me."

Fierce joy surged through her at that admission. Nadia didn't excite him, but *she,* Emma Gavin, did.

"I don't excite her, either, so we're not tempted by sex. One day, we'll create the union that will benefit our families, but not yet."

"It seems so cold and calculated, Aidan."

"It's my duty." He cupped her cheek and gazed at her, his eyes growing more wolflike with every passing moment. "And you're running out of time. Will you let me take you, Emma Gavin?"

She thought she'd die if he didn't. "Will the sofa hold us?"

Standing, he scooped her up in his arms and headed for her bedroom. "Not for what I have in mind."

Her heart beat wildly in anticipation. No man had

ever made her feel like this, as if she were a prize he'd won and now intended to savor to the fullest. But Aidan wasn't a man, she reminded herself. As he'd said, the wolf was always there.

He tumbled with her onto the bed, which was still in disarray from the night before. He rolled her onto her back, and then rolled again, pulling her on top of him. Her robe loosened, and he dispensed with the tie in one swift tug.

"There." His white teeth gleamed as he cupped her breasts, urging her down to his waiting mouth.

But they were human teeth, not a wolf's sharp canines. Bracing her hands on either side of his head, she leaned down so that he could suckle. He was a man, his fingers long and lean as he massaged her breasts. Straddling him, she lowered her hips until her throbbing clit brushed the hard ridge of his penis straining against the black jersey of his sweats.

He made a sound low in his throat, and it was the groan of a lusty man, not the growl of a mating wolf. But in another time and place, he would become that wolf. Nadia, his chosen companion, would be able to join with him as both wolf and woman. Emma hated knowing that she could not.

Yet she had him with her now. That would have to be enough.

Slowly she rotated her hips, rubbing against him, teasing him with what he could have if he removed that barrier of cloth that separated them. With another soft groan, he released her breasts, leaving them damp and quivering. Shoving his sweats to his knees, he put his hands around her waist.

"Ride me, Emma." His voice was rough with desire as he started to lift her.

"Not yet." Wiggling out of his grasp, she slid back along his powerful thighs and felt his muscles bunch. When she wrapped her hand around his thick penis, he arched toward her and his breath hissed between his teeth.

"Maybe I'm into revenge, after all," she said. "This is payback for what you did to me while I was lying on the living room rug Friday night." Then she lowered her mouth to his cock.

The wild, erotic taste of him nearly made her come. She tried to tell herself that in human form he was no different from any other well-endowed man. But that wasn't true. His flavor was different, his scent was different, and as she made slow, deliberate love to that most male part of his human body, his groan became a low growl. The wolf was there.

He combed his fingers through her hair, lightly pressing them to her scalp. He trembled as if cradling her so gently took great restraint. The pressure of his fingers increased a little more as she took him deep into her mouth and massaged his balls.

His rapid breathing told her he was skating along the edge of release. As she teased and caressed him, coaxing him to let go, she wondered whether he'd allow himself that much loss of control.

Then his grip tightened. "No more."

She decided to honor his wish, but she took her time releasing him. Her upward progress included numerous licks and nibbles that prompted him to swear softly under his breath. But he didn't pull her away, and she loved knowing he loved every second even though he had to battle for control.

At last, with one lingering kiss on the tip of his glorious penis, she lifted her head and met his gaze. "Revenge is sweet."

"Come here." Continuing to cup her head in both hands, he urged her forward.

She looked into his eyes as she crawled toward him and allowed him to draw her close for a long, hot kiss. The seductive movement of his lips and tongue pulled her down, down, into a whirling vortex of sensation. She missed the moment when he transferred his grip from her head to her hips.

Without interrupting the kiss, he guided her into position, sliding his cock into her with such fluid grace that it felt like dancing. When they were locked together, he sighed against her mouth. "I could stay like this . . . forever."

The words, so sweet and sincere, pierced the armor she'd been vainly constructing around her heart. She lifted her head to gaze down at him. "Don't you dare fall for me, Aidan."

"I can't." But the truth was there to see in his golden eyes. He was going down for the count, just as she was.

"I can't fall for you, either."

He kneaded her bottom with his talented fingers. "So, don't."

"I definitely won't." She closed her eyes because it was the only way she could lie to him. "I'm only here for the sex."

"Yeah." His voice was husky. "Me, too."

She opened her eyes and smiled at him. "And the research." Then she began to move, showing him with her body how she felt, even if she couldn't say the words. Her gaze locked with his as she began a steady rhythm. The glow in his golden eyes reflected the same emotion she felt, the one neither of them could name.

Gradually she increased the pace and watched the fire build in his eyes. He held her hips loosely, allowing her to be in control. Even as his jaw clenched and his breathing grew labored, his touch remained gentle.

Surely that took effort. Her trust grew as she began to understand how deeply his protective instincts ran. Man or wolf, he would go to great lengths to keep her from harm. And her trust was returned. In this moment of intimacy, he'd surrendered completely, allowing her to be in command.

She shifted the angle slightly and felt him begin to tremble beneath her. "Let go, Aidan," she murmured.

He struggled to breathe. "Will you?"

"Yes . . . soon." She pumped faster. "Come with me."

"Emma . . ." He rose to meet her, his movements in perfect cadence with hers.

"I'm here." She began to pant as her womb tightened. "Now, Aidan. *Now.*"

With a groan, he held her still and surged upward. She climaxed at the moment of impact, and his name fell from her lips in a cry of pure joy as his orgasm flowed into hers.

They rode the wave together, freed for that brief moment from the forces that conspired to keep them apart. Despite those forces, she knew they'd forged a bond . . . and it was growing stronger.

He had to know it, too. Quivering in the aftermath, she looked once more into his beautiful eyes. The emotion she'd glimpsed before was still there. Vibrant and strong, it said more than words ever could.

And it would have to be enough.

Chapter 22

We're in big trouble. Aidan had suspected it from the moment he'd realized his attraction to Emma, but as she smiled and tucked herself into his arms with a contented sigh, he began to understand the full extent of the problem.

This petite blond woman—with a mind that had intrigued him from the beginning and a body he desired beyond all reason—could be his downfall. Or he would be hers, depending on how this all played out.

Roarke had warned him, but Aidan hadn't listened. Worst of all, he didn't regret a single minute he'd spent with Emma. As he stroked her silky hair and wondered how the hell he'd ever dig himself out of this mess, the bedside phone rang.

"I've got it." Emma propped herself on his chest and reached for the receiver.

"Maybe I should—"

"Never mind. I have it." Resuming her snuggle position, she put the phone to her ear. "Hello? Oh, hello, Nadia."

Aidan squeezed his eyes shut. Not the person he needed to be talking to right now.

"Sure, he's right here." Emma shifted her position slightly so she could hand him the receiver, but otherwise she continued to nestle close.

If Aidan didn't know better, he'd think Emma was guarding her territory. But she wouldn't stake a claim to him . . . would she?

He put the phone to his ear. "Hi, Nadia."

"Hi, yourself. When Emma said you were right there, she wasn't kidding. I take it she doesn't scare easily."

"Guess not."

"Are you two in bed?"

"Sorry. I didn't catch that. Must be some static on the line. What can I do for you this morning?" He grabbed Emma's hand as she began tickling him.

"There's static on the line," Nadia said. "And it's you trying to blow smoke. I tried your cell phone, and you didn't answer, so that's when I called your room. I'm downstairs in the lobby."

"Oh! Um, I'll be right down."

Emma scooted up and began nibbling his earlobe.

"Don't come down," Nadia said. "I'll be glad to come to you. In fact, I'd prefer that. Because we already have a Henderson bodyguard stationed outside your door, the hotel gave me a key to access the elevator, but I thought providing you with some advance warning would be a classy gesture."

"Thanks, Nadia. You're welcome to come up here, but could you give me ten minutes?"

Emma pushed herself to a sitting position and frowned at him.

Nadia chuckled. "Yeah, sure, lover boy."

"See you in ten."

Emma scrambled out of bed. "You should have asked for twenty," she said over her shoulder as she headed for the bathroom.

"It wouldn't matter," he called after her. "She's figured out we're involved. And you weren't helping, by the way, by tickling me and nibbling on my ear."

Emma paused and turned back to him. She looked like a wood sprite—naked, rosy, and ready for more of what they'd just enjoyed. "Aidan, I have to say this, and then I'll shut up about it. It's a crime against nature for someone as passionate as you to spend a lifetime with someone you're not excited about."

"It's my—"

"Your duty. I know. You said that. And if you're hell-bent on doing your duty, I guess there's nothing more to discuss. But if your parents truly care about you, I can't imagine them wanting you to make such a sacrifice. In fact, I can't imagine Nadia making that sacrifice, either, or expecting you to."

"But—"

"And just so you know, this isn't about you and me. Being the crown prince and all, you probably still have to hook up with a female werewolf, and that's cool. But at least pick someone you have some chemistry with."

He opened his mouth to argue the point, but she'd already disappeared into the bathroom and turned on the shower. He'd do well to follow her example and make himself presentable before Nadia showed up. He headed toward his own bathroom.

Nine minutes later, he walked into the penthouse living room dressed in slacks and a white dress shirt open at the collar. He'd chosen typical work clothes because he needed to stop the fun and games and get down to business. His hair was slightly damp, and he'd nicked himself while shaving, but other than that, he looked reasonably respectable.

The door to Emma's bedroom was closed, and he could hear the hair dryer. Apparently coming in contact with Theo's head the night before hadn't broken it. Aidan wondered whether Nadia believed the hammer story. Probably not, but he was very curious as to why she'd come here today.

Right on time, she rapped on the door, and he hurried to open it. Having a chance to talk to her before Emma came into the room would be a good thing. No telling what would come out of Emma's mouth.

Nadia smiled as she entered the room with her usual graceful stride. Under a black goose-down jacket, she wore a metallic gold running suit.

He helped her off with her coat. "You're looking great, as always."

"Thanks. You're looking happier."

"Happier than what?" He'd never given much thought as to whether he looked happy or sad.

"Happier than you usually do. I think Emma must be good for you." She stopped him as he started to put her coat in the closet by the foyer. "Don't bother. I'll keep it with me. I won't stay long." Her gaze swept the room and lingered on the coffee table where the remains of Emma's breakfast sat on one side and his untouched plate sat on the other.

Aidan figured she'd have no trouble reconstructing the scene—obviously they'd started out eating breakfast and ended up abandoning the meal to jump into bed. He hadn't given himself time to clear away the evidence, but then again, so what if Nadia saw this? It wasn't as if she hadn't suspected.

"Please, have a seat." He gestured toward the two sofas. "I'll order up some fresh coffee."

She walked over and sat down on the right-hand sofa, the one he'd chosen for eating the breakfast he'd never touched. "No coffee for me. Thanks." She glanced up at him. "I came to warn you that my father's swallowed Theo's ridiculous story—hook, line, and hammer."

"That's what my dad said."

"I know Theo's lying, but it's too bad both of you ended up shifting in front of Emma."

"It was the only way I could effectively fight him, but you're right. It's not good." Aidan thought about the benefit he'd derived—being able to have sex with Emma without a condom—and realized he wasn't as sorry as he should be.

"How did she take it?"

"She . . ." He hadn't really thought about that, either. "She's fascinated—which, now that you bring it up, is remarkable. You'd expect her to run screaming into the night, but she didn't. She wants to learn more."

"But the more she learns, the more she could reveal about us."

"Yeah." Aidan paced in front of the fireplace. "I'm not sure how that's going to be resolved."

"Obviously, my father's frantic, which is why he posted that guard. What steps have you taken so far?"

Aidan outlined the cobbled-together plan of substituting a virtual book tour for the in-person one and whisking Emma away to Upstate New York. "Her mother thinks we're madly in love and I'm taking her to an undisclosed tropical hideaway," he added.

"The first part of that story appears to be true."

He hoped she was making a wild guess and his obsession with Emma hadn't turned into a flashing neon sign above his head. "It's not."

"Okay. You would know."

Aidan grabbed the first change of topic he could think of. "How's your brother?"

"Obnoxious as always. But he has a pretty big knot on the back of his head. I don't buy the hammer story, but what happened?"

Emma came out of her bedroom wearing black slacks and a soft white turtleneck. "I bonked him with the hotel hair dryer, which still works, amazingly enough. I wish I could say I'm sorry I smacked him, but I'm not. He was trying to hamstring Aidan."

Nadia glanced from Aidan to Emma. "You were defending him, even when you knew he was a werewolf?"

"What difference does that make? He was still Aidan under all that fur, and he'd come to my rescue when Theo shifted. I wasn't about to stand by and watch him get hurt."

Nadia's eyebrows lifted, and her gaze swung to Aidan as if to say, *See? Madly in love, both of you.* Then she turned her attention back to Emma. "Aidan says you're curious about our lifestyle."

"That's putting it mildly." Emma walked over and sat on the sofa opposite Nadia. "I could get so many ideas for my books! You're a creative person, so I'm sure you can understand how exploring the actual world of Weres would provide unlimited inspiration for my work."

Nadia leaned forward, and her voice was warm with empathy. "I do understand, but . . . having you know so much is a danger to us, Emma."

A chill slid down Aidan's spine. "She won't be. I've promised everyone that."

"And I'll promise, too!" Emma looked so earnest, so eager. "I can be trusted with this information. And I could help with your PR image. Not to brag or anything, but my books sell pretty well. Aidan said he was happy to find a writer who portrayed Weres in such a positive light."

"I'm sure he was, but whether a writer presents a good picture or a bad one doesn't really matter if we remain a secret society. And we're committed to that, or I should say most of us are."

"Theo isn't," Emma said.

Nadia sighed. "No, he isn't. He'd like to have us all uncloak ourselves and stage a massive takeover. I'm sure he thought you'd help him because your books are so sympathetic to Weres."

"Dear God." Emma recoiled in horror. "By writing my books, I caused the Wallaces to put me under surveillance and Theo to crank up his takeover scheme. All I wanted was to create an entertaining fantasy that would earn me enough to live on."

Her plaintive tone caused Aidan to round the sofa and sit next to her. "Theo was headed off the deep end before you came along," he said. He longed to take her in his arms and reassure her, but he wasn't going to do that in front of Nadia.

"Yes, he was," Nadia agreed. "But I'm afraid he's changed your life forever, Emma."

Aidan winced. He'd been trying to avoid saying it so baldly.

"I know." Emma sounded brave and resolute. "But no matter how my life has changed, I need to have two things stay the same. I want to continue my publishing career, and I want to be able to see my mother. Those two things are nonnegotiable."

Nadia exchanged a glance with Aidan. They both knew Emma was in no position to dictate terms.

Yet Aidan also knew at that moment that he would stake his reputation—no, that wasn't right. He would stake his *life* on seeing that Emma got what she wanted. He couldn't allow Theo, or himself, for that matter, to be responsible for ending her career or her relationship with her mother.

"And as long as I'm making pronouncements," Emma said, "I might as well get this off my chest, Nadia. I think this marriage pact you and Aidan have going on is ridiculous."

Aidan groaned. "Emma, let's not get into—"

"Yes, let's do," Nadia said. "Because Emma's right. Until this weekend I had assumed that both of us were so committed to uniting the two packs that we couldn't allow ourselves to feel deeply for someone else. I thought we were programmed that way from the day our parents decided to give us names that were mirror images of each other."

"I am committed to that," Aidan said quietly. "I have been ever since I was old enough to understand."

Nadia met his gaze. "Then you have a greater talent for self-sacrifice than I do." She stood. "That's mostly why I came up here, to see for myself what I sensed was a growing bond between you two. Now that I'm convinced how strong it is, I'm renouncing you as a potential mate, Aidan. You're free."

Although a huge weight lifted from his heart at her words, Aidan couldn't let it go at that. He came to his feet. "You can't just go against the wishes of the packs and throw away the proposed merger of our families."

"Yes, I can. It was never a great idea to begin with."

Emma stood and raised both fists in the air. "Hallelujah, a woman with common sense! Excuse my terminology. I should probably say a werewolf-slash-woman with common sense."

Nadia laughed. "I think it's the woman part that's making this stand. My werewolf side always wants to go the traditional route, but at the moment my twenty-first-century emancipated female is in charge, and she wants to kick this outdated custom to the curb."

"Good." Emma folded her arms and smiled in obvious satisfaction.

"There will be hell to pay," Aidan said. "Your father—"

"My father and your father will have to deal with this and realize they're asking the impossible. Besides, I plan to blame the whole thing on Theo and his shenanigans, and I would advise you to do the same. The threat of Theo forced you into proximity with Emma, which ignited your mutual attraction."

Aidan sighed. "The fallout will be significant, but in reality they can't do much about it, I guess."

"Nope. They can rant and rave, but it's our decision." She paused. "Still, I need to warn you that, although I'll try to hang this on Theo, everyone will probably blame you and Emma, and mostly Emma, because she's not a Were, which makes her an easy target."

Aidan moved closer to Emma, as if he might have to start defending her at any moment. "But that's so unfair. She didn't ask for any of—"

"It's okay." Emma laid a hand on his arm. "I don't mind taking the fall if it means you're free to marry for love."

"In a perfect world," Nadia said gently, "he'd be free to marry you. But all things considered . . ."

"I know that, too." Emma lifted her chin. "I'm a human, and the pack will despise me for leading their crown prince astray. As I said before, all I want is my career and the freedom to see my mother."

"And you'll get that," Aidan said. "No matter what I have to do, I promise you'll get that."

Chapter 23

No sooner had Nadia left than Roarke called Aidan, and Emma watched in awe as the Wallace team went into action. Howard Wallace contacted his old pal Roger Claymore, and before Emma could turn around, her book tour had been rearranged. The Internet and Skype would allow her to appear at each bookstore on a computer monitor, and fans would be able to talk to her as if she were there in person.

Emma fielded a call from Jenny and gave her publicist the phony tropical getaway story Aidan had concocted. Emma tried not to feel like a lying piece of crap for misleading yet another trusting *person* in her life.

But the truth would put Jenny at risk, just as it would her mother. Emma had never aspired to a cloak-and-dagger life, but she'd been thrust into one anyway. She preferred her conflicts on the page, but she couldn't figure out how to dial back the drama.

The Wallaces in action provided drama to burn. Once the runways were cleared, the Wallace corporate Learjet was dispatched from New York to collect Emma and

Aidan. By midafternoon they were in Barry's town car, flying the Wallace flag on the way to the airport. Emma smiled grimly to herself when she thought about that flag. No wonder it had wolves on it.

Naturally, the town car took them straight out onto the tarmac, where the jet waited, stairs lowered. A broad-shouldered man in a topcoat stood beside the steps, his blond hair tossed by the winter wind. Emma recognized Roarke, who'd probably been sent to make sure Emma got on the plane.

Aidan kept telling her she was a guest, not a prisoner, but Roarke's forbidding expression indicated otherwise. She kept up her courage by thinking of this as more research. She tried to imagine what it would be like to live this way all the time, whisked around in town cars and private jets before being transported to a secret multimillion-dollar mansion.

The werewolves in her books were loyal, decent creatures loaded with sex appeal, but it hadn't occurred to her to give them piles of money. She had to admit that a wealthy werewolf added a whole other dimension to the fantasy.

Thinking about that, she glanced at Aidan before Barry helped her out of the town car. "Got your watch?"

He held up his wrist to display it in all its glory.

She nodded. "Just checking that you didn't leave it on the dresser. I figure we're in enough trouble without adding a lost watch that cost more than an Ivy League education."

Aidan reached over and squeezed her hand. "Don't worry. Everything's going to be fine."

"If that's true, then what's with Roarke? I've seen friendlier-looking guys on *America's Most Wanted*."

"That's his game face. He thinks it makes him look older and scarier."

"Well, he's right. It does." Emma climbed out of the car and tightened the belt on her trench coat. The wind was biting cold. If she'd been traveling commercial, she'd walk through a cozy Jetway that would protect her from the wind on the way to the plane.

But before she took her first step, Aidan was beside her.

"Damn, it's cold." He put a sheltering arm around her shoulders. "Stay close."

Okay, so maybe a Jetway wasn't so great, after all. Being tucked in beside a warm hunk like Aidan had definite advantages.

When they reached the steps, Roarke's gaze remained chilly. He inclined his head. "Aidan. Emma."

Whoa. Emma wondered whether this would be her reception from everyone in the werewolf community. If so, she could be in for a tough few days.

But instead of responding in kind, Aidan laughed. "You're enjoying the hell out of this, aren't you, bro?"

Roarke's mouth was set in a grim line as he stared at Aidan. "Yep." Then his expression began to shift, until a wide grin transformed his handsome face. "It's not every day I get to say, *I told you so,* to the big brother who always thinks he knows best."

"Don't get too comfortable in that smug suit you're wearing, Roarke. I intend to pull this one out of the fire."

"That I have to see, considering you're in some serious shit. Now if we're finished with verbal sparring, could we go inside? I've been out here doing the disapproval stance long enough to freeze my privates."

The tension in Emma's stomach eased a little. Yes,

she was about to visit a pack of werewolves, but in the final analysis, they were a family, with the normal dynamics of any family. As the oldest, Aidan was expected to do the right thing.

When he screwed up, his brother grabbed the chance to gloat. If Aidan's mother and father could be typical parents, Emma might not feel so out of place, after all. Then again, she wasn't sure how typical the family could be when they all had the ability to shift into wolf form and race around in the woods.

As she climbed the steps, she shivered.

"You'll be warm in a minute," Aidan said as he climbed the steps behind her.

"I know." But her shivers had less to do with the cold wind and more to do with anticipation of what she'd find at the Wallace estate. And whether they intended to ever let her leave.

Aidan could sense Emma's nervousness despite her attempts to appear calm and in control. She took great interest in the plane's white leather seats, which swiveled, reclined, and even folded flat for sleeping.

Or . . . they could be folded flat for other, more interesting activities. Aidan shocked himself by having X-rated thoughts about Emma naked at thirty thousand feet. He'd helped her off with her coat once they'd boarded, and for the first time today, he had the leisure to admire the fit of her soft white sweater and black slacks.

He liked the way she looked in them, but he'd love the way she looked out of them. It wouldn't be happening, even though they had a certain amount of privacy. Normally a flight attendant traveled with the jet, but apparently Roarke hadn't thought it necessary for this trip.

Roarke himself had immediately headed for the cockpit, obviously hoping to take the controls on the way home. Theoretically, Aidan and Emma were alone in the cabin, but that didn't mean they could strip and have at it. In fact, sex with Emma might be a luxury he would never enjoy again, and he had to come to grips with that.

In the next day or two, he needed to convince his parents that Emma could be placed on something resembling parole, where she'd be allowed the freedom to do her work and see her mother as she'd requested. Aidan had to assure his mother and father that Emma could be trusted not to compromise the pack. If his parents thought lust was clouding his judgment, they'd never go along with his recommendations.

"I can see why you like flying this way." Emma chose a seat and strapped herself in. "Even if you do have to duck your head when you move around in here."

"There's still more of a feeling of space." He chose the seat facing her and fastened his seat belt. A Lucite pedestal table separated them, but his knees came very close to touching hers. "I like space around me."

She settled back into the seat. "Is that a personal preference or a werewolf trait?"

"Both, but the need seems to be stronger in me than most Weres. Roarke, for instance, drives a sports car and loves the cockpit of this plane. I'd hate both things. His tolerance for small spaces is obviously greater than mine."

"In other words, no two werewolves are created alike," she said with a smile.

"No." That smile of hers could be his undoing. Now that he'd kissed her so thoroughly and often, her smile made him want to do it again.

If he could kiss her now, he wouldn't mind the dreaded takeoff so much. But they both needed to be belted in, and besides, kissing her would only begin a process he couldn't finish, which might initiate a shift. He wasn't about to give Roarke the satisfaction of witnessing an embarrassing episode like that.

So he'd white-knuckle the takeoff. As the plane taxied down the runway and the familiar panic clawed at his insides, he closed his eyes and gripped the armrests.

Then her scent enveloped him, and his eyes snapped open. She'd settled on his lap. "Emma, you should be—"

"Right here. You hate the takeoff, and I can help. There's no bossy flight attendant to make me buckle up, so why not?"

He wrapped both arms around her because he couldn't help himself. "I'll tell you why not." He gazed at her. "You sitting on my lap is a disaster waiting to happen."

"I think we have more control than that."

"I'm not sure. I'd no sooner demonstrated to you how the seats fold flat than I pictured you naked on one."

Her lips curved in a saucy smile. "So, I have totally corrupted you."

" 'Fraid so." He couldn't resist that mouth, so he cupped her head and pulled her lips down to meet his. *Ah.* Kissing was one of the things he loved most about his human form. The missionary position was another. Call him sentimental, but he liked looking into his partner's eyes during sex. He specifically liked looking into Emma's eyes.

Kissing her sucked the panic right out of him and replaced it with good old-fashioned desire. His fear of flying had disappeared, but now he had another problem.

The backs of his hands were starting to itch, and his tail-bone ached. This was not good at thirty thousand feet.

He'd never shifted midair, and he wasn't about to now. But how he'd avoid doing so was somewhat of a challenge. If Emma had worn a skirt instead of slacks, they might have quietly accomplished the deed, but he didn't relish having either of them take off articles of clothing with Roarke and the pilot not far away.

Emma lifted her mouth from his. "I can feel your teeth growing."

"That would be a sign that we have a slight problem."

"I'll take care of it."

"Emma, I'm not sure—"

"Is anybody ever sure of anything?" Climbing out of his lap, she crawled under the Lucite table. "That's the nature of life, isn't it? Uncertainty."

"I'm certain this is a really bad idea." He knew exactly what she had in mind, and while he was wildly excited at the prospect, he could think of a thousand ways it could backfire.

"It's a great idea. You're facing the cockpit, so you can warn me if anyone shows up, but we're still climbing, so there's no chance either of those guys will wander back until we reach altitude."

"You must have flown a lot if you know these things."

"I have, but never in a Learjet. And never while giving someone a blowjob." She unzipped his slacks.

His heart hammered against his ribs. "I should tell you to stop."

"If I stop, you grow fur. Am I right?"

"Yes, damn it."

"Then relax and leave the driving to me." She freed his penis and drew it into her mouth.

His eyes rolled back in his head. The vibration of the plane combined with her attention to his cock produced a surreal buzz of excitement that traveled from his toes to the roots of his hair. On the plus side, the backs of his hands didn't itch anymore. On the other plus side, he'd found a way to enjoy the experience of flight.

Contrary to her seductively lazy method the previous night, she got right down to business. He understood. She had limited time before the plane leveled off and someone, either the pilot or Roarke, might wander back to the cabin for a chat.

Between the novelty of the experience and Emma's dedication to her task, Aidan knew he wouldn't last long anyway. Then he realized that the Lucite table allowed him to view exactly what was going on, and the visual of Emma with her sweet mouth working his dick put him over the top. Somehow he clenched his jaw tight enough to muffle his groan of pleasure when he came.

His acute hearing picked up the sound of her soft swallow. If he hadn't pledged his honor and his life to her before, he would have done it then as she carefully adjusted his briefs and closed his zipper. As it was, he could pledge only his undying gratitude.

The woman had heart and spirit. His werewolf soul rejoiced in that. In the natural order of things, Emma would mate with her own kind and Aidan would do the same. But his entire being rebelled at the thought.

Easing out from under the table, she stood and balanced in the aisle as the plane swooped upward.

"Emma, that was . . ."

"Yeah." She grinned. "Wasn't it?"

He took in her flushed cheeks and sparkling eyes. "Did you come?"

"Yes, as a matter of fact. One of those spontaneous

things because I was so excited for you." She stretched. "I'm not *nearly* as tense and worried about meeting your parents." She returned to her seat and buckled herself in.

"Don't worry about my parents." He was worried enough for both of them.

"You could help by telling me something about them. I've heard a little about your dad, but I know nothing about your mom. What's she like?"

"Fierce." Her look of dismay had him scrambling to modify that word. "I mean fiercely protective." No, that wasn't any better. "She's very loving," he said at last, hoping that would help.

"I'm sure she is"—Emma looked pale, but she met his gaze—"to those she cares about."

Aidan wanted his mother to care about Emma, but that might be a tall order. Emma held the key to their destruction, and in addition to that, she was a human. She'd also been the catalyst that had ended any hope that he'd marry Nadia. He wondered whether that news had filtered over to the Wallace camp yet.

"Let's back up," Emma said. "I'm a visual person, and I need a mental picture. Tell me your mom's name and what she looks like."

"Her name's Fiona, and she has dark hair that's short and curly. In human form she's five-seven, and I think she looks fine, but she's always complaining that she needs to lose ten pounds."

"Do werewolves go gray?"

"Sometimes, when we're very old. My mom's forty-seven, and she doesn't have a single gray hair."

Emma sighed. "So much to learn. I had my werewolves going gray like people do, but that's wrong."

"Maybe it's better if your books have a few mistakes

in them." Aidan's mind leaped ahead. Limited freedom for Emma would mean she could keep publishing, but the Were community might think of her as a time bomb ready to go off at any moment. If her books were less accurate, that might help alleviate the concern.

"But if I know how the world actually functions, I'll want to write it that way."

Aidan blew out a breath. "One of your conditions was continuing with your writing career, right?"

"Absolutely. If the werewolf community wants to muzzle me, you might as well put a gun to my head and pull the trigger."

"What's your definition of muzzling?"

"Just what you'd think. Preventing me from writing, obviously, but censoring what I write would be almost as bad."

Aidan's head began to ache. If he could convince his parents to allow Emma to continue her career, he could almost guarantee that his father would demand to read every word she wrote before she sent it to her publisher.

"You think your parents are going to want censorship privileges, don't you?"

Leaning both forearms on the table, he met her gaze. "Yes."

"Haven't they ever heard of the First Amendment?"

"They answer to a law older than the Bill of Rights, Emma. That document was created for humans. You're not dealing with humans."

"I understand that, but if you think I'm going to be intimidated into giving up my right to free expression, you've misjudged me, Aidan."

He didn't think for a minute he'd misjudged her. He'd always known she was an independent, headstrong woman. Despite being alone in the midst of an alien population, she planned to stick up for herself and her Constitutional rights, even if no one around her gave a flip for those things. He didn't look forward to mediating the coming confrontation between Emma Gavin and his parents.

Chapter 24

Emma talked a good game, but maintaining a courageous front became increasingly difficult after the Learjet landed and an imposing black SUV picked them up for the trip to the Wallace estate.

She recognized Ralph, Aidan's driver, who greeted her with a reserved smile. He must have known she was now considered a bona fide security risk, to be handled with care. Roarke took the front passenger seat while Aidan and Emma took the back.

Once Emma's orange suitcase and laptop were stowed and they were on the highway headed north, she had the uneasy feeling this could be the road of no return. Aidan had promised her that wouldn't be the case, but she still suffered an attack of nerves.

Gathering research was the only antidote she could think of, so she tapped the window next to her. "Is this bulletproof?"

Aidan's eyebrows lifted. "Why? Are you worried about getting shot?"

"No. I've never been in a bulletproof car before, and

if any vehicle ever looked like it should be bulletproof, this thing does. So I'm asking. For research."

"Yes, it's bulletproof," Aidan said. "It's a precaution many wealthy people take, not because we expect to be shot, but to foil kidnappers."

"Oh." Emma thought about that for a while. "I pity the unsuspecting kidnapper who snatched one of you guys. Panic City."

"It's really more for the kids."

"Right. Because they can't shift." She leaned forward. "Ralph, are you trained in defensive driving?"

"Yes." Ralph glanced at her in the rearview mirror. "All the drivers are."

"Wow. I'd love to see you in action."

"When we get on the two-lane, I could show you some moves."

"Or not." Roarke sent the driver a quelling glance.

Ralph shrugged. "Or not."

Roarke turned in his seat and glanced back at Emma. "Here's a tip for when you meet the 'rents, Emma. You might want to put a lid on the curious questions."

"But—"

"Roarke has a point," Aidan said. "The goal is to calm their fears that you're going to run out and tell everything you know to the *Enquirer.*"

Along with her nerves, Emma's patience was being stretched. "That would be the act of a terminally stupid person. The humans would accuse me of either being crazy or on drugs, and the Weres would be howling for my blood. Why would I want to risk bringing all that down on myself?"

"That sounds like a logical argument," Roarke said, "but if you'd somehow collected evidence, you might convince somebody to listen, and the rodeo would begin. Which reminds me. Aidan, do you have her Black-Berry?"

Emma clutched her purse to her chest. "No, he doesn't, and he's not getting it." That cell phone was her emergency weapon, a way to contact the outside world and arrange for her escape if the Wallaces tried to keep her at the estate.

Roarke glanced at his brother. "She's gotta give it up."

"I know." Aidan sighed and turned to Emma. "I can't let you onto the estate with your phone in your purse. You have to understand that no human has ever been there before, and—"

"*Never?* Cool beans! I'm like a pioneer! I'm like the first astronaut to set foot on the moon!" She gazed at Aidan. "But you can't have my phone."

Roarke cleared his throat. "Bro, you have to take the phone away from her. That's the first thing Dad will ask about."

"Yeah. Ralph, pull over."

Emma gasped as Ralph hit the accelerator, cut across two lanes of traffic doing at least ninety, and swerved to a stop on the shoulder of the highway. *Defensive-driving demonstration: check.*

Aidan unsnapped his seat belt. "We're getting out, Emma."

"Out? Why?" She had a sudden vision of being frog-marched through the snow into a stand of leafless trees and shot through the head. But Aidan wouldn't do that. Surely not, and if he would, then she sincerely regretted giving him oral sex on the plane.

"We need to have a talk."

"Is that code for using physical force to get my phone? Because that's the only way you'll get it, wolf boy."

From the front seat, Roarke groaned. "Good luck, brother of mine."

"Thanks." Aidan glanced at Emma. "Are you coming?"

"What if I don't want to?"

His hand closed over her arm and his golden eyes grew intense. "Get out of the car, Emma." He paused, as if the next word cost him a great deal. "Please."

He was scaring her a little. "Okay, but only because you used the P-word." She unfastened her seat belt.

"I have a P-word for you, bro," Roarke muttered. "Puss—"

"Zip it, Roarke." Aidan kept his grip on Emma's arm as she scooted across the seat. Before she could step out, he put both hands around her waist and lifted her over a drift left by a snowplow. She dangled in the air for a moment before he set her down on a small spot of dry asphalt. "Stay there."

She had no inclination to move. Snow and ice surrounded her. Eighteen-wheelers roared past on the highway, and on her other side, the shoulder of the road sloped down to a gully of rocks and more snow. The trees beyond, where Aidan would have to take her if he intended to do away with her and leave her body, were a good twenty yards from where she stood.

Aidan stepped over the snowdrift. Then he scooped her up in his arms and carried her down the slope without slipping or even breathing very hard. Being carried a few feet into the bedroom was one thing, but this . . .

She'd underestimated his strength by quite a bit. Obviously if he wanted to kill her, he wouldn't need a gun. He could use his bare hands. Taking her phone wouldn't be any kind of challenge at all.

"See if you can stand here okay." He lowered her slowly to the rocks and snow of the gully.

She teetered a little bit, but found her balance. "Sure,

but I don't know what all this is about." Her breath fogged the air. "I realize now you could have taken my purse away while we were in the SUV. Why go through all this if all you want is the phone?"

"Because I want more than the phone."

She gazed up at him. "What's that supposed to mean?"

His golden eyes softened. "Emma, I—"

"You'd better not be getting frisky, because I have my limits. By the side of the road in the snow is not my idea of a good time."

"Oh, for God's sake! Do you think everything I do is motivated by sex?"

She opened her mouth to respond.

"Don't answer that." He scrubbed a hand over his face, but his other hand continued to grip her forearm, maybe to steady her, and maybe to keep her prisoner. "Look, I've made no secret of my sexual needs, but I am capable of other emotions besides lust when it comes to you."

"Like what?"

"Like empathy. I know you're nervous and scared about what's going to happen next. I also imagine that you're worried about being confined on the estate for some undisclosed amount of time."

"Let me keep my phone and I won't be so worried."

He blew out a breath. "I can't do that."

"Then you'll have to take it from me by force." She clutched her purse with both hands. "And I warn you, I'll put up a fight. I won't win, of course, but I'm not about to turn over my only means of communicating with the outside world without a struggle." She had a sudden insight. "You didn't want them to see you manhandle me. That's why we're down here."

"No, that's not why. Do you trust me at all?"

"Should I?"

"I'm the only one you can trust. I got you into this, and I've promised to get you back out. Do you understand what that promise is worth?"

"I don't know, Aidan. You're about to go up against your parents at the very least, and the entire werewolf community at the very most. You may be powerful, but—"

"I will handle it." His grip tightened on her arm. "I *will* keep you safe and get you out, no matter what the personal sacrifice might be."

"Yes, but—"

"Look at me, Emma."

She met his gaze.

"I need you to know this, to believe this." His golden eyes blazed with purpose. "Here's the bottom line. I will protect you with everything I have . . . including my life."

Her breath caught. All righty, then. She was going to be okay. And if she wasn't okay because something terrible happened to Aidan, she realized she wouldn't much care if something happened to her, as well.

Although her fingers were numb from the cold, she managed to open her purse and pull out her BlackBerry. Silently she handed it to him.

"Thank you." He took it and slipped it in his coat pocket. Without another word, he scooped her into his arms and carried her back to the SUV.

For the rest of the trip, Emma stayed fairly quiet, and Aidan kind of missed her barrage of research questions. Apparently their discussion in the gully had sobered her considerably. He was sorry if he'd scared her, but she had to start relying on him and stop being so damned independent, or she'd get them in worse trouble than they were in already. She didn't know the world they were about to enter. He did.

She perked up a little bit when they reached the rushing stream and Ralph activated the dam.

"You operate the dam by remote control?" She stared at the quickly diminishing flow. "What if the water freezes? Come to think of it, shouldn't the water be frozen now?"

"Very perceptive." Roarke sounded impressed by the question.

That was a good thing in Aidan's estimation. If Roarke came to respect Emma's brain, then he'd be less likely to side with those who wanted to end her publishing career, so Emma would have another ally besides him.

"So why isn't it frozen?" Emma asked.

"We heat the water in the wintertime," Aidan said. "Not much, and we use a solar system to cut back on the environmental impact, but we have to keep it from freezing and wrecking the whole program."

"That's amazing." Emma peered out as Ralph took the SUV through the damp streambed. "Can we park on the other side so I can watch it come back?"

"We always do, anyway," Aidan said. "We never drive off and assume it's working. This stream is one of the most important security features on the estate. We monitor it constantly. There's a camera upstream that gives us a picture of what's going on with the water."

Emma turned so she could look out the back window as the water came rushing back, giving it a flash-flood effect. "I suppose you have cameras all over the place," she said quietly.

"Yes." Aidan had installed an upgraded system two years ago after researching various options. The cameras were top-of-the-line, and one room in the mansion housed the screens that were monitored twenty-four-seven. A squirrel couldn't climb a tree without getting its progress recorded.

There would be no need to lock Emma in during her stay. She couldn't go anywhere on the estate without being observed. The concept had to be intimidating for her, but there was no help for it. He'd do his best to make her stay short and sweet.

That wouldn't be the end of it, of course. Somebody from the Were world would be keeping track of her for a long time, maybe even the rest of her life. She was, unfortunately, a woman who knew too much. But that somebody watching her wouldn't be him. He'd learned the hard way that he was not the werewolf for the job.

The road leading to the mansion was filled with ruts, although anyone who drove it often enough could avoid all the really bad spots. Roarke had become an expert at steering his Ferrari around them without throwing his precious car out of alignment. Ralph knew the road well, too, but still a certain amount of bumping was unavoidable.

One particular spot caused Aidan and Emma to jostle each other. Even that small contact sent a shiver of desire through him. When they had their discussion by the side of the road and he had to hold on to her to make sure she didn't bolt, he'd wanted to carry her off into the woods.

The closer they came to the mansion, the stronger the urge became. Life in the city tended to blunt his werewolf instincts, but he always felt a little wilder out here, a little more primitive. As the mansion came into view around a bend and through the trees, he smiled to himself. No one looking at the imposing stone facade would think of it as a wolf's den, but that's exactly what it was.

"Oh, my goodness," Emma said. "It's huge."

"It needs to be for pack gatherings," Aidan said. "You can't see them from here, but there are stone cottages scattered all over the estate. That's where the aunts, uncles, and cousins live. Some have places in the city and use the cottage for a vacation getaway. Others are here year-round."

Emma swallowed. "Am I—am I going to be brought in front of some kind of werewolf tribunal?"

"God, no." He realized that a person with her imagination could be coming up with a million scenarios. "We're keeping this low-key. The only Weres you'll be meeting at this point besides Ralph and my brother are my parents."

Roarke snorted. "The 'rents are scary enough."

"Hey." Aidan glared at his brother. "She's already nervous. You don't have to make it worse."

"Yeah, but she shouldn't be blindsided, either. FYI, Mom and Dad know that Nadia's bailed on the Henderson-Wallace unification plan."

Aidan tensed. "And?"

"Hard to tell how they feel about it. Dad didn't say much, although he's not happy with anybody named Henderson these days, so that could help your cause. Mom looked sort of sad. She's always been partial to Nadia."

"I know. Nadia's great. She . . ." Aidan gazed at Roarke as a brilliant idea began to form. "Listen, she really *is* great. You two would get along. That would solve—"

"That would solve nothing because it isn't going to happen."

"Don't reject it out of hand, Roarke." Aidan was proud of his idea. "Nadia is gorgeous, intelligent, talented. Sure, she's a couple of years older than you, but—"

"Back off, big brother. I have no interest in getting hooked up with anyone, let alone allow myself to be tied down to some arranged deal to unite the two packs. I always thought that was bogus."

"See?" Emma nudged Aidan with her elbow. "Even your own brother thinks it's a dumb idea."

"I do," Roarke said, "but Mom and Dad have always been very high on it. They and the Hendersons had the whole mirror image–name thing going on. Thank God nobody tried that with me. Besides, my mirror-image sweetie would have to be named Ekraor, which just doesn't work, does it?"

Aidan sighed. "One brilliant idea, shot to hell."

"One crappy idea, relegated to the round file where it belongs."

"Then again, Nadia probably wouldn't have you." Aidan grinned at his brother. "She's particular."

Roarke made a grab for him, and Aidan ducked.

Ralph cleared his throat. "Your parents are standing at the front door. You two might want to knock it off."

Aidan straightened and discovered that Ralph was correct. His mother and father, both wearing their warmest navy wool coats, stood outside the mansion's massive front door much like diplomats waiting to greet visiting dignitaries. Obviously, they'd been alerted by the security team that the SUV had arrived.

His father stood like the imposing alpha he was, his back straight and his expression stoic. His mother had linked her arm through her husband's as if needing some support for this meeting. She looked regal, as always, but even from this distance, Aidan detected anxiety in her expression.

Their presence at the door underscored the importance of this moment for them. He was bringing a human into their midst, and that had never been done before. He reminded himself that they were the ones who'd demanded that Emma be brought here.

"That's weird," Roarke said. "They don't usually do the welcome-committee routine."

"There's nothing usual about this visit." Aidan reached for Emma's hand, which was ice-cold. He squeezed it and hoped that gave her some reassurance. Then again, maybe he was the one looking for reassurance.

Until now, he'd been the golden boy, the Were everyone expected to take over leadership of the pack when his father stepped down. He'd been groomed for that position his entire life. He'd looked forward to assuming his duties.

Although he hadn't always pleased his parents, he'd never given them any major problems . . . until now. Bringing a human to the estate was an issue of great magnitude. No matter how many times he tried to convince himself that he hadn't caused this breach in security, he still felt responsible for it.

And yet, he knew that the real problem wasn't the security breach. The real problem was the bond developing between him and Emma. Even he wasn't certain how strong it had become. He was afraid to test it and find out.

Chapter 25

Research, Emma repeated as a silent mantra when Aidan helped her out of the SUV. The cobblestoned drive curved in front of the house, and as Emma walked along it toward the distinguished couple standing by the front door, she was reminded of a tour of Hollywood homes she'd taken while on a vacation in LA several years ago.

This elegant two-story mansion would be suitable for any major movie star in the country. Or any head of state in any foreign country. Jane Austen would have loved this house, but a Regency home would have been surrounded by formal gardens. Instead, the forest hovered all around the house, protecting it from prying eyes.

For this place wasn't owned by a head of state or a member of the English nobility. It was owned by a pack of werewolves, and no human had seen it since they'd moved in. Unless she broke the trust Aidan had placed in her, no other human would ever see it besides her.

Although she had to be careful not to behave like a reporter gathering information, she felt a certain responsibility to record every detail she could remember. She wouldn't ever present it as fact, but she could certainly disguise it as fiction. She would get to write about this house and the werewolves who lived here, because Aidan had promised that her publishing career would continue. She was choosing to believe he'd make good on that promise.

So she took in the butterscotch color of the stone, the steep pitch of the red slate roof dusted with snow, the twin chimneys rising high into the air, the multipaned windows catching stray beams from the setting sun, and the twin wrought iron balconies at each end of the house. She wondered whether she'd be given a bedroom with a balcony. The romantic in her had always yearned for one.

As she neared the front door, Fiona Wallace stepped forward and held out her hand. "Welcome to our home, Emma Gavin."

Emma clasped Fiona's hand and felt quiet strength there. Aidan's mother had yellow-gold eyes very similar to her son's, but Aidan had inherited his high cheekbones and square jaw from his father. After Emma shook hands with Fiona, Howard Wallace extended his hand to her.

His grip spoke of power that was all the more intimidating because he didn't flaunt it with a crushing handshake. Here was a man used to being in command, and she sensed that he didn't like losing control of a situation the way he'd obviously lost control of this one.

"Thank you for coming," he said simply. His gray eyes seemed to see right through her.

She doubted he missed much, so she'd be wise to be perfectly honest with him. "I don't know that I had a choice."

His laugh was deep and infectious, rumbling upward from his barrel chest. "True enough. But now that you're here, let's get you inside and find some wine and a warm fire, shall we?"

Emma could see why Aidan's father was such a successful businessman. He operated on the assumption that everyone agreed with his plan, whatever that might be. In this case, Emma found herself ushered inside and guided along a marble hallway.

Someone took her coat, and then seamlessly, she found herself in a cozy sitting room where a cheerful blaze crackled in a large stone fireplace. She chose what turned out to be an infinitely comfortable easy chair, sat down, and took stock of her surroundings. Fine art, predominantly landscapes, adorned the walls. The furniture looked very Ethan Allen, but Emma suspected it was far older than that.

She couldn't have scripted a gracious welcome any better if she'd written it herself. Someone, perhaps a butler of sorts, appeared at her elbow and asked whether she preferred red or white. She chose red, and shortly thereafter was sipping an exceptional wine as yet another person—female werewolf, probably—served some kind of wonderful pâté on thin slices of rustic bread.

Searching for Aidan, she found him leaning against the mantel, wineglass in hand, as he talked with his father and Roarke. Emma had been spared the burden of making any conversation for the time being, and she was grateful to be allowed to get her bearings. But such a period of calm couldn't last.

Fiona took a seat in the chair next to Emma's, settled back with a sigh, and took a hefty swallow of her white wine. "How was your trip from Chicago?"

A memory of the oral sex with Aidan flashed into

Emma's mind, and she quickly squelched it. "Fascinating," she said. "I've never flown in a private jet before."

"Aidan hates flying. When he was a little boy I used to sing nursery rhymes to him during the entire flight so he wouldn't freak out."

Emma decided sharing her method for soothing a jumpy Aidan wouldn't be a great idea. She angled herself so she could look squarely at Fiona, mother of Aidan, wife of Howard, matriarch of the Wallace pack.

If Emma left out the last part of that description, she'd have no problem picturing the nursery-rhyme singing going on. But trying to imagine a werewolf mother singing "Ring Around the Rosie" blew her circuits.

"You look dubious," Fiona said.

Being a vocabulary junkie, Emma appreciated the use of the word *dubious*. She might get along with Fiona, except she'd never get the chance. "I'll admit I'm in over my head. I thought werewolves—you, basically—were imaginary."

"I'm sorry you discovered otherwise, Emma. It complicates things."

The wine on a somewhat empty stomach had apparently affected Emma's good judgment, because she leaned toward Fiona and asked, quite clearly, "Will I be killed?"

Fiona recoiled in obvious horror. "Good heavens, no. Did someone say that?"

"Yes, as a matter of fact. Aidan told me some pack members were suggesting that was the best way to handle the problem."

Fiona *tsk-tsk*ed and shook her head. "It's certainly not. You're a well-known author. There would be all kinds of media interest and police investigations if you turned up dead."

Emma blinked. So it was fear of reprisal that kept her from ending up in a shallow grave on the Wallace estate. She supposed that was some comfort.

"Emma, I have to know . . ." Fiona lowered her voice. "I have to know exactly how you feel about my son."

Emma decided to hedge on that one. "What do you mean?" She still might not be out of the woods, so to speak.

If she admitted to having a major crush on Aidan, she might be wiped out on the grounds of sheer audacity. She'd figured out from the fact that no humans had set foot in this house that humans shouldn't be jonesing on werewolves. It just wasn't done.

"I've seen the way he looks at you," Fiona said. "And I've seen the way you look at him. Unless my instincts are off, which is always possible now that I'm going through menopause, you two have forged a bond."

"Not exactly." Better to diffuse this potential bomb. "Aidan needs to find a werewolf mate, and I would never want to interfere with that in any way."

"Bullshit."

"Excuse me?"

"Emma Gavin, you're crazy in love with my son, and if you could figure out a way to be with him permanently, you'd grab it. Am I right?"

"Oh, God." Emma drained her wineglass.

"Am I right?"

Emma turned her head to discover Fiona watching her the way a hawk watches a rabbit. "Yes, you're right. But I'm not an idiot. I realize Aidan is the crown prince of the Wallace pack. Hooking up with me gets him absolutely nowhere. In fact, it causes him an untold amount of problems. So all I want is to disappear from his life so he can get on with finding the perfect she-wolf, or whatever it is you call his mate."

Fiona nodded. "That would indeed be wonderful and a great solution to the sticky situation we're in, except for one thing."

"Which is?"

"My son is crazy in love with you."

Everything in Emma rebelled at that idea. She shook her head violently. "No, no, he's not. That would be a disaster." *I will protect you with my life.* But that was duty, not love. Wasn't it?

"I completely agree it's a disaster," Fiona said. "You're miles away from the daughter-in-law I had in mind. Nadia is the daughter-in-law of my dreams."

Emma didn't like that any better than the concept of Aidan being crazy in love with her. "He doesn't love Nadia, at least not in the way a man should love a woman he plans to marry and spend his life with. I'd go so far as to say he never will love Nadia that way. To think of him marrying Nadia would be a tragedy."

"Hm." Fiona sipped her wine. "So what's he supposed to do, be a lone wolf with nobody to keep him warm at night?"

"Of course not. There are plenty of fish in the sea. Or werewolves in the woods. I'm sure there's a perfect mate out there waiting for him, once he no longer has the responsibility of Nadia hanging like an albatross around his neck."

"Hm," Fiona said again. She finished her wine and signaled to someone on the other side of the room. "I don't think you understand the werewolf way, my dear."

"No, but I'd like to. Roarke warned me not to ask

too many questions, but I'm a writer. I'm all about the questions." She accepted another glass of wine from the butler-type person who arrived with red for her and white for Fiona.

"Then let me tell you how a werewolf chooses a mate." Fiona took another hefty swallow of her wine.

"Fiona, are we going to have dinner soon? Because I haven't had a lot to eat today and this wine is potent stuff."

"We'll have dinner in about fifteen minutes. Drink up."

"Okay." Emma took another sip. She didn't want to waste wine that tasted so good that she wouldn't be surprised if it was several hundred dollars a bottle.

Fiona raised a finger. "Werewolf-Mate Selection 101."

"I'm listening." Emma chalked this up as the absolute weirdest evening she'd ever had in her life. But it made for great research.

"The first thing is the smell."

"Oh." Emma couldn't ignore all the references Aidan had made to her scent.

"Howard chose me on scent alone. He also liked the way I looked, fortunately, because that has a bearing on how the children will turn out, but my scent is what closed the deal."

That got her attention. "You and Howard didn't marry for political expediency?"

"No, we married for lust and love and pheromones. Why do you ask?"

"Because you expected Aidan to make a practical, politically beneficial marriage! How could you?"

Fiona drank more wine. "Logically, the chemistry should have been there. We had both their birth charts done. We brought them together several times as children so they'd have a shared history. They're both beautiful. It should have worked."

"It did, in a way. They're fast friends."

"I still wonder, though, if you hadn't come along . . ."

Emma shook her head. "You can pin lots of things on me, but I'm the savior in that situation. Those two would have had a boring, miserable life together, fulfilling what they saw as their duty to both packs. You would have made your son into a martyr, and I can already tell you're not the kind of mother who would want that."

"No, I'm not. I'm the kind of mother who wants the best for her son." She gazed at Emma over the top of her wineglass. "And whether I like it or not, he seems to have chosen you."

"No, he hasn't."

"Yes, he has, Emma. That's what I've been trying to tell you. First there's the attraction of scent, and then there's the sexual exploration phase. Last of all there's the binding."

"The binding?"

"Yes. If you have to ask what that is, it hasn't happened between you two yet. But I predict it won't be long, judging from Aidan's behavior. He shows all the signs of a werewolf seeking a binding experience."

The wine had definitely taken its toll and loosened Emma's tongue. "The thing is, Aidan's promised me I won't end up having to stay here." She realized belatedly that sounded ungracious. "Not that it isn't lovely, but I have a whole other life."

Fiona laid a hand on her arm. "Emma, much as it pains me to say this, I predict your life is about to be joined with Aidan's."

Emma opened her mouth to protest that unsettling prediction, but dinner was announced. Aidan came to take her in, and after two glasses of wine, she was glad for a strong arm to lean on. She had much to think about. If Aidan truly loved her and wanted her to stay, would she? Would she have to give up everything else— her career, her mother, her friends? Fiona almost made it sound as if she wouldn't have a choice in the matter, but she wasn't about to abandon her independence, not even for Aidan.

"I caught a little of the conversation you were having with my mother, but not all of it," he said as they walked into the dining room with an immensely long table. Fortunately, the places had been grouped at one end so they wouldn't have to shout at one another during the meal.

"All things considered, she's been very gracious." Emma glanced up at him. "Although she's not happy about it, she claims you show all the signs of a werewolf seeking a binding, whatever that is."

His eyes widened.

"Of course, I have no idea what she's talking about."

"I do." Aidan helped her into a chair at the table. "And she's wrong."

"That's what I thought." Of course he wouldn't consider marriage to a non-Were. That simplified things, and no, she wasn't disappointed to discover she was right and Fiona was wrong. Well, maybe a little, but this was for the best. Deciding to live for the moment, she proceeded to enjoy one of the most delicious meals she'd ever had the pleasure of eating.

A binding. As always, his mother could read his moods better than anyone. He'd been fantasizing about that very thing ever since that first night of sex with Emma, but he was determined to reject the concept.

Fiona had some good reasons for being unhappy with

the idea, and he would honor those reasons. No human had ever been bound to a member of the Wallace pack, and Aidan wasn't about to be the groundbreaker with that concept. He wasn't about to put his parents through the drama of it.

As the meal progressed, Emma seemed to be having a great time, but one family dinner didn't a lifetime make. She would always be an outsider here, and she'd never accept the kinds of restrictions on her lifestyle that a binding would dictate.

As his mate, she'd be privy to all the secrets of the pack, and pack members wouldn't be at all happy with that. They'd demand that she be sequestered here on the estate, and his parents would probably demand it, as well. Emma already knew more than was good for her. Binding her to him would be a supreme act of selfishness on his part.

Wine flowed during dinner as it had before. His parents were excellent hosts, and Aidan remembered many a dinner party where the entire table had been filled . . . with Weres. After dinner the tradition was for pack members to shift and take a run through the woods.

As the plates were cleared after dessert and the after-dinner liqueurs were being savored, Aidan's mother rose and came around to his chair. "I'm sure Emma must be tired."

Aidan glanced over at Emma. "Are you tired?"

"Not particularly."

"Even so." Fiona's voice was gently insistent. "I think it's time Aidan showed you to your room." The message was clear. It was time for the outsider to make herself scarce.

Aidan braced himself for an argument from Emma. To his surprise, she smilingly agreed and pushed back her chair with a convincing and ladylike yawn. The tension eased from his shoulders. If she'd take all her cues that willingly, convincing his parents to grant her freedom might not be so difficult.

Aidan tucked his linen napkin beside his plate and stood.

"I had Angelina put Emma's things in the blue room," his mother said.

"All right." The blue room was at the opposite end of the house from his room, and his mother had surely done that on purpose.

"What a fabulous meal," Emma said as he walked with her toward the winding stone staircase leading up to the second floor. "I wasn't quite sure what to expect."

"Did you think we'd throw some bloody bones on the floor and start gnawing on them?"

"No, of course not." She glanced at him as they mounted the wide staircase side by side. "Well, maybe. You're free to do whatever you want here, after all."

"And what we want is a civilized meal, complete with the good silver and excellent wine. We gave up raw meat two hundred years ago."

"I didn't mean to be insulting."

"No insult taken." But he was in a mood, and he knew it. He was facing sexual deprivation, and he'd discovered that he didn't like the idea one damned bit.

"Aidan, I know this must be awkward for you. Just so you know, I plan to keep well away from you for however many days I'm here."

They reached the top of the stairs and he turned to her. "That won't be hard to do. The bedroom my mother chose for you is at the end of the hall going that way." He pointed to his left. "And mine is at the end of the hall going that way." He pointed to his right.

"And there are hidden cameras in the chandeliers."

"Uh-huh. Placed there by yours truly. Unless I want to be caught on camera, I won't be paying you a visit tonight."

"That's for the best."

"Easy for you to say. Come on. I'll show you to your room." He started down the carpeted hallway lined with antique sconces and old photographs.

"Oh, wait!" She paused in front of a sepia-toned picture. "This looks like a bunch of prospectors!"

"My prospecting ancestors. The Alaska Gold Rush made them rich."

"These prospectors are werewolves?"

"A little-known fact of history. Or make that a carefully guarded secret of history. Werewolves make excellent prospectors and miners. They can smell the gold, and they have the endurance to live under primitive conditions."

"So who's this guy?" She pointed to a formal picture of a man in a gray morning coat and pin-striped trousers.

"That's Irving Gentry. He moved his pack from Alaska down to the Portland area around the turn of the twentieth century. Made a mint in shipping. His descendants are involved in several Pacific Rim business ventures."

"Do the Gentrys own a chunk of Portland, then?"

"I think that's fair to say. They're pretty influential there, and I think a branch of the pack is now in Seattle, too."

"What other cities are dominated by Weres?"

He hesitated. "I wonder how much of this I should be telling you."

"You brought up trust earlier today. It goes both

ways, Aidan. You have to trust me, too. After monitoring my life for three months, you must have some idea of my trustworthiness."

"You're right. I know you're trustworthy. I just have some other people to convince."

"I know."

"Anyway, to answer your question, San Francisco and Denver. The Stillmans have holdings all over Colorado, in fact. I've heard rumors of a Stillman split because one faction wants to expand to Salt Lake City and another one likes the Jackson Hole area of Wyoming. Weres go where there are deep woods and plenty of economic opportunity."

Emma nodded. "Makes sense." Then her eyes widened. "Oh, my God. Are there werewolves in Congress?"

That made him laugh. "No. We contribute to campaigns, but we stay completely out of politics."

"Why?"

"Think about it. The media follows politicians everywhere. We don't need that kind of attention."

"No, I suppose not." She wandered to the next picture. "Who's—"

"Emma, I don't mean to hustle you along, but unless I'm back downstairs soon, I'll be asked what took me so long. Then I'm screwed no matter what I say. If I tell them the truth, they'll worry that I've given you too much information about our history. If I'm evasive, they'll think we were up here making out."

"Then let's get going." She turned immediately and started down the hall. "Is it the room on the left or the room on the right?"

"On the left."

"Oh! Does that mean I have a balcony?"

She sounded so eager about it that his foul mood lifted a little. "Yes, Juliet, you have a balcony." And that gave him an idea that lifted his mood a little more.

Cameras were trained on the house, of course, and on each balcony, as well, but the lens didn't pick up every single inch of the railing. And he knew where the blind spots were.

Chapter 26

Aidan left without kissing her, which Emma thought was very wise. He didn't need to go back downstairs with extra hair curling out the front of his shirt. These people—or rather, these werewolves—were his family. They knew better than anyone that he had a genetic predisposition to shift when aroused.

Poor werewolf. Guys had it tough anyway, having to worry about whether a telltale bulge in their jeans would announce their intentions. In addition to that, Aidan had to worry about growing hair and fangs.

Closing the door to the room that had been assigned to her, Emma took a look around. Now *this* was what she called a bedroom. A large and ornate four-poster with a canopy was to be expected in a mansion, she supposed. The deep blue velvet hangings tied back with gold cords that could be released to create a cocoon of luxury must be standard mansion decor.

But the bed was only the beginning. It took up about a third of the space, which left room for a cozy seating area in front of a blazing fire. Bookshelves on either side of the fireplace contained both leather-bound classics and current bestsellers in hardback. Many of her favorites were there, along with some she'd been meaning to read.

The blaze in the marble fireplace was real, and a small supply of wood in a copper tub on the hearth invited her to enjoy the fire through the night. Two wingback chairs upholstered in a blue-and-white print flanked a small walnut coffee table. The table held a tray containing an insulated carafe filled with—if her nose didn't deceive her—fresh coffee. A small pitcher of cream sat next to the carafe, along with a plate of six chocolate truffles on a white paper doily. Emma bit into one and discovered it was her favorite flavor, espresso. Aidan had indeed been paying attention during those three months of surveillance.

Taking another small bite of the truffle, she wandered over to the door leading into the bathroom and sighed with pleasure. A claw-foot tub was another item on her wish list, and this one looked deep enough for her to sink up to her chin in bubbles. A dark wood and marble vanity surrounded a sink hand-painted with forget-me-nots.

All the amenities she could ever want were clustered in a basket on the vanity, including bubble bath. A thick white robe hung on a hook next to the tub. If she couldn't have Aidan tonight, she could relax in a warm bath and sit in front of the fire with a book, a cup of hot coffee, and the rest of the truffles.

She might as well unpack and get comfy. Back in the room, she opened a closet and found her orange suitcase and her laptop case on a shelf. Her clothes had been neatly hung in a row, with the exception of what she'd already worn. No doubt, those items were in the mansion's laundry being washed and pressed.

Because her makeup bag was nowhere in sight, she returned to the bathroom and opened a drawer in the vanity. Sure enough, there it was, along with a hair dryer. She'd bet the mansion had its own generator and water supply so that the place could be totally self-sufficient.

She was literally out in the middle of nowhere. No one—not her mother, her girlfriends, or her publisher—knew where she was or would even be worried about her. They thought she'd been spirited away to a tropical island by one of NYC's most eligible bachelors.

Her isolation wasn't causing her to freak out exactly, but she was impressed by how thoroughly the Wallaces were able to close themselves off from the rest of the world, except . . . *for the Internet.*

Racing back to the closet, she flung open the door and grabbed her laptop case where it sat on the shelf next to her suitcase. It felt too light. Heart pounding, she unzipped it, knowing that she'd find it empty. They'd taken her laptop.

She checked the pocket where she kept her backup flash drive, and that was gone, too.

Not cool. They'd stolen her book ideas. They'd swiped her research notes and e-mails, which she needed to answer, and . . . damn it! Taking her laptop and flash drive was like ripping out her heart, and she wasn't putting up with that for even one second, let alone a whole night.

She'd been a good sport up until now, but they were going to give her back that laptop, and they were going to do it tout de suite or heads would roll. She didn't care whether Aidan's mother had implied that Emma should go to her room like a good little girl and stay there until

morning. She wasn't going to rest until she had her laptop back.

As she walked into the hallway, she listened for the
sound of voices and heard nothing. But the house was huge,
so not hearing voices didn't mean the place was empty.
She'd start with Aidan's bedroom.

Marching to the end of the hall, she took her best
guess and opened the door to her right, which would be
the other balcony room. The minute she stepped inside,
she knew it belonged to Aidan. She was no werewolf
when it came to scent, but she'd grown fond of his, and
she picked it up immediately.

A light was on beside the large bed, a four-poster and
canopy similar to hers. The room was appointed much
like hers, too, although manly greens and browns predominated. Aidan had a balcony, too, and a fireplace
with two wingbacks and a coffee table arranged in front
of it. Logs were laid for a fire, but it wasn't lit, and the
room felt vacant.

Even so, she called his name. No one answered. Then
she noticed something she'd missed in her first scan of
her surroundings. The white dress shirt and dark slacks
he'd had on when he'd left her in her room were draped
across the end of the bed.

But there was no light on in the bathroom and no
sound of splashing water. Then, from somewhere outside, she heard a wolf howl. She ran to the French doors
leading to the balcony and found them unlocked. With
the best security system money could buy, the Wallaces
didn't need locks.

She opened the doors and stepped out, gasping as a
cold wind sliced through her. Below her on the cobblestoned driveway, three wolves paced restlessly by the

front door. She forgot the cold as she stood watching them, totally mesmerized.

Only a short while ago, she'd sat at an elegantly appointed table and held a conversation about world events with these three. And now . . . they were wolves. Despite never seeing any of them in this form, Emma instantly identified each one.

Howard had to be the large white wolf, who kept watching the front door, while Fiona, smaller and sporting a gleaming black coat, stayed close by. Roarke's blond fur made him look ghostly white in the lamp's glow as he romped around in playful abandon, as if enjoying the fresh night air. The white wolf howled again, impatiently.

Then Aidan joined them, his dark brown coat tipped with silver, looking as magnificent as she remembered. He hadn't come through the front door, so she had to assume there was another way in and out. *Instead of a doggy door, they must have a wolfy door.*

One of these wolves knew where her laptop was, but she couldn't exactly call out and ask them. Making her presence known at all might cause all sorts of bad things to happen, including imminent death, which she would very much like to avoid. Aidan wouldn't kill her, but she wasn't so sure about the other three.

As if some signal had passed through the group, they loped off into the dark woods, with the white wolf in the lead. Aidan was easily as big as his father, and Emma found some comfort in that. Howard had seniority, though, and in a wolf pack, that counted for quite a bit. She'd researched it.

When they were out of sight, she retreated into Aidan's bedroom and closed the French doors. Man, it was cold out there. How could they stand it? But she supposed as wolves they had those gorgeous fur coats.

If they'd gone for a run in the woods, that gave her a chance to search for her laptop. Moving quickly, she left Aidan's bedroom and headed for the stairs. During dinner she'd learned the mansion had ten bedrooms in addition to the obligatory billiard room, library, and conservatory, which she had to assume contained a bunch of exotic plants. She felt like Miss Scarlet in a game of Clue.

But if she were the person who'd confiscated her laptop, she wouldn't leave it under a potted orchid or shoved between books on a library shelf. She'd put it in Howard Wallace's office, so she decided to look for that room first. It didn't take her long to find it on the ground floor.

The room smelled of leather, imported cigars, and brandy. But if it contained her laptop, she wasn't going to get it without a hacksaw or a blowtorch. Howard's heavy wooden desk was locked, as was the wall safe she found behind a painting that looked like a Van Gogh original.

Finally she realized that she was on a needle-in-a-haystack mission and her best strategy would involve returning to Aidan's room and waiting for him to come back from his family-togetherness run. She climbed the stairs and made a quick trip to her room for a book to read before walking back down the hall.

Without a fire going, his room was decidedly colder than hers, so she slipped off her shoes and climbed onto his bed. Propping several pillows behind her back, she pulled the fluffy comforter over her knees. He might not be happy to find her here in his bed. Then again, he might be delighted.

If he turned out to be happy to see her, she'd need to remind him that the security cameras had surely recorded her every move. She didn't much care whether they had and whether everyone knew she'd prowled through the mansion after they were gone. She wanted her laptop, and she would get it before the night was over, by God. If Aidan wanted sex, he could jolly well produce her laptop first.

Aidan stood in the moonlit clearing, hackles raised, as he faced all three family members. His father's low growl had intimidated him in the past, but he wouldn't let it intimidate him now.

They'd run for nearly an hour, stretching their legs, glorying in their strong animal bodies. But Aidan had known the run would end here, at the clearing where every important decision had been made since he could remember. He'd known that this would be where his resolve to protect Emma would be tested.

I don't give a damn what you promised her. His father's words came through loud and clear in the telepathic manner of Weres. *She's a danger to the pack, and our duty is clear. We must keep her on the estate.*

For how long?

I'll decide that.

Aidan's answering growl was as strong as his father's. *You'd imprison her?*

She'll be given the best of care.

Then you might as well kill her now because you will have taken away everything that she values—her bond with her mother, her writing career, her independence. She won't give a damn about the luxurious surroundings if she doesn't have those things. Are you prepared to take her life? Aidan knew he wouldn't let that happen, but he had to throw out the challenge to make a point.

Howard glared at his son. *I won't have her blood on my hands, and you know it.*

Then you'll have mine. I'll leave with her, and if you want to stop us, you'll have to kill me.

Fiona stepped forward. *Will you two cut it out? There's no need for the histrionics. We—*

Howard snarled a warning. *This pup is challenging me. I won't have it!* He lunged forward and closed his powerful jaws over Aidan's neck.

Aidan threw him off but felt the skin tear. He circled his father, looking for an opening, ready to do what he had to for Emma.

Stop it! Fiona threw herself between them, snapping and growling until both wolves backed away.

Fiona stood between them, panting. *I won't have this!*

A rumbling growl rose from deep in Howard's throat as he glared at Aidan. *Your mother has always coddled you boys. I've never approved.*

Then tell her to step aside, and we'll settle this.

Howard turned to his mate. *You heard your son. This is between Aidan and me.*

Roarke circled the group until he was shoulder to shoulder with Aidan. *And me. I stand with my brother. He's made a promise. Let him keep it. Emma won't betray us.*

Aidan's heart swelled with gratitude. Although he didn't look at his brother, he hoped Roarke knew how much the support meant to him.

His father snarled defiantly. *And if she does betray us?*

Aidan met his father's steely gaze. *You will turn me over to the pack, and they will seek their revenge according to pack law.*

You would lay down your life for this human female?

Yes.

Fiona moved forward again. *Then bind her, Aidan.*

Howard whirled toward her. *No! Aidan's the eldest son. He can't mate with a human!*

Fiona stood calmly facing her life's partner. *I don't like it any more than you, but it's obvious he's made his choice. And if she's going to hold our fate in her hands, she needs to be one of us.*

But their offspring might not be Were!

We have to take that chance. Fiona turned her attention back to Aidan. *Bind her.*

No. She wouldn't want that.

His mother gazed up at the night sky. *Males are all alike. They think they know everything.* She looked at him. *Ask her.*

And if she says no?

His mother's gaze softened. *She won't.*

But if she does?

His father snorted. *Then I'll be saved the humiliation of having my eldest son muted to a human.* His gaze swung to Roarke. *I'm counting on you to give me Were grandchildren now that Aidan's lost his mind.*

Not anytime soon, I hope. Roarke broke ranks and wandered off to sniff something in the bushes. *I'm extremely busy sowing my wild oats.*

Don't be sowing them in the wrong field. Howard glanced around the clearing. *Are we done here? I'm ready for a warm fire and a warm bed.*

Aidan faced his father one more time. *Just so we're clear. Whether I bind Emma or not, she'll be free to see her mother, continue with her writing career, and—*

Yes, yes. But I'll want to approve all her manuscripts.

I can begin on that first thing. Her laptop and flash drive have been confiscated.

Aidan's blood ran cold. *Confiscated?*

Roarke brought me her laptop and her flash drive from her room.

Aidan turned to where his brother browsed through the weeds. *Roarke?*

They're in the safe in Dad's office. I figured we needed to know what she—

Shit. Aidan took off at a run. Maybe she'd been too tired to check her computer case. Maybe she'd enjoyed a bubble bath and some coffee and chocolates before climbing into her big bed.

That was wishful thinking. If he had to guess, he'd say that she was, at this very moment, ransacking every room in search of the most important piece of equipment in her creative life. No telling what sort of panic she'd go into because she'd been separated from that laptop.

Roarke and his father had no clue what they'd done, but Aidan had studied Emma's habits for three solid months. She wouldn't take the theft of her laptop lying down.

Chapter 27

Emma did her level best to stay awake. She was furious about her laptop being snatched, and she struggled to hang on to her fury, but she'd had a long day. A long weekend, for that matter. The craziness was catching up with her.

Several times the book slipped from her grasp, but she snatched it upright again and rubbed her eyes. She'd grabbed a book at random and should have chosen more carefully. Something involving murder and mayhem would have been good.

Once Aidan showed up, her anger would reappear. She was sure of that. But he wasn't here. Instead he was off racing through snowy woods with his immediate family. His laptop-stealing family.

In their absence, the house was very, very quiet. And Aidan's bed was very, very cozy. A girl couldn't be blamed for snuggling down on pillows that were probably covered in thousand-thread-count cases. Or whatever the top thread count was these days. She'd have to research that, because if she intended to make her next batch of werewolves rich—no, *wealthy*—she'd have to know her glitz and glamour.

First, though, she had to get her hands on her laptop, and then she might chain it to her wrist. *Aidan should be back soon.* Or maybe werewolves stayed out all night and slept all day. There was so much to learn . . .

Despite her best efforts, her eyelids closed. But just as she started to drift off, she heard a noise. Forcing her eyes open again, she saw Aidan standing in the bedroom doorway. Only it was Aidan the wolf, not Aidan the man. She blinked, just to make sure. *Yep, Aidan the wolf.*

Even though she knew he was behind those golden eyes, her heartbeat kicked into high gear as she slowly sat up to gaze at him. He was a very big wolf, and she was a very small human. She wasn't afraid, exactly.

But she had a complaint, and even if he was a wolf right now, he would be able to understand her. "They took my laptop," she said. "You have to get it back, Aidan."

He blinked once, turned around and left the room.

Emma rubbed her hands over her face. "Dear God, I feel as if I've just given Lassie instructions to fetch a rope from the barn so we can pull little Timmy out of the well."

Would Aidan return with her laptop in his teeth? She hoped not. That wouldn't be good for his teeth or her laptop. No, of course he wouldn't do it that way.

He was too logical, and logically, he'd have to shift back into human form to retrieve her laptop. That would leave him wandering through the mansion naked because the clothes he'd worn today lay over the end of the bed. If she'd been thinking, she would have tossed those at him before he left. But how a person was supposed to anticipate these situations and be prepared for them was a mystery to her. Maybe given enough time, she'd get used to the wolf-to-man-to-wolf thing, but she wasn't there yet.

The room seemed colder than it had before, and she was antsy waiting for Aidan. She decided to light the fire. After climbing out of bed, she used a small butane torch she found in the copper tub. The wood caught right away, which was lucky because she was a city girl who knew diddly-squat about making fires.

She'd like to learn, though. There was something satisfying about watching the flames lick the wood and something sensual about the heat. She also loved the sweet smell of the smoke. Except the smoke was becoming a little overpowering and made her eyes water.

"Good God! Are you trying to burn the place down?" Aidan rushed into the room holding her laptop and waving the smoke away with his free hand. "Did you open the flue?"

"What's a flue?" Even through the smoke, she could see that he'd found a pair of brown sweats to put on, probably swiped from Roarke's room.

He tossed the laptop on the bed and crouched in front of the fireplace. Then he stuck his hand into the flames. "Ouch! Shit, that's hot!"

"Aidan! You'll burn yourself up!" Coughing from all the smoke in the air, she tried to pull him away from the fireplace.

"Got it." He withdrew his hand. "Open the French doors, and air it out in here. I'm going to the kitchen for some mustard for my fingers. They're a little toasty."

"Your neck! You're bleeding!"

"Am I?" He swiped his unburned hand over his throat

and it came away smeared with blood. "I'll pick up some antiseptic ointment on my way back." He pinned her with a look. "Stay here. Don't leave this room."

"Okay." The wound on his neck scared the bejesus out of her. The last time he'd had a wound like that had been on his leg after he'd tangled with Theo. Just now he'd been out in the woods with his family.

She shivered. Had one of his own family members attacked him? And had she been the reason?

After opening the French doors and trying to wave the smoke out, she abandoned the effort. *Might as well just leave the doors open and let the night air suck out the smoke.* Hugging herself to ward off the cold, she began to pace. Despite that jovial evening meal she'd shared with the Wallaces, she had to believe they were sharply divided about how to handle her.

Aidan had pledged to protect her freedom. Had his demands on her behalf prompted an attack? Her tummy ached as she tried to imagine what had taken place in the woods. Had Aidan retaliated? How much blood had been spilled in her name?

"We can close the French doors, now." Aidan returned with gauze wrapped around the first two fingers of his right hand and a damp cloth pressed to his neck.

"You bet." She rushed to do it. "I'm so sorry. I was trying to warm up the room."

"I know." He nudged the hall door closed with his foot. "You have to open the flue in order for the smoke to—"

"Of course!" She slapped her forehead. "Duh. I've read the Harry Potter books. They talked about flues all the time. But I've lived in apartments all my life, and none of them had fireplaces." She walked toward him, her tummy still doing a very unpleasant dance. "Let me see your neck."

"It's nothing."

"Don't go all Bruce Willis on me. Let me look."

With a sigh of resignation, he took the cloth away.

The blood had stopped oozing from the jagged tear on his neck. The wound didn't look deep, thank God. "What happened?"

"Never mind." He walked into the bathroom and dropped the cloth in the sink before returning to the bedroom. "It's over."

Her gaze flew to his. "What do you mean by *over*? Is anyone else hurt or—"

"No." He cupped her face in his bandaged hand and wrapped his arm around her waist. "Relax, Emma. Everyone's fine."

"You swear?" She could smell the mustard he'd put on his fingers before wrapping them in gauze. "Nobody else is even bleeding?"

"Just me, and this is only a scratch."

"Who attacked you?"

He hesitated.

"Please tell me."

"My dad. I don't think he meant to break the skin, but his reflexes aren't as good as they were when he was thirty-five." Aidan brushed his thumb across her cheek. "Have you checked your laptop? Is it okay?"

Her throat felt tight and angry tears threatened to fall. "Who cares? You were out in the woods fighting with your father because of me. What if he'd misjudged and severed an artery?"

"But he didn't."

"Not this time, but I can see this pledging-with-your-life crap is real, and I don't want you doing it anymore! Don't you dare risk your life for me ever again, Aidan Wallace. Promise me you won't."

He smiled gently. "Sorry, but I can't promise that."

"Sure you can. People retract promises all the time."

"A werewolf doesn't."

"Okay, but you made the promise to me, and I release you from it. I'll sign a document, swear in front of witnesses, whatever it takes."

"You don't have that power, Emma. You could sign a hundred documents in front of a thousand witnesses, and my life would still be yours."

"Oh, Aidan." She was going to start leaking tears any second, and she didn't want that. "You may be the bravest person—*werewolf*—in the world, but I'm a rotten coward, and I don't want anything bad to happen to you, ever."

"I don't expect anything bad to happen to me. For one thing, I trust you not to betray the pack, no matter where you go or what you do. And you're free to go, Emma. Ralph can take you back to your loft tomorrow if you want."

That should have made her ecstatically happy, but leaving him sounded like a horrible idea. Besides, something about that plan didn't sound right. "They'll just let me go? What sort of guarantee do they have that I won't blow the whistle on all of you?" She was afraid she knew the answer.

"Me. I'm the guarantee."

She closed her eyes. "So if I slip somehow, they'll come after you." *They'll kill you.* She couldn't make herself say that part.

"You won't slip, Emma. I have great faith in you."

She opened her eyes to gaze into his beloved face.

"Look, I know you'll end up with a Were wife someday soon, and I'm cool with that, but—"

"Are you?"

"No, but it seems like the right thing to say. You obviously want me out of here ASAP, so I thought it would be classy to wish you a happy life. But the thing is, I don't want to lose touch, because communicating with you will help me remember not to screw up accidentally. You're like my lucky charm."

"Your lucky charm." He didn't seem all that pleased with that.

"All right. You mean a lot more to me than a four-leaf clover embedded in a plastic key ring, but since we'll be going our separate ways, I think we should—"

"Do you want to go your separate way, Emma?"

She looked into his eyes, searching for the wolf and finding the warm gaze of a man, instead. "Do I have a choice?"

Slowly he nodded.

Her breath caught. "But I'm human. And your mother hates me."

"No, she doesn't. She's the one who advised me to bind you. And the sooner, the better."

That jacked up her heart rate. "You'll have to define this binding thing." Tension coiled within her, and she tried to ease it with a joke. "If it's whips and chains, then I'm not interested." She didn't think that for a minute.

He touched his thumb to her lower lip and stroked softly back and forth. "We came close to it that first night in the hotel. I made sure we never came that close again."

She gulped.

"If we make love that way tonight, you'll be bound to me forever, and I to you. It's the strongest bond possible, stronger than anything forged in a church or a law office, stronger even than blood. In our world, there's no such thing as divorce. A wolf mates for life."

She began to tremble, but clutching his muscled shoulders did a lot to steady her. And arouse her. "Does a wolf mate for love?"

"Apparently this one does."

She sighed. *Right answer.*

"I've fought it with every breath in my body, Emma, but I can't fight it anymore. I love you. And because I do, I must give you the choice to walk away. I want what's best for you."

She cradled the back of his head in both hands. "I'm thinking that would be you, hotshot."

His steady gaze didn't waver. "You need to consider your answer carefully. Living my life wouldn't be easy."

"I'll say. Riding around in town cars, staying in luxury hotels, eating truffles. But just so you know, if anybody gives me a watch worth eight hundred large, I'm hawking it and donating the money to charity."

Still, he didn't crack a smile. "You'll have to be alert at all times so you don't accidentally give away our secret. You can't tell anyone, not even your mother or your best friend."

She knew better than to joke about that. "I understand."

"You could face antagonism from the other Weres, although no one would dare snub you when I'm around. Still, I can't promise that the Were community will ever accept you."

"Maybe not, but think of the research possibilities."

Finally he gave up and grinned. "Is that all I am to you? A research assistant?"

She massaged the back of his neck. "Research assistant, dance partner, cabana boy . . . love of my life."

His grin faded, and heat flickered in his gaze. "Say that last part again."

"Love of my life. I love you, Aidan. Whatever this binding process is, I want it."

The wolf emerged from the golden depths of his eyes. "You could get pregnant."

"Will our children be Were?"

"We won't know. Can you—can you live with the uncertainty?"

Her heart beat so fast she grew dizzy. "The only certainty I need is that you love me."

"I do."

Stepping away from him, she pulled her sweater over her head. "Then show me, Aidan." She stripped off her slacks and dispensed with her bra and panties. "Show me how a Were binds his mate."

And so he did.

She'd expected wild and primitive. Instead he was tender and slow. He guided her down in front of the fire, and as the heat caressed her quivering body, he took her slowly from behind, easing into her with murmured words of praise and gratitude.

The slow rhythm spoke of passion, but also of intense emotion. He took his time loving her, holding her hips steady for each firm thrust. As her orgasm drew near, he seemed to sense it.

With a low growl, he increased the pace. This was more what she'd expected. She'd braced her hands on the floor, and he placed his hands on top of hers. His chest brushed her spine and his thighs slapped hers with ever faster strokes.

She cried out when the first spasm of her climax hit.

Lifting his hand from hers, he combed her hair away from her neck. As she rode the waves of the most intense orgasm of her life, he surged forward and raked the back of her neck with his teeth. Then he came, shuddering silently against her and gasping for breath.

"It is done." He gulped for air. "We are bound." Gently he pulled her down to the rug and curled his body around hers. "I love you, Emma." He kissed the spot where his teeth had been.

She took a long, shaky breath. "I love you, too, Aidan. And when I recover sufficiently, I'm biting you back." She felt his smile against her skin.

"Anytime, my love. Absolutely anytime."

Epilogue

"Well, big brother, looks like you've pulled off the society wedding of the year." As stirring organ music filled the church, Roarke stood next to Aidan and gazed out at the expectant faces of New York City's A-list. "If only they knew this is a mere formality."

"Some of them do," Aidan said. His father had invited his friends from each of the other packs, so the room was a mix of humans and Weres.

"So far they've all been pretty cool about Emma."

"Yeah. That's saved me from having to kick some ass."

"Which I know you're fully prepared to do. I just about plotzed when you took on the old man that night."

"And I'll always remember that you backed me up, Roarke. I owe you one."

"You owe me several. Let's not forget making me stand up here in this monkey suit. I wouldn't be doing that by choice, either."

"Yeah, you would. You love it. You'll have your pick of the women at the reception."

"There's a pleasant thought." Roarke smiled. "Will you look at the 'rents sitting out there, proud as punch, both acting like they've won the lottery? After all the bitching and moaning about their new daughter-in-law's lineage, they're totally on board. Emma's won them over."

"I never doubted it."

"Liar."

"Okay, there were some dicey moments." He thought back over the fight with Theo, the disapproval of his parents, the ultimate confrontation with his father.

"Well, you're about to have the payoff for sticking it out. Here's a moment for you, bro. Your lady love approacheth."

Roarke didn't have to tell him that. Aidan had caught Emma's scent the moment she'd stepped out of the chamber where she and her mother had finished preparing for the ceremony. She walked arm in arm with her mother, who served as her only escort and attendant, just as Roarke was his.

Aidan hadn't been allowed to see Emma since yesterday, and the night had been long, indeed. Now he drank in the sight of her like a man presented with a feast after starving for days. Everyone else became a blur as he focused all his senses on her.

Her lace dress flowed in a graceful column down her still-slim body, and her veil, also of hand-woven lace, cascaded down her back. She'd chosen not to cover her face, and he applauded that choice. The joy of impending motherhood made her skin glow and her blue eyes sparkle.

He was the only one who knew that she was three months pregnant with the child they'd conceived the night of the binding, and he liked knowing they shared the secret. They would tell it when they were ready. Emma was good at keeping secrets.

He hadn't realized what a great secret keeper she was until he'd watched her provide partial truths to her inquisitive mother. Thanks to Emma's talent for fiction, Betty Gavin believed that her daughter was marrying a wealthy bachelor whose parents traveled outside the country frequently, often taking Aidan and Emma with them. That was the story Emma had created to explain why the Wallaces were only occasionally in the city and why they preferred having rooms at the Waldorf to owning a place in Manhattan.

The life that Aidan had feared would become a burden to Emma had proven to be an exciting challenge instead. Her fascination with the Were community won her more converts every day. Some Weres were already suggesting plots and characters for future projects.

His father still insisted on reading everything she wrote, but she'd taken that with good grace. She said she actually found some of his literary comments helpful in developing her stories. Now instead of resenting him as a censor, she seemed to enjoy him as an editor. Aidan was learning from her that confrontation wasn't always the best way around his father.

He'd learned much from his mate, in fact, and knew that in the years ahead, he'd become wiser still. Sometimes when he was with her, he even took the subway.

But they would not ride the subway today. A white limo waiting outside the church would take them to the Rainbow Room and the Waldorf. Later tonight, it would transport them to a private runway where the corporate jet would fly them in style to St. Barts.

On some things he refused to compromise, and when

it came to giving Emma a day to remember and the honeymoon of her dreams, he would shower her with luxury.

Most of all, though, he would shower her with love. When he took her hand and turned to the minister, his heart was so full that he wasn't sure he'd be able to voice the required responses. But when the time came and the minister asked whether he would take this woman, he found the words came easily.

He gazed down at Emma's smiling face and poured every ounce of his love into his pledge. "I will."

Please read on for an excerpt from
the next Wild About You Novel,

A Werewolf in the North Woods

Coming from Signet Eclipse in October 2011.

Maybe Bigfoot was watching her.

Abby Winchell had loved imagining that from the time she'd been old enough to wander alone on her grandfather's property, about thirty miles outside Portland. As she trudged through the early-morning mist, damp leaves squished under her hiking boots and the evergreens dripped in a steady, familiar rhythm. Otherwise, the forest was quiet, but she kept her hand on the camera tucked inside her jacket pocket, just in case she saw something big and furry.

Ten days ago, after a lifetime of fruitless searching, Grandpa Earl Dooley had seen not one, but *two* big furry creatures. A Bigfoot mated pair! But his evidence was maddeningly inconclusive. His single grainy shot could easily have been a picture of two very tall hikers wearing hooded sweatshirts. Two exceedingly smelly hikers. Grandpa Earl claimed the stench had been overpowering, even from a hundred yards away.

While Earl had struggled to attach his zoom lens, the creatures had loped off. Earl's arthritis had kept him from giving chase, and a heavy rain had washed out any footprints. That left Earl with only one bad picture to corroborate his story.

It had been enough for the Bigfoot faithful. Earl had made the trip to town and told everyone down at his favorite bar, Flannigan's. News had spread quickly among the cryptozoology crowd. As happy as he'd been about finally realizing his dream of a Bigfoot sighting, Grandpa Earl hadn't been all that pleased with the consequences.

With the exception of Abby, his family down in Arizona had thought he was losing his marbles. Curiosity seekers had trespassed on his property. And his wealthy neighbors, the Gentrys, had flown in some big-deal NYU professor to label the sighting bogus. Having Dr. Roarke Wallace challenge Earl's claim had cut down on the trespassers, but Abby's grandfather smarted under the insinuation that he was either gullible or a nutcase.

Abby had volunteered to take a week off from her job as an insurance-claims adjuster in Phoenix to check on Grandpa Earl. She'd promised the rest of the family that she'd convince him to sell the land and the general store with its attached living quarters so he could move to the desert, where his loved ones could keep an eye on him. He might have agreed to do it, too, now that he'd seen Bigfoot and possibly Bigfoot's mate.

But that damned professor had gotten her grandfather's hackles up, and he wanted to prove the stuffed shirt wrong. Grandpa Earl was also convinced the Gentrys had been smearing his reputation on purpose, because they hoped he'd leave and they could buy his land. He didn't want to give them the satisfaction.

Abby didn't blame him. The Gentrys had been trying to buy out the Dooleys for at least seventy years. Both pieces of property backed up to a wilderness area, so if the Gentrys got Grandpa Earl's land, they'd be sitting on one of the most secluded private estates around.

And the Gentrys loved their seclusion. She could imagine how horrified those highbrows must have been to hear about the Bigfoot sighting. Flying in a Ph.D. from some Eastern school had fit the Gentry mentality. No doubt the guy was a condescending jerk.

The Gentrys were like royalty in Portland, and as a kid, Abby had often climbed a rocky promontory on Dooley land because it provided a view of the obnoxiously huge Gentry mansion. She had decided to do that again this morning for old time's sake. The estate was off-limits to all but a selected few, so spying on them had always appealed to her sense of mischief.

Other than this view from the promontory, the heavily wooded estate couldn't be seen except from the air. A tall iron gate at the main road barred anyone from driving up to the mansion unannounced, and a sheer rock wall dropped fifty feet below the promontory. The steep cliff continued along the property line for about half a mile, neatly dividing Gentry land from Dooley land.

Grandpa Earl's property ended at a rushing stream that tumbled over the cliff in a beautiful waterfall. The far side of the stream marked the beginning of the wilderness area. That was where Grandpa Earl had spotted the Bigfoot pair.

Abby was puffing by the time she reached the top of the outcropping, which meant she'd spent too much time sitting at a desk lately. Looking across to Gentry land, she noticed lazy curls of smoke rising from two of the Gentry mansion's six chimneys. Trees hid a good part of the building, giving it an air of mystery.

Abby trained her camera on the mansion and zoomed in to admire the stonework and the massive bulk of the place. Surely a family this powerful wouldn't sabotage some old guy's reputation in order to get what they wanted. They already had plenty of holdings in the Portland area.

Standing on the rocky outcropping looking down at the mansion, she wondered why the Dooley land was so important to the Gentrys. Maybe they knew something Grandpa Earl didn't, like the presence of mineral deposits. Or what if the prize was this very spot? What if they hated the idea that someone could watch them from here?

Fascinated by that thought, Abby began scanning with her zoom to evaluate how much she could see of the place. A cherry red Corvette convertible sat in the circular cobblestone drive, but no people were around. Slowly she panned toward the back of the house, with its formal gardens, neatly trimmed hedges, and a large collection of marble statuary. As she did, she caught a movement in the trees.

Focusing on that spot strained the limits of her little camera, but she managed to identify what looked like a large dog. It behaved more like a wild animal than a domestic dog, though, as it glided through the trees. A coyote, maybe? No, it was too big, and its coat was an unusual pale blond.

The body shape reminded her of a wolf, but that was impossible. There were no wolves on the west coast of Oregon, and even if one had somehow migrated over here, it wouldn't have been this color. She'd heard of white wolves, but not blond ones. Knowing the Gentrys, she thought the animal could be some sort of exotic hybrid.

Grandpa Earl wouldn't be happy if the Gentrys had decided to keep dogs on their property. Her grandfather and great-grandfather had always avoided adopting any, because they didn't want dogs around to scare off Bigfoot. In all her visits to her grandfather's place, she'd never heard the sound of barking dogs coming from the Gentry estate, either.

She snapped a couple of pictures, even though she knew they wouldn't be very clear. Grandpa Earl would want to know about this. Maybe the wolf-dog was another tactic to annoy him.

As she considered that, she deleted the pictures. No sense in stirring up her grandfather even more. That wouldn't fit with the plan that was gradually forming in her mind.

Much as she'd love for her grandfather to stick it to the Gentrys and stay on the land for another ten or fifteen years, that wasn't in his best interest. His arthritis wouldn't bother him nearly as much in Arizona, and she sensed that Grandma Olive's death a year ago had left him lonelier than he admitted.

Therefore she needed to contact the stuffed-shirt anthropology professor and convince him to change his tactics. If the professor would support Earl's belief in Bigfoot instead of challenging it, everyone might get what they wanted. Grandpa Earl would relax, sell his land, and move to Arizona, and the Gentrys would get her grandfather's property. Grandpa Earl said the professor was staying with the Gentrys. But Abby didn't relish driving up to the gate in Grandpa Earl's ancient pickup with the battered camper shell on the back and asking for admittance to the estate. Too demeaning. But she was a member of Rotary Club International, so she could attend a meeting today at a hotel in Portland, where the guest speaker just happened to be Dr. Roarke Wallace.

Taking one last look through her camera's viewfinder,

she was startled to notice that the blond animal was staring at her. Then he wheeled and ran into the trees, moving with a fluid grace that looked far more wild and wolflike than doglike.

What in hell had she seen down there?

Also Available

FROM

Vicki Lewis Thompson

The Babes on Brooms Novels

Blonde with a Wand

Sexy witch Anica Revere has one rule: never under any circumstances get involved with a man before telling him she's a witch. Still, what's one silly rule? Especially when the guy in question is as cute as Jasper Danes. But when Anica and Jasper have a spat, she breaks an ever bigger rule of witchcraft and turns him into a cat. Bad news for him. Worse for her...

Chick with a Charm

Lily Revere is free-spirited and fun loving—two dangerous qualities in a witch. Especially while planning her sister's engagement party, and she needs a date! She's determined to bring hot Griffin Taylor, but he's a divorce lawyer who claims his job has warned him off romance. He may pretend he's just not into her, but she knows better— he only needs a nudge in the right direction.

Slipping a love elixir into Griffin's drink may not be the noble thing to do—but it sure works! Lily's dreamboat drops all defenses and the two discover they're perfectly matched in every way. There's just one problem: Are Griffin's feelings the result of some truly good witchcraft—or is he really in love?

**Available wherever books are sold
or at penguin.com**

S0004

Also Available

FROM

Vicki Lewis Thompson

Wild & Hexy

After gaining twenty pounds, former Dairy Festival Queen Annie Winston dreads going back to Big Knob, Indiana, feeling like a dairy cow. But if Annie has changed, so has her quirky home town. A matchaking witch and wizard have moved into the neighborhood—and they've found the perfect man for Annie.

Shy computer whiz Jeremy Dunstan secretly lusted after Annie when they were teenagers, but he never had the courage to pursue her. Now he has a second chance, but only if he can unleash his wild side. It's the sort of transformation that requires confidence, determination—and a little hex.

Available wherever books are sold
or at penguin.com